Children's Literature
Volume 19

Volume 19

Annual of
The Modern Language Association
Division on Children's Literature
and The Children's Literature
Association

Yale University Press

New Haven and London

1991

Children's Literature

The editors gratefully acknowledge support from the University of Connecticut.

Editorial correspondence should be addressed to:
The Editors, *Children's Literature*
University of Connecticut
Department of English, U–25
337 Mansfield Road, Room 442
Storrs, Connecticut 06269–1025

PN
1009
.A1
C514
v.19

Manuscripts submitted should conform to the new *MLA* style. An original on non-erasable bond with two copies, a self-addressed envelope, and return postage are requested. Yale University Press does not accept dot-matrix printouts, and it requires double-spacing throughout text and notes. Unjustified margins are preferred.

Volumes 1–7 of *Children's Literature* can be obtained directly from John C. Wandell, The Children's Literature Foundation, Box 370, Windham Center, Connecticut 06280. Volumes 8–18 can be obtained from Yale University Press, 92A Yale Station, New Haven, Connecticut 06520, or from Yale University Press, 23 Pond Street, Hampstead, London NW3 2PN, England.

Library of Congress catalog card number: 79–66588
ISBN: 0–300–04972–2 (cloth); 0–300–04973–0 (paper)

Set in Baskerville type by Tseng Information Systems, Inc., Durham, N.C. Printed in the United States of America by Vail-Ballou Press, Binghamton, N.Y.

Published with assistance from the Louis Stern Memorial Fund.

10   9   8   7   6   5   4   3   2   1

Contents

The Eye and the I: Identification and First-Person Narratives in Picture Books

Perry Nodelman

There is an essential doubleness about stories told in books containing sequences both of words and of pictures. They are unlike movies or television narratives, which provide us with simultaneous access to both visual and verbal information, for we cannot simultaneously read the words and observe the pictures in a picture book and must alternate our attention between them. Even when children hear a picture-book text read to them by someone else as they look at the pictures, they experience the words and the pictures as two separate and distinct streams of information. Moreover, as listening children look at the book, they have no choice but to see not just the pictures but also the visual signs of the words they are hearing. Even those children who can't read must separate these two sources of visual information—discard the visual signs for the words in order to make proper sense of the pictures.

Furthermore, the basic differences in the nature of the two media mean that pictures inevitably convey a different kind of information from words, and do it in different ways. These differences stem from the fact that pictures, which occupy space rather than time, lack an easy means of expressing the temporal relationships of cause and effect, dominance and subordination, and possibility and actuality that the grammar of language so readily expresses. Our knowledge of grammar allows us to understand immediately how the words in a sentence relate to each other, to words in previous sentences, and to the real objects and ideas they represent; a picture can't tell us directly how the objects in it relate to each other, to objects in previous pictures, or to the real objects or ideas they represent.

Pictures communicate this sort of information by other, less specific means—through conventions of the meanings of particular visual objects and of the implications of their spatial relationships to each other, through references to a repertoire of conventional

Children's Literature 19, ed. Francelia Butler, Barbara Rosen, and Jean Marsden (Yale University Press, © 1991 by The Children's Literature Foundation, Inc.).

assumptions about the meanings of shapes, colors, and styles, and, most significantly, through verbal information—through titles, captions, and verbal descriptions that focus our attention on specific details of pictures in specific ways (see my *Words about Pictures*). Words cannot easily communicate the detail and depth of information about the overall appearance of physical objects that pictures so readily convey; even the most complete verbal description of a face or a setting is far more focused on the implications of specific details than the most simple caricature, which readily conveys the sense of a visual whole.

Because words and pictures communicate different kinds of relationships in different ways, the doubleness of picture books is not simply the repetition of the same information in a different form. The pictures inevitably convey a different story from the words. As a result, any given picture book contains at least three stories: the one told by the words, the one implied by the pictures, and the one that results from the combination of the first two. This last story tends to emerge from ironies created by differences between the first two. In a discussion of the different ways in which different media communicate, Susanne Langer says, "There are no happy marriages in art—only successful rape" (86). Picture books represent this sort of rape.

The doubleness of picture books is nowhere more apparent than in books containing texts with first-person narrators. In most such stories in picture books, the first-person narrators tell of events they themselves are centrally involved in; these are examples of the kind of narrative text that Gérard Genette calls "autodiegetic" (245). In verbal narratives of this sort the distinctness of the speaker's perceptions of what happens to himself or herself is always a matter of interest, a focus of a reader's attention; but a picture, even one in a narrative picture book that contains an autodiegetic verbal narrative, cannot so directly and so obviously focus a viewer's attention on the distinctness of its narrator's perceptions of the same events.

This does not mean that pictures cannot be told, or shown, in the first person. In fact, they never do anything else, and we tend to value visual art based on the extent to which its style and its form express the individuality of an artist's perception. Nevertheless, pictures rarely convey the effect of an autodiegetic first-person narration in which the same person is both the teller of the story and a key figure within it—where what Genette calls "oneness of person of the narrator and the hero" (198) occurs.

The rare exceptions are those paintings labeled as self-portraits. It's not insignificant that we need the label to perceive the doubleness, the knowledge that the artist is observing him- or herself. Even then, what the picture shows is not what the artist usually sees. Self-portraits conventionally depict faces and eyes—aspects of ourselves that are physically impossible for us to see except on those relatively rare occasions when we look into mirrors. A more legitimate form of self-portrait might be an attempt to depict the spaces an artist occupies as the artist sees them—as Van Gogh did when he painted his room in Arles.

Unlike that Van Gogh painting, picture books in which narrators tell of events they are significantly involved in almost always express an acute doubleness by implying in the pictures what they don't imply in their texts: an objective observer who perceives the speaker performing the events the speaker describes from some distance. In purely verbal narratives, Genette distinguishes between the person who speaks (the person who tells the story) and the person who sees (the focalization, or the person from whose point of view the events in the story are seen) (186). In an autodiegetic verbal narrative, the two are one and the same; but in most picture books with auto-diegetic texts, "who speaks" is not "who sees." In books like Ellen Raskin's *Nothing Ever Happens on My Block* and Mercer Mayer's *I Am a Hunter*, the words are in the first person but the pictures seem to be in the third.

As an adult reader with some consciousness of the subtle implications of narrative point of view, I find this odd. The intended audience of books I'm talking about consists of the least experienced of readers and viewers; yet these books combine two quite different forms of focalization, each of which requires a subtle understanding of a different set of assumptions. Of particular significance is the common belief that these different focalizations demand greatly varying degrees of empathy from readers. The many adults who believe that young readers "identify" with characters in texts whom they see as being like themselves think they are especially likely to identify with autodiegetic narrators: the "I" who tells the story becomes the "I" who reads it. To complicate this already complex situation by combining a text that demands empathy with pictures that imply the objectivity of distance would seem to demand far too much of young readers. But that is just what most picture books with autodiegetic texts do.

The oddities of such books might easily cause confusion. In a book intended for the youngest of readers, John Burningham's *The Baby*, a first-person narrator declares, "There is a baby in our house"; the accompanying picture shows three people, seen from some distance away—a baby, an older child, and an adult. Although we might logically assume from the set-up of the picture that the speaker is somebody outside it, the author clearly expects us to understand that the words are being spoken by one of the people in the picture. Even so, unless we automatically assume an identification between a child reader and the child depicted, we need to ask who it is. It's clearly not the baby, but it might well be either of the two other people; it isn't until the speaker speaks of helping Mummy some pages later that we know for sure that it's the child.

A similar confusion develops in the relationship between G. Max Ross's text and Ingrid Fetz's pictures for *When Lucy Went Away*— and it is never resolved. One of my students wrote, "The narrator is one of the children who belong to the family that takes care of the cat Lucy. The reason I say one of the children is because there are two children involved but I am never sure which of the two is explaining the situation in the story. When I am introduced to the child telling the story . . . the picture does not help to distinguish whether it is the girl or the boy." Like Burningham, Fetz and Ross have combined a first-person verbal narrative with a third-person visual one without considering the implications of doing so.

Clearly, then, this combination is a convention of children's picture books—and, like all the unspoken conventions that writers, illustrators, and adult readers take for granted, its implications do need to be considered. Such conventions require a knowledge of interpretive strategies that adults simply take for granted but that children may not yet possess. A survey of some picture books with first-person narrators should not only reveal the presence or absence of a number of such conventions but also suggest the need for adults to work more actively than we currently tend to do to equip children with strategies for making sense of these books and deriving pleasure from them.

A very few picture books with autodiegetic texts do attempt to show in the pictures the same subjective point of view expressed in the words. Ann Jonas's *Now We Can Go* begins conventionally; the text says, "Wait a minute! I'm not ready," and we see the child who must be speaking these words from some distance. But then there's a switch. As the child moves objects from a box to a bag, we no longer see the child; instead, we see the box on the left side of each succeeding double-page spread and the bag on the right side, both shown in extreme close-up and from an angle most easily understood as suggesting what the child who speaks would see (fig. 1). In a sense, these are autodiegetic pictures—what we see is what the person who speaks sees. I find it revealing that this book made me, a mature viewer with a wide experience of picture books, uncomfortable on first viewing: its autodiegetic pictures transgress the admittedly less logical but much more common practice of showing the speaker rather than what the speaker sees.

Jonas's *Holes and Peeks* represents a subtle compromise between the two possibilities. The narrator is again a child, seen from a distance on the cover and again on the first page. As the text says, "I don't like holes," the child disappears from view, and we shift to a view of what the child sees—close-ups of the drainhole in a bathtub and of a toilet. But surprisingly, we then pull back to see the child *in* the picture again, as it peeks from underneath a towel. This makes sense in terms of the basic idea of the book. "Holes" are what the child sees; but since "peeks" are what the child does with a hole it can look through, we must see the child doing it in order to understand the concept. Nevertheless—and perhaps even more surprisingly—we are still seeing the child from a child's point of view, or at least that of someone short; as the text says, "I can watch my daddy through a peek," we see the complete child but daddy only from the waist down, as another child might view him (fig. 2). So the book shifts between the narrator's view of objects and what appears to be another child's view of the narrator; it implies a third party, another child not mentioned in the text but nevertheless taking part in the action. What we see is not exactly what the person who speaks sees, but something quite a bit like it.

Diane Paterson's *Smile for Auntie* also uses close-ups to imply a child's point of view. But while this book has a first-person speaker who is involved in the story, it's not that person's point of view that we see in the pictures; it's the point of view of another person, of someone looking *at* the speaker. As Auntie tries unsuccessfully to make a baby smile, we do occasionally see the baby; but most of the time we see Auntie herself, from so close up that her face seems to be sticking uncomfortably out of the picture. The pictures make it clear that the first-person words of the text come from the mouth

Fig 1. An "autodiegetic" picture—we see what the speaker sees. From *Now We Can Go* by Ann Jonas. Copyright © 1986 by Ann Jonas. Reprinted by permission of Greenwillow Books (a division of William Morrow & Co.).

I need my bag,

Fig 2. An implied child-sized viewer observes the child who speaks. From *Holes and Peeks* by Ann Jonas. Copyright © 1984 by Ann Jonas. Reprinted by permission of Greenwillow Books (a division of William Morrow & Co.).

Fig 3. Why are the words of the nursery rhyme placed in speech balloons and assigned to just one of many characters performing similar activities? The answer comes only later, when the use of the word "I" implies an autodiegetic narrator involved in the events he relates. From *Come Out to Play* by Jeanette Winter. Copyright © 1986. Reprinted by permission of Alfred A. Knopf.

of the person we're looking at—just as happens in real life, or in the simulations of real life that take place on a stage or screen. Although we usually assume that readers, particularly young ones, tend to identify with first-person narrators, we can feel no particular closeness to Auntie, for the pictures force us to view her, and thus to understand her words, as other and distant. In other words, the pictures undercut the autodiegetic quality of the text, and make the words part of a larger narrative that can best be described by Genette's term "heterodiegetic"—as in drama, the narrator is absent from the story he tells.

A similar heterodiegetic quality develops in many of the picture books which imply—usually through the use of speech balloons— that, as in our experience of drama, the words of their texts are actually emerging from the mouths of characters we are seeing from some distance. Jeannette Winter's *Come Out to Play* (fig. 3) is an interesting example. When considered on its own, the Mother Goose rhyme that begins, "Girls and boys, come out to play," seems like general advice, not words spoken by any one particular speaker in a particular situation; so on first glancing at Winter's picture-book version of the rhyme, we might wonder why she has put the words in speech balloons, thus implying that the rhyme is actually the speech of one specific boy chosen apparently at random from the group of children depicted. The reason becomes clear later in the rhyme, when the grammar demands our consciousness of a particular speaker; "You'll find milk, and *I'll* find flour" (italics mine). Having specified an "I," the text suddenly becomes a first-person narrative, which it apparently was all along. By placing the words inside speech balloons, Winter makes the narrator a character involved in the events from the beginning—and just one of many characters observed from some distance; this makes sense of the relationship between the words and the pictures.

But apart from books containing speech balloons, most picture books with autodiegetic narrators do demand a closer identification with the speaker. Judith Viorst's *Alexander, Who Used to Be Rich Last Sunday* begins, "It isn't fair that my brother Anthony has two dollars and three quarters and one dime and seven nickels and eighteen pennies." The person speaking to us is the central character in the story that follows. He presents himself sympathetically—and the text provides no evidence to suggest that we shouldn't adopt his point of view and sympathize with him. Alexander is like a first-person narrator in a story by Katherine Anne Porter described by Wayne Booth:

> Very little heightening of her character is needed to make us unite with her against the hostile world around her; simply because she is the only sensitive person visible . . . she wins us irresistibly. . . . She must be accepted at her own estimate from the beginning, and that estimate must, for greatest effect, be as close as possible to the reader's estimate of his own importance. Whether we call this effect identification or not, it is certainly the closest that literature can come to making us feel events as if they were happening to ourselves. [276–77]

It is exactly this effect of identification that elicits praise for books like *Alexander*.

Yet if we try to consider their implications without reference to our usual assumptions about how children read, we have to acknowledge that the pictures accompanying Viorst's text do much to destroy the identification. If the pictures paralleled the text, they would also show us the world as the narrator views it; presumably, then, the words about Anthony's money should be accompanied by a picture of Anthony gloating over his money. But what we see in Ray Cruz's picture is not a gloating child, but an unhappy-looking one with his hands jammed into his obviously empty pockets; we are obviously looking at the narrator himself, rather than seeing what he sees. The picture implies something that a conventional third-person verbal narrator might: an objective onlooker, someone who observes the central character from an uninvolved distance. From that distance, furthermore, the narrator is seen as comical. The cartoon style of the drawing focuses our attention on how cute and silly this narrator looks in his despair, in a way that undercuts the validity of the despair itself.

As I suggested earlier, this combination of sympathetic first-person verbal narrative with uninvolved third-person visual narrative is so typical of picture books that we tend to disregard its oddity. But the ways in which such books allow two different points of view to undercut each other defies our usual assumptions about first-person narratives written for children.

Many novels for inexperienced readers are in the first person because we believe that children find it easier to identify with—or, to use a suggestive metaphor, see themselves in—characters who tell their own stories. The basic strategy required for reading books like Judy Blume's *Are You There, God? It's Me, Margaret* is absolute sympathy with the narrator. Interestingly, such sympathy is often difficult for adult readers, who not only approach such novels with a broader sense of the meaning of experience than that available to Margaret and those of her readers who do identify with her, but who also have more sophisticated expectations of fiction and more sophisticated strategies for reading it. Indeed, for sophisticated readers, the central pleasure of first-person narratives is an ability, as another suggestive metaphor says, to see through them, to understand the events we are being told about differently from the way in which the narrator perceives them; and writers often leave clues in the narrations of first-person narrators that clearly imply the inaccuracy of the only words we actually read. Someone who reads *Are You There, God?* in the light of a previous experience of more sophisticated fictions and with knowledge of the strategies required to read them may well see Margaret as a self-pitying and self-indulgent little brat, and believe that Blume has managed to create a "self-portrait" of a typical adolescent that cleverly reveals the limited vision of adolescents.

But, of course, that wasn't Blume's intention; she rightly assumes an unsophisticated audience unlikely to perceive ironies. Even so, many members of that audience are likely to have read (and enjoyed) books like Viorst's *Alexander, Who Used to Be Rich* in which the pictures provide an ironic objective counterpoint to the subjective identification being demanded by the text. Apparently these simple picture books require a more complicated response than many novels intended for older, more experienced readers; yet younger children do respond to these books with as much enthusiasm and as appropriate an understanding of their tone as older children respond to those apparently more simple novels. Either our understanding of the process of identification is wrong or else we need to understand more about such picture books.

We can explore both possibilities by looking at those picture books that require the most concentrated form of identification —not first-person narratives, but second-person ones, in which a reader seems to be asked to believe that the events of the story are happening to what Genette calls the "narratee"—the audience implied by the narration. These are, quite literally, stories about "you,"

and because "you" is, most reasonably, the person actually reading the book, such stories imply particularly unsettling relationships between narrator and reader. A person who calls me "you" is
clearly separate from myself; yet this other person not myself is in
the process of telling me about what are purported to be my own
experiences, described exactly as I might myself experience and
describe them.

This is a passage from Robert McCloskey's *Time of Wonder*, describing how a rainstorm develops over Penobscot Bay:

> The rain comes closer and closer.
> Now you hear a million splashes.
> Now you even see the drops
> on the water . . .
> IT'S RAINING ON YOU!

For me, indeed for most readers, this is a lie. As we read the book,
we do not in fact get wet.

But of course, my effort to read without reference to conventions
has made me too literal. Once realizing that, I might more sensibly
assume that this is meant to be not a description of real, present
events but an evocation of possible ones. The beginning of the book
provides a context which suggests just that: "Out on the islands that
poke their rocky shores above the waters of Penobscot Bay, you can
watch the time of the world go by, from minute to minute, hour
to hour, season to season." The anonymous person speaking to me
here is asking me to experience as I read—that is, imagine myself
experiencing—something I have never actually experienced.

I can guess that the anonymous person actually has experienced
it, though; the passage would make perfectly good sense if "you"
were replaced by "I." Indeed, the thrust of the passage is to make
me as reader share another person's experience—to allow me to
feel as I read what he or she has felt in actuality. In a sense, then,
this text demands absolute identification. It demands that "you" as
reader cease to be conscious of your own past and become one with,
and thus totally empathize with, the feelings and perceptions of the
narrator.

In order for this to work pictorially, "you" would have to see the
scene as the narrator sees it. In looking at the pictures accompanying the passage about the rain over Penobscot Bay, you may believe
you do—at least to begin with. The first picture, which accompa-

nies a text about how "you can watch a cloud peep over the Camden Hills, thirty miles away," shows the scene as viewed from what appears to be high on a hill, looking down across the bay and over to distant hills beneath the cloud the text describes; and on the next page, the picture does show how "the rain comes closer and closer."

But the point of view of this picture is slightly different from that of the previous picture. We seem to have come down from the high hill in order to view the scene from a lower angle, even though the text hasn't described any movement on the part of "you." The next picture (fig. 4), accompanying the words "IT'S RAINING ON YOU!" implies an even more disconcerting switch. Instead of seeing the bay from the shore, I seem to be seeing the shore from the bay; I must assume that I am standing in the water and getting my feet wet (or perhaps more accurately, considering the specific angle of the picture, hovering a few feet over it). It's obvious that McCloskey has no qualms about showing what "you" see from points of view "you" aren't likely to take.

Even more unsettlingly, this picture of the shore shows two girls and a dog. If I apply a conventional understanding derived from other picture books to this, I must reach the conclusion that the "you" it is raining on are now being visually depicted. "You" are these children and this dog—not me, but the characters I am seeing, two quite unique and distinct human beings, separate from myself. The text, which first seemed to be addressed to any "you" who read it, actually has a specific audience in mind—these children are its narratees, not me. The identification the text demands is disrupted by the picture. Once again, the pictures transform the narrative implications of an apparently autodiegetic text and give it the heterodiegetic quality of a drama: we appear now to be eavesdropping on one side of a conversation between the narrator and the children depicted in the picture.

And yet the text does ask a reader to empathize with the sensuous experience it works to evoke. We might conclude that child readers would simply identify with the young children depicted in the picture, and so achieve that empathy. But the specific details of their appearance as viewed with the objectivity of distance make the possibility of identification more theoretical than actual. Readers can imagine being in similar situations, but not in the exact same one—even though that's exactly what the text seems to be demanding of us. Unless we imagine that the text is explicitly addressed

Fig 4. As the visual point of view shifts from that of earlier pictures, this picture changes the meaning of the words by specifying a narratee separate from the actual reader. From *Time of Wonder* by Robert McCloskey. Copyright © 1957 by Robert McCloskey. Used by permission of Viking Penguin, a division of Penguin USA Inc.

by a clearly defined narrator to two real human beings who look exactly like the two girls depicted in the picture, the words and pictures imply quite different points of view that contradict each other disconcertingly.

Yet, paradoxically—and revealingly—each does accomplish what this book seems to have set out to do. As its title suggests, *Time of Wonder* is an attempt to evoke in readers a Wordsworthian experience of the implications of the beauty of natural objects and landscapes, an experience the text conveys most immediately through its use of the second person; it is literally a story about you and the wonder you yourself might feel in response to nature. Even though pictures can convey such responses, they cannot be so literal. A picture that showed us only what our eyes would actually see while rain falls on us could not show the state of mind or metaphysical conclusion we might reach as a result of feeling rain fall on us. Such a picture could express only the appearance of rain as we would see it, and since it would then necessarily be falling only on objects we could see—that is, objects other than ourselves—it could not easily convey our response to it.

Of course, impressionistic drawings like those in *Time of Wonder* can convey more about such responses than literal photographs might. As I suggest in *Words about Pictures*, artists can imply something of the response they desire to a scene by the way they choose to depict it. For those familiar with the conventional meanings of particular shadings and combinations of color, of varying intensities of line and shading, of patterns of shapes and light sources, pictures communicate surprisingly specific emotional responses to the objects they depict. Throughout *Time of Wonder*, consequently, McCloskey does reveal much about how he expects us to respond to the beauty of the landscape simply by the way in which he depicts it—through the colors, lines, and patterns he chooses.

But he does something else, too, something that conveys much more specific feelings—as we see, for instance, in the picture accompanying the words, "In the quiet of the night one hundred pairs of eyes are watching you, while one pair of eyes is watching over all." A picture showing nothing but what one would see while sitting in a boat and looking at the stars shining over a lake might convey a beautiful peacefulness, but it could not readily express a particular response to the meaning and significance of that beauty and peace—the complex sense of feeling small in relation to nature's immensity but having faith in one's security that McCloskey implies in his reference to the "one pair of eyes." What does express that double sense of security and immensity visually is nothing so literal as the actual depiction of an invisible pair of eyes; it is the inclusion in the picture of a relatively small figure of a boat, dwarfed by its surroundings but still, because its singleness makes it stand out, the part of the picture most likely to attract a viewer's attention. In a sense, this picture turns us as viewers into the "one pair of eyes . . . watching over all" but with a specific concern for the human figures we see; if we then identify with those human figures, as the text demands, we must temper their sense of insignificance with our own consciousness of the protective viewpoint of immensity. This outsider's distant view of the "you" the text describes may appear to be at odds with the immediacy of the text; but it nevertheless allows a different medium to express a parallel state of mind. The pictures in *Time of Wonder* clearly convey how we might feel about what we see by showing other people seeing and feeling it.

Paradoxically, then, pictures seem best able to convey complex emotional responses we might identify with by showing other people experiencing them. The extent to which that is true becomes even clearer in another book in the second person—this time in the second-person imperative. Betty Miles's text in *A Day of Autumn* consists of a series of commands; for instance:

> Listen—a morning in autumn.
> Hear doors bang, cars start,
> Birds call, bottles clink.
> Hear the wind blowing.
> Listen—a clock rings.
> Time to get up!

As we have learned to expect, Marjorie Auerbach's picture for this text shows not just a bedroom as seen by an awakening child but an awakening child. The pictures once again change the implications of the text by specifying a narratee; the instructions seem to be directed specifically to the child depicted, and the voice of the narrator becomes less a one-sided exhortation than a contributing part of a heterodiegetic drama.

In this case, the heterodiegesis is particularly necessary, for it would be impossible for a picture to show through visual means what the text asks us to perceive: the nonvisual experience of sounds. Throughout this book the text instructs readers to enter into experiences that cannot be visualized in pictures: not just "Listen" and "Hear" a number of times, but also "Taste the sweet juice" and, perhaps least visually depictable of all, "Sleep through the autumn night." The text of this book is unillustratable except by indirect means; and the pictures, which show figures as solid blocks of color, so that mauve children sit at a brown desk cutting orange paper, do not directly evoke the way things look. The pictures use other visual means—exaggerations of shape and line, conventional implications of color—to convey the moods the words directly assert and demand. As these pictures reveal, it makes sense that third-person pictures should accompany first-person texts, especially when those texts demand emotional empathy from a reader— for it is exactly such emotions that the visual conventions of "objective" pictures can convey.

Nevertheless, the mere fact that the same emotions are communicated in two different ways inevitably changes the nature of the communication. As we've seen again and again, the presence of pictures turns first-person narratives into heterodiegetic dramas that establish the extent to which reading a picture book is more like watching a play than reading a novel. In their essential doubleness, picture books are as inherently dialogical, as dependent on ironic relationships between different forms of information, as theater is.

If we return to *Alexander, Who Used to Be Rich* in the light of what we have learned from these second-person narratives, we can see how theatrical it is. The pictures don't merely disrupt the intentions of the text; as do the setting and costumes of a play, they affect our response to the text in a way that subtly changes its meaning. Alexander is not simply an intensely sympathetic person telling his own story, but a person telling his own story in a context that surrounds him with specific scenes and people and separates him from us. Rather than becoming immersed in his words, we tend to respond to them as we do to the dialogue of a play—or as we do to words in speech balloons. There may be identification, but it can't be the absolute empathy which we assume to arise between young readers and a sympathetic first-person narrator who is not also shown in pictures. Instead, we adopt a double-sided perspective on Alexander that mirrors the doubleness of words and pictures. We sympathize with him even as we see through the exaggerated significance he gives to his situation and laugh at him. We both see ourselves in Alexander and see him as someone separate from ourselves.

As I suggested earlier, this doubleness would seem to separate such picture books from novels like Blume's *Are You There, God?* But if we stop to think about such novels in the light of these picture books, we will realize that they are not so different after all. No reader ever experiences complete empathy with a fictional character, even one so determinedly "typical" and therefore so widely identifiable with, as Margaret is. The simple existence of specific names like Margaret, specific family situations, and specific locales that differ from one's own creates some distance between readers and characters; and even those who claim to share Margaret's feelings will always be conscious of other feelings of their own that Margaret does not share.

Indeed, the inevitability of that sort of difference is one of the main reasons why we read fiction. Real life is mysteriously random and endlessly complex: what happens to us in life may be interpreted in an infinite number of ways and may or may not make sense in terms of our previous actions and expectations. But our understanding of fictional characters is always limited by the specific context of the text in which they appear, and they always make sense in terms of their previous actions and expectations as reported to us; even characters whose lives are meant to suggest that life is mysteriously random have only a limited number of experiences that suggest randomness. The inevitable limitation of fiction allows us insight into our own situations exactly because it simplifies and clarifies—because it differs from our own actual experience to the extent that it is a limited, orderly construct. Suggesting that all art represents a reduction of reality either in scale or in terms of the number of properties depicted, Claude Lévi-Strauss says that "this quantitative transposition extends and diversifies our power over a homologue of a thing, and by means of it the latter can be grasped, assessed, and apprehended at a glance" (23).

Fictional characters may not always be quite so easily grasped. But to "identify" with them is nevertheless an act of self-understanding that depends on our seeing them as homologues and applying a simpler model to our own more complex experience; we could not identify with characters we truly understood to be exactly the same as ourselves because they would no longer offer us the order and clarity of fiction. Paradoxically, Blume offers young readers that order and clarity exactly to the extent to which her novels seem oversimple to more mature readers; but even young readers must experience these novels as fiction—that is, as more orderly and more limited than reality—before they can indulge in the process we label as "identifying."

Furthermore, Blume wants readers to "identify" so that they can learn better ways of handling their problems—so that they can see them from a different, more mature, and more objective perspective, as the events of her story bring Margaret to do. In other words, such fictional identification is designed to bring readers to the same two-sided perspective, the same combination of subjective self-indulgence and objective understanding, that third-person pictures bring to first-person texts. The picture books turn out to be not so different from the novels after all.

If we return to picture books with the idea that the objective distance implied by their pictures is a source of strength rather than a disruptive weakness, we can explore that distance with greater understanding of its effects. In *Alexander, Who Used to Be Rich*, for instance, we can note that the distance shifts in intensity throughout the book. While the text of the first page implies that Alexander is speaking to us, the picture shows him with his mouth closed. We might conclude that he is actually *thinking* rather than speaking these words. If that is so, then the divergence between picture and text becomes even greater: while the picture keeps us at a distance, the words invite us into private thoughts. Later in the book, however, other pictures imply different relationships. As Alexander is saying, "And most of the time what I've mostly got is . . . bus tokens," he looks out of the picture toward us, as if he knew we were there. Since his mouth is still not open, we know he is not talking to us directly; but he does seem to be conscious of our presence and making an appeal for our sympathy—which requires our consciousness of him as separate from ourselves. But then, as Alexander tells us on the next page that he used to be rich, the picture shows not just his daydreaming face but also, floating behind his head, another image of him, happy and surrounded by toys and chocolate bars (fig. 5). This must be Alexander's image of himself: so we *do* see into his mind in this picture, and we presumably feel less distance. But then we can understand that we are seeing into his mind only by also seeing what Alexander cannot see—himself and the expression on his face as he pursues this memory. These

Fig 5. By showing both Alexander's thoughts and Alexander himself, the picture qualifies a reader's empathy with him. Reprinted with permission of Atheneum Publishers, an imprint of Macmillan Publishing Company, from the illustration by Ray Cruz in *Alexander, Who Used to Be Rich Last Sunday*, by Judith Viorst. Illustrations copyright © 1978 by Ray Cruz.

shifts subtly imply variations in the intensity of a reader's intimacy with and objective assessment of Alexander.

There is less variation later in the book. As Alexander describes what happened to him earlier in the week, the pictures show us the remembered scenes. Alexander is in those scenes, just as he was earlier in the book; but now this implies a more obvious relationship with the first-person point of view of the text: we can assume that we see the scenes as he sees them in his memory. Although this doesn't change the book's subtle combination of intimacy and distance, it does lessen the chance for confusion or misunderstanding. Not surprisingly, a similar convention operates in many picture books with an autodiegetic narration in the past tense; and despite its relative simplicity, clever illustrators still manage to create evocative manipulations of point of view while using it.

The first picture in Molly Bang's *Dawn* shows a man whom we must take to be the speaker of its text talking to a young girl. But the text makes it clear that it is not we as readers who are being addressed here: "A long time ago, Dawn, before you were born, I used to build ships." We are overhearing a conversation, just as we overhear conversation in the theater, so there is nothing unsettling in the fact that we see the speaker of these words from the same sort of distance from which we view actors in a theater. Since the text that follows is the speaker's reminiscence, we must assume that the pictures are, too, even though the artist uses no obvious convention to suggest any difference between the reality of the first picture and that of the later ones. Indeed, some of the pictures imply points of view impossible for the speaker to have taken—we see, for example, a sailboat which is supposed to contain him and his family from a great height above. But there are subtle differences in some of the pictures that do suggest the specificity of the point of view. Many of the memory pictures, including almost all the ones showing the strange young woman who came to live with the speaker, do not depict the speaker himself but imply the point of view he might take if he were watching the scene himself—as obviously, in his deep love for her, he did spend much time looking at her. Furthermore, she returns his regard; in three separate instances she stares directly and lovingly out of the picture, presumably at the person observing her.

Chris Van Allsburg's *Wreck of the Zephyr* is also a reminiscence—indeed, two reminiscences, for the original narrator's story is about how he once heard a story told by someone else. On the first page a first-person narrator says, "I followed a path out of the village, uphill to some cliffs high above the sea. At the edge of this cliff was a most unusual sight—the wreck of a small sailboat." The accompanying picture shows a man in a brown suit, presumably the speaker, looking at a sailboat. As in *Dawn*, the text implies a speaker, conscious of an audience, telling about events he himself was once involved in; the picture then represents what he remembers as he remembers it. So does the last picture in the book; as this original speaker comes to talk of himself again, we again see the brown-suited figure.

Both images of the narrator show him from behind, as he looks into the picture at the significant objects mentioned in the text: the sailboat in the first picture and an old man limping in the last. Although we see the narrator in the scene, our attention is drawn away from what he looks like to an outsider and (if we assume that backs are less interesting and less evocative of personality than faces) onto what he sees. Something similar happens in the first of Deborah Ray's illustrations for Jeanne Whitehouse Peterson's *I Have a Sister—My Sister is Deaf*, which depicts two young girls, most likely the narrator and her deaf sister; we can tell which is which because one of them has her back turned to us and looks into the picture toward the other (fig. 6). Such pictures seem to create the peculiar fiction that we identify ourselves with those whose backs are turned toward us.

Most of *Wreck of the Zephyr* is the story the original narrator once heard from an old man. The story seems to be about a third person, a boy who is neither of the two narrators; since this doesn't seem to be autodiegetic, there's a great distance between the voice of the narration and the visually depicted events. But some of that distance may be illusory; the last page of text hints that the boy might actually have been the old man who tells of him, who would then have been deliberately creating an artificial distance between himself and the person we see in the pictures that represent his story. But even then, the fact that this narrative is embedded in another narrative demands our distance from it and objective understanding of it. Perhaps that is why Van Allsburg has balanced the distancing effect by making the frame narrator a less distanced "I." Or perhaps, by insisting that he himself did actually hear this story, he is only trying to imply the truthfulness of what is clearly imaginary.

Much of the pleasure of books like *Dawn* and *The Wreck of the Zephyr* is their ability to make fantasies seem real. In terms of narrative voice, words and pictures seem to work to that end through opposing techniques. Words are more convincing when spoken by an "I"—and both Bang and Van Allsburg provide us with first-person narrators to bring an aura of conviction to their fantastic stories. But both also present highly detailed, apparently objective pictures which show their characters as viewed from a distance that implies the uninvolved objectivity of truth.

Van Allsburg pushes this combination of first-person narrative and third-person visual information to an extreme in *The Polar Express*, where we see the events described by the first-person narrator

Fig 6. In accordance with a frequently used convention, the person who speaks the words of the text has her back to us. From *I Have a Sister—My Sister is Deaf* by Jeanne Whitehouse Peterson, illustration copyright © 1977. Reprinted by permission of Harper and Row.

in pictures that not only include him but often present the scenes he speaks of from angles he could not possibly have seen them from. One picture of the interior of the train as he would have seen it accompanies his description of his trip, but there are also a number of pictures showing the train as seen by a distant observer—sometimes so distant that the train is merely a tiny line in the background.

Such pictures force our attention onto the ambiguous differences between pictures and texts in order to assert the reality of their fantasies; but many picture books with first-person narrators present fantasy situations which are clearly meant to be seen as fantastic. The pleasure is not in considering the possibility that the impossible might have happened; it is in understanding that the impossible never did happen, that it was all in the mind of one person—the narrator. Such books are the clearest examples of how pictures can transform autodiegetic texts into heterodiegetic dramas.

In Steven Kellogg's *Much Bigger than Martin*, as the narrator tells how his brother has victimized him by giving him uncomfortable roles in imaginative games, the pictures move between real, remembered scenes and imaginary versions of them—depictions of the characters inside the fantasy worlds of their games. Once we accept as a convention the idea that we are sometimes seeing the world as it is seen in the mind of the narrator, then this movement between fantasy and reality makes good sense; sometimes the narrator's mind sees what his eyes see, and sometimes it imagines quite different scenes.

The relationship between imagined visual scenes and first-person narratives is not always so clear-cut. As the narrator of Mercer Mayer's *I Am a Hunter* first tells us, "I am a hunter, and I hunt a snake in my backyard," the picture shows a child, presumably the narrator, about to take an ax to a vicious-looking giant snake. Since it's hard to accept this situation as literal fact, the most logical explanation is that the picture shows what the narrator imagines. On the next page, as the narrator says, "But my father doesn't like me to go hunting," we see the same ax-wielding child, only now beside a chopped-up garden hose and in the company of an angry-looking man. This is obviously the same scene from an objective outsider's point of view. This alternation between the narrator's view and that of an objective outsider continues throughout the book; the effect is like a joke, a move from confirmation of imagined reality to destruction of it, a constant dispersal of the personal vision with the cold light of objectivity.

But if these switches are meant to undercut the fantasy, the ending of the book is a surprise. The narrator tells us that he is a sea captain, and the picture confirms that he is on a ship; and, as expected, when the next page tells us that he's really only taking a bath, we see him in the tub. But when he says his last words, "But I am a sea captain, and I just sail away," the picture shows a disconcerting combination of real and imaginary vision, the boy sailing in his bathtub as the bathroom actually turns into an ocean. The last page returns firmly to fantasy, as we again see the boy on the ship, sailing off over his imaginary ocean. Or is it imaginary? If it is, why are we still seeing it? We might conclude that we are viewing the world of the narrator's mind once more; but if so, then the book becomes a chilling portrayal of schizophrenic withdrawal. Alternatively, we might assume that the story is literally true—that we must trust the evidence of our eyes and conclude that this apparently imaginary event is not imaginary at all.

Two books by Ann Jonas are similarly ambiguous. As the narrator of *The Quilt* says, "I have a new quilt," the pictures show a young girl, obviously the speaker, pointing to the patches in the quilt that she mentions. The pictures imply that she is conscious of being observed, and that her words are explanations for our benefit. But then the child falls asleep—and as she does, we see stars dance through the window and the quilt change into a landscape. It seems that we are now in the middle of the child's dream. As rarely happens in picture books, these pictures show us the world from a first-person speaker's perspective—since the child is no longer conscious of an audience, the effect of an outside observer disappears, and we look down on the scenes from above, just as the child looks down on her quilt from her pillow.

The switch from external observer to first-person point of view would be less ambiguous if it were not for the one picture in which the transition between quilt and landscape occurs. In this picture, as in the picture of objectively perceptible reality on the page preceding it, we are observers looking down on the child's bed from somewhere behind its head: we see the quilt and the child's arm holding a stuffed toy. But we also see the quilt transforming, so that we are both inside the child's dream and outside of it at the same time. This gives the dream itself a mysterious ambiguity.

Jonas also establishes a world somewhere between subjective and objective reality in *The Trek*. As the narrator says that her mother "doesn't know that we live on the edge of a jungle," we see the shapes of exotic animals lurking everywhere from shrubs to storefronts and front stoops in her apparently urban world. But we also see the narrator herself, and this gives what she claims to see herself the same degree of reality as our own objective knowledge of her visibility. The speaker's friend, whom we can also see in the pictures, also shares the fantasy; furthermore, the speaker never names the creatures she claims to see, but since we ourselves can see them clearly enough to identify them and provide them with their appropriate names, we have to acknowledge the visible reality of their existence.

But the speaker says of someone we can see in one of the pictures, "That woman doesn't know about the animals. If she did, she'd be scared." This amounts to a kind of teasing, an admission that what we see might not in fact be seeable—might not really be there at all. Other picture books with first-person narratives push this sort of questioning of the speaker's reality even farther: the pictures create an intensely dramatic situation by deliberately contradicting the information and the point of view provided by the text.

Faced by this sort of contradiction, we inevitably accept the objective truth of what our eyes see and doubt the truth of a text clearly spoken by one specific person who claims to see something different. We refuse to accept the narrator's brave claims in Dr. Seuss's *I Can Lick 30 Tigers Today*, simply because the pictures show us the look of dismay on his face as he regards the thirty malevolent tigers he claims he can lick. And in Ellen Raskin's *Nothing Ever Happens on My Block*, we know that Chester Filbert's claim that his block is a boring place is wrong because our own eyes can see the interesting things happening behind his back. Our acceptance of the truthfulness of visible actions is so strong that we happily doubt Chester's version of events, even though many of the things that he *doesn't* see but we can—trees that grow huge almost instantaneously, multiplying witches—are improbable, even impossible.

These books use the differences between the subjectivity of a first-person narrator and the distanced objectivity of third-person pictures in a decidedly ironic way; but in less extreme ways, so have all the books I've discussed here. The pleasure all these books offer depends on our perception of how the different implications of text and picture combine to create a third, far more dramatically dialogical story. In this specific and unusual way, these books duplicate the effects of more complex literature: our sympathy with any given character is qualified by our understanding of the context of the whole. There are still unanswered questions about the ways children can be taught to cope with the sophistications of point of view in picture books. But to read well is always to read with a sense of the doubleness of literature, which requires us to become involved in, even to identify with, its characters and situations but also to stand back and understand those characters and situations with some objectivity. In the clear-cut doubleness of their words and pictures, picture books like these can offer inexperienced readers an introduction to one of the most basic and most rewarding of literary competences.

Works Cited

Bang, Molly. *Dawn*. New York: William Morrow, 1983.
Blume, Judy. *Are You There, God? It's Me, Margaret*. Englewood Cliffs, N.J.: Bradbury, 1970.
Booth, Wayne C. *The Rhetoric of Fiction*. Chicago: University of Chicago Press, 1961.
Burningham, John. *The Baby*. London: Jonathan Cape, 1974.
Genette, Gérard. *Narrative Discourse: An Essay in Method*. Trans. Jane E. Lewin. Ithaca: Cornell University Press, 1980.
Jonas, Ann. *Holes and Peeks*. New York: Greenwillow, 1984.
———. *The Quilt*. New York: Greenwillow, 1984.
———. *The Trek*. New York: Greenwillow, 1985.
———. *Now We Can Go*. New York: Greenwillow, 1986.
Kellogg, Steven. *Much Bigger than Martin*. New York: Dial, 1976.
Langer, Susanne. *Problems of Art: Ten Philosophical Lectures*. New York: Scribner's, 1957.
Lévi-Strauss, Claude. *The Savage Mind*. Chicago: University of Chicago Press, 1966.
McCloskey, Robert. *Time of Wonder*. New York: Viking, 1957.
Mayer, Mercer. *I Am a Hunter*. New York: Dial, 1969.
Miles, Betty. *A Day of Autumn*. Illus. Marjorie Auerbach. New York: Knopf, 1967.
Nodelman, Perry. *Words about Pictures: The Narrative Art of Children's Picture Books*. Athens: University of Georgia Press, 1988.
Paterson, Diane. *Smile for Auntie*. New York: Dial, 1976.
Peterson, Jeanne Whitehouse. *I Have a Sister—My Sister Is Deaf*. Illus. Deborah Ray. New York: Harper and Row, 1977.
Raskin, Ellen. *Nothing Ever Happens on My Block*. New York: Atheneum, 1966.
Ross, G. Max. *When Lucy Went Away*. Illus. Ingrid Fetz. New York: Dutton, 1976.
Seuss, Dr. *I Can Lick 30 Tigers Today and Other Stories*. New York: Random House, 1969.
Van Allsburg, Chris. *The Wreck of the Zephyr*. Boston: Houghton Mifflin, 1983.
———. *The Polar Express*. Boston: Houghton Mifflin, 1985.
Viorst, Judith. *Alexander, Who Used to Be Rich Last Sunday*. Illus. Ray Cruz. New York: Atheneum, 1978.
Winter, Jeanette. *Come Out to Play*. New York: Knopf, 1986.

Devouring the Text:
The Subversive Image in Jules Ratte

Paulo Medeiros

In the middle of the night a band of rats invades a town and one of them eats all but one of the books in a little girl's house, as she is to discover in the morning. With this nightmarish scenario Peter Hacks begins the story of how Jule Janke, the little girl, traps the rat who has eaten all the books and then relies on the rat to give her the answers she needs for school, until it disappears and the girl's ignorance is found out. At first sight the text of this picture book can be seen as a cautionary tale intended to instill in its young readers the virtues of self-reliance, as implied in the proverbial quality of the subtitle, *Selber lernen macht schlau* (learning on your own makes you smart), and reinforced in the concluding verses:

> Nur eigne Weisheit macht den Weisen.
> Ratgeber können mal verreisen.
> Der kluge Freund läßt dich im Stich.
> Dann fragst du wen?
> Dann fragst du dich.

> Only your own wisdom makes you wise.
> Counselors can go away sometime.
> The smart friend deserts you.
> Then whom do you ask?
> Then you ask yourself.

Even if it is not strictly a product of socialist realism, this story still serves a clearly delineated purpose in educating children to rely on their own work instead of fantastical help. Klaus Ensikat's illustrations, on the other hand, give *Jules Ratte* a completely different dimension as they subvert the conformity demanded by the textual message.

Peter Hacks is a known and respected, if controversial, author. Although his reputation is based mainly on his drama, since 1956 he has published a large number of works for children.[1] After his

Children's Literature 19, ed. Francelia Butler, Barbara Rosen, and Jean Marsden (Yale University Press, © 1991 by The Children's Literature Foundation, Inc.).

student days at Munich and his move to the German Democratic Republic in 1955, his early literary career presents an intricate mingling of ideological confrontation and involvement with children's literature.[2] His work has not always conformed to the political expectations of the leaders of the GDR, as the severe governmental criticism of *Die Sorgen und die Macht* (1959), a play for adults dealing with the contemporary situation in the GDR, makes clear; it is nonetheless evident that Hacks for the most part has embraced the tenets of literary production in a socialist society.

Party ideology reinforces the notion that children's literature is an integral part of literature in general, and it makes the same demands on children's books as on adult works: ideological soundness, a stress on community interests prevailing over individual ones, and the depiction of the development of the people within a socialist regime.[3] Children's literature in the GDR had, from the beginning, to work against the fascist influences of the all-too-recent past and prepare youth for a new society. This essentially didactic function is reflected throughout Hacks's work (Di Napoli, 1987, 19), and *Jules Ratte*, far from being an exception, could be looked upon as paradigmatic.

The illustrator Klaus Ensikat has collaborated with Peter Hacks in the production of two books and a story.[4] His work has been appreciated outside of the GDR: a West German edition of *Jules Ratte* included his illustrations rather than those of a previous illustrator,[5] and two other books illustrated by him have been published in English.[6] Even if Ensikat is not the most prolific of the illustrators who have worked with Hacks, there seems to be a good relationship between the two, and he is the illustrator for a forthcoming anthology of all of Hacks's work for children.[7] Hacks sharply censured Heinz Edelman's illustrations for his *Meta Morfoß*, which "depict incidents which simply do not occur in the story or . . . distort those scenes that do occur . . . and in fact even compromise the text."[8] So we may infer that Hacks was pleased with the illustrations Ensikat provided for *Jules Ratte*.

Yet a close comparison between the illustrations and the text they accompany demonstrates that Ensikat's illustrations do not conform to the story in important points and that they create an alternative narrative which not only contradicts the textual one but subverts it as well. According to the text, Jule's deviancy is quickly detected by an enforcing agency which restores order. The images instead concern themselves much more with maximizing the act of seeing which turns into observing. In the end, using a print by M.C. Escher as model, Ensikat establishes a pictorial intertextuality that is independent of the written text.

Traditionally, picture books have been conceived of as a symbiotic whole in which text and image work together to establish meaning. Sheila Egoff, tracing the evolution of picture books, says of this "classic" conception of the picture book: "It was this era, the 1930s to the 1960s, that gave rise to the classic definition of a picture book: 'a perfect balance between text and pictures,' a work that evoked a total response. Neither the text nor the pictures worked as well separately as they did together. The illustrations could reinforce the story, as in Marjorie Flack's *Angus* books of the 1930s, or play with it as in Wanda Gág's *Millions of Cats* (1928), but the pictures stayed in their place, as it were, never overshadowing the printed word" (249). Commenting on the difficulty of producing a picture book, Maurice Sendak points out just this ideal of the symbiotic relation between text and image: "the illustrations have as much to say as the text; the trick is to say the same thing, but in a different way" (Lorraine 327).

Conversely, Perry Nodelman in his pioneering essay on "How Picture Books Work" advances the notion that there is always an implied and explicit distance between the text and the images. In reference to Pat Hutchins's *Rosie's Walk*, for instance, Nodelman asserts that "the pictures force us to be conscious of the inadequacies of the text and, in fact, to enjoy them; it is the distance between the story the words tell and the story the pictures tell that makes the book interesting. That distance is inevitable. Pictures always change the meanings of words by interpreting them in a specific way; they always tell a different story. Like Hutchins, many illustrators turn that into a game, in which our pleasure derives from our consciousness of the distance" (60). Nodelman's concept of an essential tension between text and image in picture books is important and could well be applied generally. It recognizes the importance of the images without dismissing the text. Yet Nodelman's concept of tension does not contradict Sendak's view of the interrelation between image and text. For, even if the gap in meaning between illustration and illustrated text is perceived as fundamental, the notion of the two working together toward a common goal is still present. As Nodelman goes on to assert, "intelligent illustrators, however,

understand and make use of the contradictory pull of words and
pictures so that the two together tell a story that depends on their
differences from each other" (62). And in a recent "Introduction to
Picturebook Codes" William Moebius notes that "we read images
and text together as the mutually complementary story of a consciousness" (141). Thus, though both illustrators and critics clearly
allow for a role separate from the text for illustrations, they still
think of the two as ideally forming a whole.

In *Jules Ratte* we read the text together with the images and it is
possible to arrive at the end with the idea of having read one story.
It is not through overt deviation from the text (as with Heinz Edelman's illustrations for *Meta Morfoβ*) nor through a playful gaming
with the words that the images assert their distance from the text.
There is no enjoyment for the reader in observing the distance between pictures and words. Yet there can be no doubt that there is
a great tension between the two modes of representation. This tension is unrelated to the expectation that Jule's scheme to do well in
school without studying will be discovered, because the text, even
as it presents a moment of uncovering, proceeds to a safe ending
with the moral to be learned. Instead, the tension results from the
anxiety inherent in the images themselves and by the gaps, small
though they might be, between the meaning of the text and the
meaning of the images. These gaps, once noticed and put together
cumulatively, present a two-fold breach against the conventional
correlation of text and image and against the textual message of
conformity. Ensikat's illustrations radically undermine the text's tale
of conformity, and in so doing, they extend far beyond their presumed task of portraying the textual story in a different way and
prevent a single consciousness from establishing itself.

The front cover illustration already contains some of the details
by which Ensikat's images subvert the text they accompany: in the
center, framed by a white, gnawed, and upturned white border, a
full-body picture of a gray rat dominates the urban background.
This rat, though standing erect and wearing a fighting cap made
out of newspaper, is only slightly anthropomorphized, and far from
"cute"; it is a threatening, realistically portrayed figure holding a
torn piece of paper, with further shreds on the ground, by its long,
drawn-out claws.[10] The rat's tail curls out of the frame, ignoring
its boundaries and invading the title of the book, resting over the
word "Ratte." One can clearly read "Ensikat" on one of the shreds

of paper, but little more is discernible. The piece held up by the rat has a paragraph sign, as if it were part of some code or law that has been shredded. On the hat the only clear word is left incomplete by the fold which hides its continuation: all that can still be read is "Gemeins," letting the reader guess at *Gemeinschaft* or some other indicator of collectiveness, while suggesting an idea of meanness with the word *gemein*. Thus the front cover presents an idea of belligerence associated with the shredding of rules and a disregard for imposed boundaries indicated by the functional semantic substitution of gemein for Gemeinschaft. The title page continues the idea of rupture from the front cover, as the grinning rat seems to poke its head through a hole in the page. The back cover takes these tendencies to some form of conclusion: it is void of text, and the rat stays within the boundary of the white frame but without any signs of anthropomorphization. This last view of the rat suggests both a primacy of the image over the (no longer present) text and the rat's animal status.

The opening of the story tells how Jule, pale with fear, discovers that all but one of her books have disappeared. It is accompanied, appropriately enough, by an illustration showing empty bookcases and a solitary book (fig. 1). A large straight arrow intrudes from above and carries the whiteness which serves as background for the verses into the colorful space of the illustration: it points directly at the figure of Jule, a red-haired girl in a striped dress standing in the middle of a room. The arrow, though not in itself an unusual image, is unconventional in its forceful intrusion, clearly commenting on the artificiality of realistic representation. The rest of the picture pushes back convention even farther. Behind Jule an open door lets the reader's vision extend into the next room. To the right another door, though closed, has been sectioned away so that one can also see the large stairway behind it. And the floor has been sawed off right at the foreground, revealing the supporting beams and diverse pipes, as well as an almost indiscernible figure crouching underneath the exact spot where Jule stands: it is the rat.

This first spread presents an uncanny maximization of vision. On the one hand it simply anticipates the text by showing the rat in direct connection with Jule; but on the other it shows too much. It does not create the idea of openness that might be expected from the open door leading into another room with a window; rather, it is as if it were showing that which is not meant to be seen: the stair-

Fig 1. Jule standing by empty bookcases directly above the rat. From *Jules Ratte* by Peter Hacks. Illustration by Klaus Ensikat. Copyright 1981 Der Kinderbuchverlag Berlin.

way behind a closed door and the underground of the house where
the rat lurks. The result is an impression of shattered privacy and
broken security.

A turn of the page brings the reader to an entirely different situation which nonetheless perpetuates the feeling of uneasiness. On
the left stands a picture by itself; on the right, the text with a picture of the rat between the lines of a strophe. The picture on the
left establishes a direct contrast with the preceding image. Whereas
the first spread shows a view from below, this clearly presents a
perspective from above. It depicts a train station by night, empty
except for a multitude of rats seen alighting from a second-class
car of a stopped train. The rats appear to be heading for the exit
with the exception of one, which, perched high on a part of the station's structure, looks straight at the reader. The text on the right
page explains the preceding picture while solving the mystery of
the books' disappearance:

> Es hatte nämlich sich begeben,
> Daß in der Nacht, als alles schlief,
> Ein Zug von Wanderratten eben
> Im städtischen Hauptbahnhof einlief.
>
> Und es war eine Wanderratte,
> Die Jules Schrank geleeret hatte
> Und nun da saß, von Weisheit fett
> Und hochzufrieden unterm Bett.
>
> For it had happened,
> That in the night, when all slept,
> A train of wandering rats
> Arrived at the city's main train station.
>
> And it was a wandering rat,
> Which had emptied Jule's closet
> And now sat there, fat with wisdom
> And highly pleased, under the bed.

The picture in the middle of the second quatrain shows a rat
holding a piece of paper torn out of a book and smoking a long
pipe. The planks above it indicate that the rat is underground, and
it is surrounded by shredded pages. Its tail again curls and ignores

the boundaries of the frame, effectively going out of the picture so as to rest above the flooring and come down once more to the level underneath.

Another turn of the page and the reader again sees two separate pictures. First, on the left, a tilted street scene, where the diminutive Jule is pointed out by another white arrow coming from the area of the text. A vintage car—"Automobile" was one of the few words that could be made out on the shred the rat held on the preceding illustration—occupies the foreground. A cut on the car's roof, shaped so as not to be misconstrued for a sunroof, lets the driver be seen, while another cut reveals a section of the engine. This image, if more reassuring because it shows people in an ordinary situation, combines the perspective from above used to portray the arrival of the rats at the train station with the view from below first employed to show a scared Jule and the rat beneath her. The unexplained ability to see through objects relegates the action mentioned in the text, Jule's purchase of a trap for the rat, to the background. There is a considerable discrepancy between text and image here: whereas the text has Jule running to buy a cage, the illustration shows neither the purchase nor the seller described in the verses; Jule is present but not running and her figure is diminutive, a part of the background.

The next illustration disregards the text in an even more blatant way. It shows a stationary book inside a cage, even though the text is filled with action:

> Und legt das Buch in das Gebauer
> Sich selbst hingegen auf die Lauer.
> Die Ratte kam beim Mondenschein,
> Roch an der Falle und ging hinein.
>
> And [she] lays the book in the cage,
> Herself, on the other hand, in wait.
> The rat came by moonlight,
> Sniffed the trap and went inside.

The illustration leaves the crucial action of the imprisonment of the rat entirely to the reader's imagination, concentrating instead on the trap. It is a trap for rats, as the little picture of a rat on the outside label of the cage makes explicit, but the reader's attention is drawn to the figure inside the cage: a man. The book used as bait is an anatomy manual, and on its open pages one clearly sees a human figure. The fact that the book is tilted at an angle not unlike that of the preceding illustration, which also shows people, further elicits a comparison between the two illustrations. Curiously enough, the one book which the text has mentioned as having escaped the rat's appetite was on *Heimatkunde* ("local studies"—history, geography, topography, and so on), not anatomy. It is clear that the choice to portray a human figure inside bars where the text would have us expect a rat is not fortuitous.

The following two pages are climactic. Not only does Jule confront the rat for the first time, but they come to the agreement that the rat will help Jule with her school work:

> Drauf sprach die Jule zu dem Tiere:
> Du Mutter der Verfressenheit,
> Wer hilft mir nun, wenn ich studiere?
> Wer rät mir bei der Schularbeit?
>
> Von meinen Büchern blieben Fetzen,
> Du sollst sie, denn du kannsts, ersetzen.
> Willst du das tun? Die Ratte will.
> Und unsre Jule lächelt still.
>
> Then Jule spoke to the animal:
> You mother of gluttony,
> Who will help me now when I study?
> Who will advise me on my schoolwork?
>
> My books are all in shreds,
> You shall, since you can, serve as a replacement.
> Will you do that? The rat agrees.
> And our Jule smiles quietly.

The accompanying two illustrations are like nothing else in the book in their symmetry and orderliness. Each picture is divided into five smaller ones labeled from a to e. Even though the intended sequence of the vignettes is not exactly duplicated, there still is a clear correspondence between the two pages. Their physical layout presents each as a mirror image of the other, so that the reader is expected to see the rat and the girl as complements of each other, if not as different aspects of the same reality.[11] In one of the small pictures (c) Jule is shown communicating with her hands, while on the other page there is a balloon over a picture (d) of the rat with a letter inside it: an inverted (as in a real mirror image) R. This can stand for *Ratte* and be interpreted as an affirmation of individuality, which is nowhere to be seen in the text. The verses, indeed, do not have the rat speak; the reader is told merely that the rat agrees to Jule's proposition. With the text in mind, a J for *Ja,* if anything, might have been expected to appear inside a balloon representing the rat's speech.

If Jule and the rat are indeed portrayed as doubles, they are not shown face to face or engaging in conversation. The text here has reached a high emotional point and the power of Hacks's verse is fully conveyed in the epithet with which Jule addresses the rat, "Du Mutter der Verfressenheit." The images, by contrast, look like simple illustrations out of a manual or comic strip, in spite of their consistently high technical quality. No emotion is evinced in the successive close-ups of Jule's face, and only the girl's open mouth indicates that she is speaking. Jule faces the reader in all five frames; the rat does so in four. In one of the smaller frames—the one reproduced on the back cover—it appears sideways.

The spread that follows is symptomatic of the relationship between text and image described so far. Hacks's verses, focusing on the relationship between Jule and the rat, are full of action and fantasy. The reader learns not only that the rat carries the knowledge of the world in its stomach but also that it directs Jule's homework. All this could have served well for a full illustration or even a series of smaller images on both pages. Instead, Ensikat combines the methods previously alluded to and shows a large scene, from above, tilted, in which one sees into the interior of buildings through walls as well as through windows. The only way in which this illustration can still be said to conform to the text it accompanies is in the centering of the two principal figures within the frame of a large circular window, with another white arrow pointing to them. Yet, in spite of their focal positioning, Jule and her rat are dwarfed by the scale of the illustration; the reader's eye is drawn more to the lower right corner of the picture where two cats peer out of a window under a skull relief.

Other illustrations stay much closer to the text. Ensikat draws seven wooden toy sheep crudely linked to an eighth by a painted plus sign to represent the addition Jule is performing with the rat's help, and he shows Jule seated at her school desk, with the rat hidden under the top, where it can give her the answers she needs. In two cases the image intervenes in the text by incorporating a line of verse. These two closely related images both portray human figures of authority: Jule's teacher and then the school examiners. The first stands at the apogee of Jule's contentment based on the knowledge lent her by the rat, but the second marks Jule's fall from grace when her ignorance is found out on account of her silence. The verses are themselves illustrative of the relationship between the two images: first, the teacher expresses contentment with Jule's supposed achievements, "Danke, Janke!" Then comes the *Schulrat* (school examiner), who comments on Jule's silence, "Das ist ja / . . . Das dümmste Mädchen, das ich sah." (This is really / . . . The dumbest girl I have seen.)

These two illustrations are noteworthy in another way, too. The image of the teacher is very disturbing. His torso is enclosed in a central vertical rectangle with only a partial rendering of the head, cut at eye level. The rest of the rectangle is filled with a larger picture of the teacher's head cut both at the chin and at the forehead. At the sides of the rectangle are a number of arms or only hands in various positions, all gesturing as if to accompany speech. One of the hands from one of the arms still attached to the body holds a book, half of which is already outside the rectangle. On its cover one can read part of a title, "HACKSens WERKE."

This surrealistic, Siva-like image stands on a proportionally smaller head that is complete down to the shoulder line and flanked by the verse "Danke, Janke!" The fragmentation of this first human figure of authority—Jule's parents are altogether absent from the book—could portray a sense of anxiety on the part of Jule which is nowhere to be found in the text, but it comes across mostly as just grotesque. The indefinite multiplication of power intimated by the image of the teacher is realized in the image of the Schulrat's committee, composed of five members, as the illustration shows—"mit einer ganzen Kommission," in Hacks's words. Only the one Schulrat member from whom the dire sentence issues in a flourished whisper is well defined and shown in full color. The other four background figures pale in comparison with their simply drawn lines; some are given a vague hue, while others remain in part mere outlines.

If these two illustrations, logically connected but sequentially separated, entwine the text to the point of incorporating it within them, their counterpart, the next pair of illustrations on facing pages, further deepens the distance between text and image. The latter pair reflects the meaning of the text—but in a way that explodes it. In the right-hand illustration the reader sees Jule sitting at her desk with arms folded in direct contrast to the exuberant movement of the flung, seemingly independent and disembodied, arms of the teacher in the left-hand one. The rat is there, too, under the top of Jule's desk, as a cross section reveals. This conforms partially to the text (printed to the left), which tells how both reacted to the teacher's praise:

> Die Ratte grinste in der Banke.
> Und Jule setzt sich wieder hin,
> Pampig wie eine Königin.

> The rat grinned in the desk.
> And Jule sat down again,
> Haughty as a queen.

Yet, although the reader would normally expect the classroom to be filled with children—and though the text reinforces this by mentioning a *Schülerschar* (crowd of pupils) before whom the teacher tests Jule—all the other seats are empty. By now the large white arrow coming from above, which almost touches Jule's head, is accepted as a given, so familiar as to be almost inconspicuous. Another detail, however, is stunning: four of the empty chair backs and a pair of resting eyeglasses sport eyes all turned toward Jule.

On one level it is possible to think of this as an effective means of conveying the impression that Jule is the center of attention. By erasing the other children the artist accentuates Jule's presence. Still, this has to be considered a radical move, for simply showing the other students looking at Jule would have achieved the same effect without such a complete denial of the text, which explicitly refers to the large number of students making up Jule's audience. The lending of watchful eyes to inanimate objects does more than simply focus attention on Jule; the sheer oddity of this detail makes it inescapable. Beyond merely lending a surreal tone to the image, the eyes convey a pervasive feeling of oppression that is reinforced by the shadowy pattern of bars cast by a window itself not depicted. Apparently aberrant, the eyes on the objects are a logical conclusion of the theme of intrusion set forth by the first spread, which originally let us see too much with its cut-outs. And there also one could already spot a pair of eyes on one of the supporting beams under the flooring. In this illustration, as in the first spread, Jule is alone except for the rat. At first she is frightened and does not know of the rat's existence; now she is supposed to feel triumphant and does know of the rat. Could the fear of the first spread still be present in this illustration, implied by the folded arms?

The page facing the one mentioned above, where the Schulrat pronounces his sentence, is also fantastical. The reader sees the five men of the commission descend in the basket of a large balloon toward the roofs of the city. The text has nothing comparable when it says that "Der Schulrat kam just an dem Tage" (The inspector of schools came right on that day), and the image totally ignores what is perhaps the most important part of the text: that the first question is addressed to Jule and that she remains silent. Not only is the balloon an unusual means of transportation, but it features a large, incongruous liquid crystal display on one of its sides.

The book's last page is mostly white and void of illustration. The last verse, in enlarged letters, dominates the space and brings home the concluding moral lesson on self-reliance. Yet immediately preceding it is a last full spread in which a tiny Jule is seen reading at a table in a huge library (fig. 2). This illustration carries Ensikat's techniques—tilting, using a perspective from above, and collapsing the distinction between closed and open space—to an extreme. Whereas up to here it was possible to maintain a fiction of separateness between what can usually be seen and what remains hidden, between inside and outside, in this image the separate realms merge, and there are no longer any cut-outs showing what usually would not be seen. The outside of the library and the reading room become one, and the flock of six birds which presumably starts flight from a ledge on the outside is actually flying within the library itself. The unreality of the scene is further reinforced by the exotic nature of the birds, which precludes the possibility of their free existence in Europe. The illustration depicts the text faithfully insofar as it shows Jule buried amid books, but it totally ignores the concomitant moral lesson.

This image is important in yet another way, as it establishes a pictorial resonance that goes beyond the fabulous nature of the text. The library in which Ensikat portrays Jule is actually a transformed image of the interior of St. Peter's in Rome; or, rather, it is a transformed image of an image, because its model is not reality, the architectural space, but the already distorted representation of it given by one of M. C. Escher's prints. Escher's *St. Peter's, Rome* (1935) was one of his last prints directly based on reality; however, in its preoccupation with the systematic repetition of geometrical forms the print could be considered transitional. A comparison of Escher's print with Ensikat's illustration reveals obvious similarities: the perspective from above, the resulting distortion, and the reduction to the level of insignificance of the human figure, which is completely overpowered by the architecture. Interestingly enough, one of the dominant visual elements in Escher's print is the inscription, which not only appears on the upper portion of the print but covers its entire span as well: "DABO CLAVES REGNI CAELO-RUM." Thus the mingling of text and image is already an important feature in Ensikat's model.

The full inscription on the cupola ring, the biblical "TU ES PETRUS ET SUPER HANC PETRAM EDIFICABO ECCLESIAM MEAM ET TIBI DABO CLAVES REGNI CAELORUM,"[12] has been shortened by Escher's perspective, although it is still recognizable. In Ensikat's version, however, the text has been far more reduced, so that one now can only read, between the fragments of two letters cut out by the frame, "AVES REGNI CA." And since the birds appear to start their flight exactly from where one reads "AVES," the shortening of the text acquires an added meaning. What starts as the institutional foundation for the church and had been shortened through Escher's perspective into its concluding promise of salvation, becomes in Ensikat's version an amusing pun (*aves* = birds) with direct reference to the image. By incorporating and modifying Escher's print, Ensikat clearly establishes a pictorial model for his own illustrations while reducing the meaning of the text contained within the image to a pun. The illustrator's approach is in some ways comparable to the process initiated by the rat: it, too, devours the text and subsequently redirects its meaning. The authority of the original text, both as performative act and as institutional and theological originator, is subverted by the "bite" imposed on it by the perspective of the image.

Taken as a whole, the images in *Jules Ratte* can be said to illustrate the text they accompany competently, but only up to a point. They refuse to follow the text at certain key passages and instead develop a meaning of their own which explodes the conventional

Fig 2. Jule dwarfed in a huge library. From *Jules Ratte*.

textual message and replaces it with another. The text has a lesson
to teach and presents an ordered universe in which the disruption
caused by the intrusion of a mysterious outside agent is eventually
corrected. But the cut-outs constantly violate the private sphere by
extending the reader's vision into places where it would not be able
to penetrate, even if given access to intimate details through the
text. Thus, while the text simply reveals the cause for the initial disappearance of the books and for Jule's success at school, the images
take us into altogether spurious sites.

The reader can in one moment feel privileged through the pene-
trating vision the images afford; yet in just another moment it
must be obvious that this maximization of seeing is unbounded and
extends everywhere, so that it may be imagined as affecting the
reader, too. And if the reader has the privilege of watching the
rats come into town, it cannot be forgotten that he or she is also
being observed, as it were, by one of the rats staring out of the
page. The concept of surveillance is pervasive: there is no place in
Jule's surroundings which escapes an invisible but all-seeing glance.
What might have appeared as mere idiosyncrasy in the first spread
is expanded to the point where even inanimate objects like chairs
have watchful eyes. By the last image, the very transparency which
makes the illustration so remarkable becomes frightening. The disintegration of normal barriers to vision equates the disintegration
of conventional meaning.

The presentation of many of the images from above reinforces
the notion of surveillance, as it keeps the reader from associating
the perspective with Jule, the rat, or her- or himself. The nature
and identity of the observing agent are never revealed, but the perspective seems to point to the Schulrat, who is first seen descending
upon town. To associate inescapable surveillance with bureaucratic
authority, then, is an easy step which has no grounding in the text
itself, being established entirely by the images. The cautionary tale
suddenly assumes a very different nature.

The story starts from a fantastical premise and ends on a down-
to-earth admonitory tone. The images, by contrast, become more
and more fantastical up to the point at which, in the last illustration, the reality of appearances is questioned on all levels. When
the text becomes fantastical—as when the rat carries the knowledge of the world in its stomach or when Jule's head figuratively
burns ("Es ist ihr Kopf, was da so raucht") while she studies by her-

self—the images ignore the fantasy. Indeed, the illustrations show few clearly fantastical elements that correspond to the text; those that do, stress an offbeat aspect of it. For example, when the verses mention the accomplishments of the rat in writing about cat traps and antidotes for rat poison, the illustration shows the rat busily writing. But this fantasy is altogether of a different order, because it empowers the rat instead of reducing the child's control and concentrates on creativity leading to a reversal in power structures. When the text narrates oppressive situations in which the child or its animal surrogate, the rat, are trapped, the images ignore it. One does not see Jule catching the rat or standing before the Schulrat.

In the choice of which fantastical elements to illustrate, the images concentrate on positive moments of empowerment for either character—itself a concept at odds with the text. Thus Jule and the rat are shown formulating their contract in a way which reinforces a supposition of equality, implied in the parallelism of the corresponding images. Also, in what is perhaps the most fantastical of the illustrations, the reader sees the rat dominating the space of the page and writing its treatise on how to capture felines, itself illustrated with an inverted—in relation to the reader—cat's head.

Nonetheless, the images do not create a pleasant substitute conclusion. The overall feeling of unavoidable vulnerability, provoked by the insistence on an undisclosed agency capable of watching everything, actively dispels the notion that all is well at the end. They also highlight another possible meaning of the text, annulled in any case by the conclusion: the rat, which, with its uncontrolled voracity ("Mutter der Verfressenheit") is able to eat, and ultimately write, itself into a position of power, can leave the city. With the coming of May, Jule's rat joins the other rats and embarks on a train, actually emigrating to Granada where it writes its books. Jule on the other hand, human as she is, must remain to face the Schulrat's interrogation. If the rat brings itself to the position of subject, appropriating the devoured books to produce its own writing, Jule is left silent. The images carry this one step farther by excluding her at the critical moment of questioning and by drawing a parallel between rat and child that precludes any facile dichotomy. The last time the reader sees Jule, she appears dwarfed by her institutional surroundings. The different techniques are combined to produce an oppressive feeling of confinement; the very openness of the space, in its excess, robs the characters of privacy. For the text's admonishing coda the images substitute another: the human figure, whether in the anatomy book or in real life, remains encaged.

Notes

1. Hacks's first published children's story was *Das Windloch*, but he had already written *Kasimir der Kinderdieb* (still unpublished) in 1951. Bio-bibliographical information was obtained from Thomas Di Napoli, *The Children's Literature of Peter Hacks*, the only systematic study of Hacks's work for children to date; see also his "Peter Hacks and Children's Literature of the GDR." A concise summary of Hacks's influence as a dramatist is provided in the *Kritisches Lexikon zur deutschsprachigen Gegenwartsliteratur*, 3:1–11.

2. Di Napoli (*Peter Hacks*) discusses Hacks's relationship to the influential West German publisher Gertraud Middelhauve, who helped him make contact, upon his move to the GDR in 1955, with Fred Rodrian, director of the Kinderbuchverlag in East Berlin.

3. On the theoretical debate surrounding children's literature in the GDR see Malte Dahrendorf's "Sonderentwicklung DDR." Di Napoli ("Thirty Years") provides an informative chronology of developments. See also Zipes for a comparative view of the situation in both Germanies from a point of view that is favorable, without being uncritical, to socialist theory.

4. The books are *Die Sonne* (1974) and *Jules Ratte* (1981). The story is "Aus dem Leben des Drachen Feuerschnief," playbill to *Armer Ritter* (1981).

5. *Jules Ratte* had previously been illustrated by Getrud Zucker when it was included in an anthology *Das Windrad: Kindergedichte aus zwei Jahrzehnten*. With Ensikat's illustrations it appeared in identical (except for publishers' imprints) East German (1981) and West German (1982) editions.

6. Alfred Koenner, *A Peacock's Wedding* (1972); Marion Koenig, *The Tale of Fancy Nancy: A Spanish Folk Tale* (1977).

7. Hacks explained to Di Napoli "that there is a plan for Ensikat to illustrate an edition of Hacks' collected stories, to be called *Kinderkurzweil*" (*The Children's Literature of Peter Hacks* 287).

8. Quoted in Di Napoli, *Peter Hacks*, 50. *Meta Morfoß* presents the story of a girl, Meta, who constantly changes her identity. It was first published in two different West German editions, one with illustrations by Heinz Edelman, and then in an East German edition with Gisela Neumann's illustrations.

9. Addressing themselves to the question of how books are received by children, Denise Escarpit, Zena Sutherland, and May Hill Arbuthnot still reiterate the need (in their view) for total correspondence between text and image. Zena Sutherland and May Hill Arbuthnot write: "Children begin as stern literalists, demanding a truthful interpretation of the text. . . . Being literal, the young child also wants a picture synchronized precisely with the text" (135). Denise Escarpit maintains that success depends on the work being a whole, with the image reinforcing the text and allowing the child's imagination to play on two registers (119).

10. Miska Miles's *Wharf Rat*, illustrated by John Schoenherr, is another exception. It, too, presents a rat realistically without *any* anthropomorphizing. The rat, however ugly and frightening, is portrayed as a natural part of an ecological system. Human beings, through an accidental oil spill, become the villains who upset the natural balance.

11. *Ratte* is a feminine noun in German, even though it applies to both male and female rats. Whether in this case the reader sees the rat as male or female, or just neuter, is of course a question of interpretation.

12. The inscription is taken from Matthew 16:18–19: "'And I tell you, you are Peter, and on this rock I will build my church, and the powers of death shall not prevail against it. I will give you the keys of the kingdom of heaven, and whatever you bind on earth shall be bound in heaven, and whatever you loose on earth shall be loosed in heaven.'" For a description of St. Peter's see, for example, Bergere 65.

Works Cited

Arnold, Heinz Ludwig, ed. *Kritisches Lexikon zur deutschsprachigen Gegenwartsliteratur.* 4 vols. Munich: Edition Text + Kritik, 1978. 3: 1–11.

Bergere, Thea and Richard. *The Story of St. Peter's.* Illustrated with photographs, prints, and with drawings by Richard Bergere. New York: Dodd, Mead & Company, 1966.

Dahrendorf, Malte. "Sonderentwicklung DDR." In *Kinder- und Jugendliteratur im bürgerlichen Zeitalter: Beiträge zu ihrer Geschichte, Kritik und Didaktik.* Königstein/Taunus: Scriptor Verlag, 1980. 92–100.

Di Napoli, Thomas. *The Children's Literature of Peter Hacks.* New York: Peter Lang, 1987.

———. "Peter Hacks and Children's Literature of the GDR." *The Germanic Review* 63 (1988): 33–40.

———. "Thirty Years of Children's Literature in the German Democratic Republic." *German Studies Review* 7 (1984): 281–300.

Egoff, Sheila A. *Thursday's Child: Trends and Patterns in Contemporary Children's Literature.* Chicago: American Library Association, 1981.

Escarpit, Denise. *La littérature d'enfance et de jeunesse en Europe: Panorama historique.* Paris: Presses universitaires de France, 1981.

Hacks, Peter. *Kasimir der Kinderdieb.* Unpublished MS, 1951.

———. *Das Windloch: Geschichten von Henriette und Onkel Titus.* Illus. Paul Flora. Munich: Gütersloh, 1956.

———. *Die Sonne.* Illus. Klaus Ensikat. Berlin: Der Kinderbuchverlag, 1974.

———. *Meta Morfoß.* In *Das Einhorn sagt zum Zweihorn: 42 Schriftsteller schreiben für Kinder,* ed. Gertraud Middelhauve. Cologne: Friedrich Middelhauve Verlag, 1974.

———. *Meta Morfoß.* Illus. Heinz Edelman. Cologne: Friedrich Middelhauve Verlag, 1975.

———. *Meta Morfoß und ein Märchen für Claudias Puppe.* Illus. Gisela Neumann. Berlin: Der Kinderbuchverlag, 1975.

———. *Jules Ratte oder Selber lernen macht schlau.* Illus. Getrud Zucker. In *Das Windrad: Kindergedichte aus zwei Jahrzehnten,* ed. Helmut Preißler. Berlin: Der Kinderbuchverlag, 1977. 45–49.

———. *Jules Ratte oder Selber lernen macht schlau.* Illus. Klaus Ensikat. Berlin: Kinderbuch Verlag, 1981. Stuttgart: Thienemann Verlag, 1982.

———. "Aus dem Leben des Drachen Feuerschnief." Playbill to *Armer Ritter.* Illus. Klaus Ensikat. Berlin: Maxim Gorky Theater, 1981.

Holtze, Sally Helmes. *Fifth Book of Junior Authors & Illustrators.* New York: H. W. Wilson, 1983.

Koenig, Marion. *The Tale of Fancy Nancy: A Spanish Folk Tale.* London: Chatto & Windus, 1977.

Koenner, Alfred. *A Peacock's Wedding.* London: Chatto & Windus, 1972.

Locher, J. L., ed. *The World of M. C. Escher.* New York: Harry N. Abrams, 1971.

Lorraine, Walter. "An Interview with Maurice Sendak." In *Only Connect: Readings on Children's Literature,* ed. Sheila Egoff, G. T. Stubbs, and L. F. Ashley. 2d ed. Toronto: Oxford University Press, 1980.

Miles, Miska. *Wharf Rat.* Illus. John Schoenherr. Boston: Atlantic Monthly Press; Little, Brown & Co., 1972.

Moebius, William. "Introduction to Picturebook Codes." *Word & Image* 2:2 (1986): 141–58.

Nodelman, Perry. "How Picture Books Work." In *Proceedings of the Eighth Annual Conference of The Children's Literature Association, University of Minnesota, March 1981*, ed. Priscilla A. Ord. Boston: The Children's Literature Association, Department of English, Northeastern University, 1982.

Sutherland, Zena, and May Hill Arbuthnot. *Children and Books.* 7th ed. Glennview, Ill.: Scott, Foresman and Co., 1986.

Zipes, Jack. "Children's Theater in East and West Germany: Theories, Practice, and Programs." *Children's Literature*, 2 (1973): 173–91.

Room with a View: Bedroom Scenes in Picture Books

William Moebius

The picture book that depends on "the drama of the turning of the page," as Barbara Bader, echoing Remy Charlip,[1] heralds it, is a sort of chamber theater, whether it opens in New York or in Moscow. Like conventional theater, it tends to play to an indoor audience, one which favors darkening rooms where the crib itself has been the first stage, the bedroom the first theater, the bedroom window the first breakthrough into the world as spectacle. In this age of homelessness, if the picture book has a corner on any market, it is the market of those who inhabit their own bedrooms, who take "home" for granted and bring picture books home. Now, as earlier, these constitute a privileged class that can afford dolls, toys, and picture books as well as the time for playing.[2] Not all picture books are bedroom material, but if their ultimate destination is the child who reads, they will have crossed the threshold of such a bedroom more than once.

A bedroom scene is generative: from it springs a certain question-marked figure of the child, the designated offspring we are invited to read about, along with that child's story or fabula and the picture book itself, which, like a notepad[3] (some people refer to their own living quarters as a pad), opening after opening, under the covers, reveals what we readers both fear and desire to *see* and to *know,* as proposed by the title of the book—for example, of Maurice Sendak's *Where the Wild Things Are,* Jean-Marie Poupart and Suzanne Duranceau's *Nuits Magiques,* Natalie Babbitt's *The Something,* or Raymond Briggs's *The Snowman.* Any book, in the right circumstances, can lull the reader to sleep. Its most vital function may be to summon up in the reader what Gaston Bachelard has called "la beauté des images premières" while simultaneously testing and challenging their interpretation in the accompanying text.

Sensitive illustrations, especially those that stage the bedroom scene, go a long way toward questioning language. Jacqueline Rose

Children's Literature 19, ed. Francelia Butler, Barbara Rosen, and Jean Marsden (Yale University Press, © 1991 by The Children's Literature Foundation, Inc.).

concludes *The Case of Peter Pan or the Impossibility of Children's Fiction* with a plea for such a questioning: "It is a questioning of language itself as the means through which subjective identity, at the level of psychic and sexual life, is constituted and then imposed and re-imposed over time" (140). Questions of self-representation, of origin and destiny, toss and turn in the picture book's bedroom scene, shaking off the word-covers, their protection against the unknown and unspeakable.

A "topo-poetics" of the picture book, then, will depend largely not on evocative text but on images, the description of which constitutes a branch of iconography. The following composite of conventional ingredients of the bedroom suite[4] as illustrated in the picture book is drawn from a reading of North American and northern European picture books. They typically include a bed (usually with headboard, sometimes with posts) and a coverlet (often a patchwork quilt), windows with flowing curtains and a view of moon and stars, a lamp, a mirror, a picture on the wall, a door, a cat or dog on or near or in the bed, a doll. The bedroom itself is usually found at the top of a flight of stairs, not in a basement or on the ground floor. The bed, positioned sometimes at a tilt on the page, is a parallelogram; still, with all its folds and wrinkles, topside, underside, head and foot, it is emphatically three-dimensional, an inanimate version of its owner or occupant, who has left an imprint or an impression on it ("someone has been sleeping in my bed"). The door and window (and the framed picture on the wall) conform, in miniature, to the rectilinear verticals and horizontals of the edge of the page. Curvilinear lines are reserved for curtains, bedclothes, and bodies.[5]

There are variations on this iconic cluster. A cave, lair, or nest may replace the bedroom; although the rectilinearity of the page is not replicated by the shape of such domains, they nonetheless fulfill certain functions similar to those of the bedroom scene. So do some box-shaped objects, such as the chest, refrigerator, or freezer (for example, in Alan Baker's *Benjamin and the Box*, Robert Munsch and Michael Martschenko's *50 Below Zero*, and *The Snowman*, respectively). I will examine this variation more closely later, after considering the temporal or syntactical relation of bedroom scenes to one another and to other scenes.

Since one explicit function of certain picture books (Margaret Wise Brown and Clement Hurd's *Good Night Moon* is a well-known example) is to prepare the child for bedtime, it is not surprising that bedroom scenes, when they do not appear throughout, should dominate their final pages. If a bedroom scene appears near or at the end—as, for example, in Bernard Waber's *Ira Sleeps Over*, *Where the Wild Things Are*, Ludwig Bemelmans' *Madeline*, Don Free-man's *Corduroy*, *The Snowman*, or even *The Story of Peter Rabbit*—one recognizes that the book is about to "shut up," that it will have nothing more to say. No matter what the book is about, the bedroom betokens the restoration of calm and the absence of confusion or anxiety. The bedroom scene is the book's (and the sleepy child's) destiny, its calling; and it is as much a testament to ultimate knowledge and certainty as its title is a call to discovery. At whatever time the story may have begun, its chronology and that of the reader come to be synchronized in this final moment, just as a wave breaks and a swimmer emerges on the shore at the same time.

Some picture books begin as well as end in the bedroom, following a venerable iconographic tradition, but nowadays without the evangelical twist provided by nineteenth-century tales.[6] To open the book is to share the character's awakening in the morning or in the night, and the beginning of a quest. In Barbara Bott-ner's *There Was Nobody There*, for example, the heroine wakes up, but "there was nobody there. I reached for the light, I fell over a chair, I moved all the plants: there was nobody there" (punctuation mine). Nobody is the object of the quest, which begins and ends in bed. Arnold Lobel's "The List" makes use of the bedroom scene as frame, as do *The Snowman* and *Where the Wild Things Are*. The first opening in *The Snowman*, (a wordless picture book) shows us the awakening child (three frames) gazing out of the window (one frame), then getting dressed to go outside (four frames) before he heads out into the snow to make the snowman. In a reprise of the first awakening, the boy is seen in the third opening being put to bed, looking out of the window, then going downstairs in pajamas to greet the snowman, who, very much alive, tips his hat to the boy. In the book's penultimate opening we are given a final reprise, when the boy wakes up once more to find the snowman quite melted. Each awakening marks another step from a new uncertainty to certainty; the bedroom can serve as both site of enigma and site of solution. That the opening scene occurs at night enhances the sense of blindness to be overcome through later insights.

Like the gate of horn, the bedroom scene often leads into and out of a dreamworld. As the borders of the dreamworld are not easily fixed, in some picture books the story begins ambiguously, in the bedroom and in some other place at the same time, and closes in the alternate site, recalling what is latent in the bedroom.[7] In Remy Charlip and Burton Supree's *Harlequin and the Gift of Many Colors*, we face such alternatives (bedroom/playroom) on the cover itself, which shows a night scene on a small stage. The title, in white letters, hovers over the figure of Harlequin, who leans forward perhaps to ask the audience for quiet. On the stage a bit behind him is a scale model of a stone house, mounted on a butler's table. Peering into a window of this house is a figure dressed in a costume of moon and stars. The backdrop depicts an Italian city (Bergamo) at twilight. The book's first opening after the inside cover repeats the night scene on the small stage. In the next opening, we find ourselves inside a bedroom where a young boy lies asleep. Peering into the window is the face of the figure dressed in moon and stars. The boy's slow awakening requires three further openings, all inside the bedroom, all without accompanying text (except for publication information and a brief historical note on Harlequin). So to start with, the book links the world of the bedroom with the world of the stage; the bedroom, the moon, and stars are all theatrical illusions. When the story is ready to end, the figure of Harlequin is shown drawing a curtain over the city at Carnival time. The view of the square in which hundreds of Harlequin's friends are shown dancing may well be the view from the bedroom. But it is also the view from the back of the theater. Dream and theatrical illusion become one and the same experience.

Robert Munsch and Michael Martschenko's *50 Below Zero* also plays with the ambiguous opening and the latency of alternate bedrooms. The book's cover (the cover illustration reappears later in the story) shows a small child standing in an open doorway, gazing out on a snow-covered wilderness; the title, in white letters, makes the moon look like a white dot above the letter *e* of "below." That wilderness forms a night scene, like the stage in *Harlequin and the Gift of Many Colors*. It is one of a series of spectacles the child will study in his quest for the sleepwalking father. The front door, drawn back like a curtain, invites us to join the boy in this quest. After a pictureless title page, and a dedication page featuring the boy in all his winter paraphernalia, we come to the opening where the story begins. Beside a picture of the boy sitting straight up in bed, his face and blonde hair starkly moonlit, are the following lines:

> In the middle of the night, Jason was asleep: zzzzz — zzzzz — zzzzz — zzzzz zzzzz.

> He woke up! He heard a sound. He said, "What's that? What's that? What's that!"

> Jason opened the door to the kitchen

only to find, as shown on the next page, his father sleeping on top of the refrigerator (new bed). Of course, when Jason goes back to his bed, the same distraction occurs, the same search for meaning, a further discovery. After Jason has rescued his sleepwalking father from the peril of a snooze outdoors in temperatures of fifty degrees below zero and thawed him out, he leaves his father "stuck in the middle of the [kitchen] floor. 'Good,' said Jason, 'That is the end of the sleepwalking. Now I can get to sleep.'" And there in the penultimate opening, the words of the first opening recur, except that Jason's mother is now the sleeper awakening to the "sound." In *50 Below Zero*, the story is launched from the boy's bed, as portrayed in the initial opening; it is relaunched from the mother's bed, which is "written about" rather than illustrated. It culminates in a picture (fig. 1) of the father sleepwalking, frozen in a sort of arabesque manquée, with the son asleep, as his father before him, on the refrigerator, and the inquisitive mother peering through the open kitchen door, as did her son in the second opening.

Although the bedroom may be the first place in which to dream or to act out the spectacles of sleep, it is not the only one. The kitchen, bathroom, garage, and great outdoors are substitutes worth exploring—anywhere, in fact, where the story of origins (whether in a "moon and stars" man, a snowman, or a stiffening father) can be detected. I will return to the matter of answers and origins associated with bedroom scenes, but first, let me round out this account of the syntactical arrangement of bedroom scenes by examining the phenomenon of "middleness."

A bedroom scene in the middle of a picture book usually serves the same function as it does in such tales as "Hansel and Gretel," "Sleeping Beauty," or "Snow White": it marks a pause and withdrawal in order to change the appearance of things. In stories about

Fig 1. It is his mother's turn to find Jason and his father asleep. Illustration by
Michael Martschenko from *50 Below Zero* by Robert Munsch and Michael Mart-
schenko. Copyright 1986 by Michael Martschenko. By permission of Annick Press
Ltd., Willowdale, Ontario, Canada.

the animal world, such as *The Fireflies* by Max Bolliger, hibernation
or pupation may be shown. Stories with human or quasi-human
subjects often use the mid-text bedroom scene as a site for con-
densing accumulated difficulties and problems. For example, in Eve
Bunting's *Barney the Beard*, the baker of this description "rushed
into the warm little room behind the bake shop and hid under his
bedcovers," vowing never to go out again because people would not
call him "Barney the Baker." At precisely the middle of *Corduroy*, it

All at once he saw something small and round.

"Why, here's my button!" he cried. And he tried to pick it up. But, like all the other buttons on the mattress, it was tied down tight.

Fig 2. The bed of his remaking, the button of new life. Illustration from *Corduroy* by Don Freeman. Copyright © 1968 by Don Freeman. Reprinted by permission of Viking Penguin, Inc.

is into an adult-size bed that we find this imperfect (he lacks a button) teddy bear crawling (fig. 2). A department store commodity, he has not won acceptance from the consumer because he doesn't look new. "'This must be a bed,' he said. 'I've always wanted to sleep in a bed.'" Lacking social acceptance, like Barney, but looking for a kind of perfection of himself, not in name but in physical appearance, he thinks he has found it in the bed: "'Why, here's my button!' he cried." But in his attempt to yank the button off the mattress, he loses his balance, and in his fall knocks over a floor lamp. The security guard is alerted, and Corduroy is discovered hiding beneath the sheets. In his search for a button, Corduroy has magnified the issue of his imperfection and demonstrated his clumsiness and vulnerability, but he has not solved the problem of acceptance by looking to a mattress to repair his image. Like Barney the Beard, he goes to bed because he is not pleased with how others read his appearance; and like him, he does not quite succeed in changing his looks.

Still, there are those who do. Harlequin, for example, back in his bedroom at the midpoint of *Harlequin and the Gift of Many Colors*, has an idea for a costume to wear to Carnival: he can put the scraps of clothing his friends have given him into a "beautiful rainbow-colored suit." At the last of the "middle" openings, he exclaims, "'It's finished!' He threw the covers off and jumped out of bed. 'Let me put it on!'" Clothed "in the love of his friends," Harlequin makes a new life out of "appearances" no one else wants. In *Nuits Magiques*, the six-year-old Marie-Luce loves to make up all kinds of adventures and to pretend that she is one or another "personnage habile et astucieux" (clever and astute personage). Near the book's midpoint, we see her getting ready for bed (fig. 3). She appears as a reflection in the mirror of her dresser, her naked abdomen and hips and one eye in view, her shoulders and the remainder of her face covered by her nightshirt. Behind her, we see the reflection of her bed and of a wallpaper pattern of flowers on a blue background. Perhaps as a clue to the impending problem of appearances, the pattern of flowered blue wallpaper reflected *in* the mirror lacks the diagonal green stripes or bars found on the otherwise identical wallpaper *behind* the mirror. In the next opening, which is precisely at the midpoint of the book, Marie-Luce is shown lying under the covers, with only her nose and wide-open eyes exposed. In this double-page spread, a window with gauze curtains has taken the place of the mirror as a "framed view." On the bed, Marie-Luce's cat sprawls on its back next to a pair of lace-trimmed underpants. Marie-Luce's own recitation of a poem accompanies this final moment of the *crépuscule* before she drops off to sleep; then the *nuit magique,* the dream-time, begins, involving Marie-Luce and her friend Guillaume, both under the spell of the witch Couche-Tard. Five openings later, her dream over, Marie-Luce is shown on her way to school; the arm and shoulder of the crossing guard loom onto the page from the right. The narrator tells us that "elle fait semblant d'avoir les idées bien en place et les deux pieds sur terre, c'est préférable; cependant, au fond d'elle-même, elle sait qu'elle est devenue lézarlapin" (she pretends she's got her head on

Fig 3. Marie-Luce prepares for bed. Illustration by Suzanne Duranceau from *Nuits Magiques* by Jean-Marie Poupart and Suzanne Duranceau, original edition in French. Copyright 1982 by Suzanne Duranceau. By permission of Les éditions la courte échelle, Montréal, Québec, Canada. All rights reserved.

straight and her feet on the ground: it's better that way; still, deep inside, she knows she's become a bunnylizard [the creature she had been in her dream]).

That the experience in bed has truly altered the appearance of things for Marie-Luce is borne out in the final episode, depicted in the last two openings. Marie-Luce observes to herself that the crossing guard is chomping on a carrot and wears a red plastic vest, which looks to her like a beautiful reptile skin. Cautiously she asks the crossing-guard, "'Vous aussi, vous devez être un lézarlapin?'"

En signe de connivence,
le vieux monsieur sourit.

Fig 4. On the book's final page, the crossing guard: psychopomp for Marie-Luce?
Illustration by Suzanne Duranceau from *Nuits Magiques* by Jean-Marie Poupart and
Suzanne Duranceau, original edition in French. Copyright 1982 by Suzanne Duran-
ceau. By permission of Les éditions la courte échelle, Montréal, Québec, Canada.
All rights reserved.

(You too, you must be a bunnylizard?). And in the final opening
(fig. 4), the guard faces us, one corner of his mouth slightly raised.
The narrator explains: "En signe de connivence, le vieux monsieur sourit" (As a sign of his collusion, the old gentleman smiles).
Although the reptilian appearance of the crossing guard is hardly
as threatening as it would be in the world of H. P. Lovecraft, his
strange wink at her and at the reader, seconded by the narrator's au-
thoritative pronouncement about *connivence,* shows us that Marie-

Luce has for herself and the reader altered the way things look. The picture book vouches for the reality of an imaginative perspective, to be realized at its core or center, "imbedded" between the beginning and the end.

Wherever bedroom scenes occur in picture books, they often seem to be surrounded by a circle of related dilemmas. It is easy to walk around this circle of troubles, skirting the issues. But as bedrooms are, off the page, the sites of romance and of naked truth, of origin and of destiny, of confinement as well as deliverance and escape, places for unnameable acts and actions as well as for profound writings and readings, the dramas to which bedrooms lend themselves on the page in picture books are centrally connected to the web of human concerns. In this final section, I should like to take a closer look at the way bedroom scenes in picture books raise such fundamental concerns.

Whether children learn or invent their own myths of origin, toying with the question of origins is as worthy a pursuit for them as it was for Plato. Chukovsky cites an anecdote sent to him by the mother of a five-year-old boy who, asked where he came from, pictures a "tiny, tiny room" on his mother's insides.[8] Piaget found the child's pre-occupation with "where things come from" worthy of prolonged study. In *The Child's Conception of the World* he concludes that "in all probability it is curiosity concerning birth which is the starting-point for questions of origin, so numerous between four and seven years, and in consequence the source of child artificialism [children's explanations of how various objects, including the sun and moon, are "made"]" (367). Oddly enough, Piaget does not concern himself with the context of such questions. More recently, Rose has taken up an anecdote Applebee had borrowed from Dorothy White's *Books before Five* (talk about origins!):

> c (appearing suddenly before me in the bathroom): How do you make things?
> d: What things?
> c: Babies and poems and things like that?[9]

For White, mention of the bathroom is an important part of the anecdote, but curiously, neither Applebee nor Rose offers a comment on it. For Rose, this anecdote focuses on the incongruous elements of the query, "in which the child momentarily holds in suspense its relationship to its own beginnings and to the coming of the word." Rose notes the "close link between the child's sexual curiosity and its access to language" (75).

Her emphasis on the child's momentary holding of language and origins "in suspense" echoes an emphasis (such as we might find in Proust) on the recovery of images and "unma(s)king of the logos" in the treatment of adult versions of origin. As Gaston Bachelard's testimony regarding the reverie of childhood points up, the search for "true" or nonverbal origins haunts the modern adult. What he has to say about it is strikingly pertinent:

> To meditate on the child we were, beyond all family history, after going beyond the zone of regrets, after dispersing all the mirages of nostalgia, we reach an anonymous childhood, a pure threshold of life, original life, original human life. And this life is within us—let us underline that once again—remains within us. . . . And when one has made the archetypal power of childhood come back to life through dreams, all the great archetypes of the paternal forces, maternal forces take on their action again. The father is there, also immobile. The mother is there, also immobile. Both escape time. Both live with us in another time. . . . And the archetypes will always remain origins of powerful images. [125]

Bachelard speaks for many "modern" writers (one thinks of Lewis Carroll and Noam Chomsky, of Lévi-Strauss and Lacan) whose fascination with primordial images has led them to ponder the gap between linguistic surfaces and deep generative structures. Children too must face this gap between "family history" and "original life," between the temporal language imposed by their elders and siblings and the spontaneous images that betoken the strength and perdurability of their own feelings and desires. In the bedroom scene, "original life" may be reawakened or reaffirmed in connection with new modes of self-representation.

Two of the picture books already mentioned—*Corduroy* and *50 Below Zero*—present the issue of self-representation in terms of something lost, something to be sought after in the bedroom and to be recovered either in speech or in silence. Whether looking for the missing button or the snoring father, both main characters are in search of a principal negative cause, of that which keeps Corduroy from a loving home and Jason from his rest. Both seek the cause through the medium of "bedland," and both seek to control that

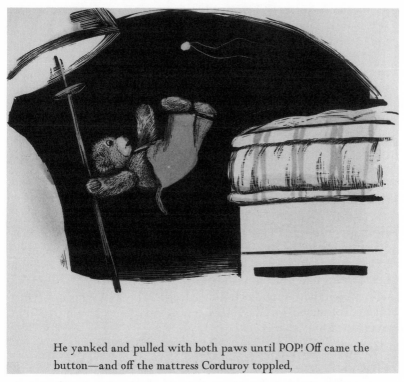

He yanked and pulled with both paws until POP! Off came the
button—and off the mattress Corduroy toppled,

Fig 5. Corduroy cannot make the mattress button his own. Illustration from *Corduroy*
by Don Freeman. Copyright © 1968 by Don Freeman. Reprinted by permission of
Viking Penguin, Inc.

cause themselves, to be the source or origin of their own destinies.
Corduroy looks for the regenerative button (a seed, albeit barren,
of his missing identity) upstairs in the department store and finds
it sewn into the mattress; although he rips it loose, he cannot make
it his (fig. 5). Jason looks first for the source of the "sound" (the
sleeper's alphabet, as it were, a destiny as well as an origin); having
found it at last (see fig. 1), he binds his father by his big toe to some
object in the kitchen. His father, looking a bit like Superman about
to fly, stands on one foot, framed (except for his extended arms
and the leg with the extended toe) by the refrigerator door. For the
first time in the book, his pajamaed figure, though presented in a
well-lit room, lacks color and line, has been drained, as it were, of

its animating juices. When Corduroy tears the button loose, he also tips over the lamp. For both, at the moment of buttoning down or unbuttoning of origins, the light changes.

At first both Jason and Corduroy are frustrated in their attempts to communicate their needs. Whereas Jason tries vainly to control his father through loud proclamations: "PAPA WAKE UP," Corduroy is simply mute, except to himself in an interior monologue. Corduroy's primary mode of self-representation at the beginning is that of speechless image, which, as we know, is diminished by its imperfection. Jason's apparent power as a speaker at the beginning is belied by the proven ineffectiveness of his commands. When Jason finally succeeds in restraining his father through physical rather than verbal means, he announces (to no one in particular, except the reader) " 'Good,' . . . 'That is the end of the sleepwalking. Now I can get to sleep.' " Like his father, he becomes mute, an attractive adult image to the mother, who will presumably reenact the cycle of attempted constraints on the unspeakable snoring of now both her husband and her son. Corduroy, on the other hand, unable to address another at the beginning except by his looks, his imperfect image, commences in the final opening what must be construed as a conversation:

"You must be a friend," said Corduroy. "I've always wanted a friend."
"Me too!" said Lisa, and gave him a big hug.

With its apotheosis of the speechless hero on top of the refrigerator-bed, *50 Below Zero* appears to privilege the silent image; *Corduroy*, on the other hand, with dialogue finally underway beneath the smallest image in the entire book (Corduroy is resting on Lisa's shoulder, and the background is entirely blanked out), seems to give the word its opportunity. In both books, the issue of self-representation, whether in word or in image, is pervasive.

A survey of other picture books will permit us to elaborate further on the network of relations surrounding the bedroom scene we have encountered in *50 Below Zero* and *Corduroy*. In *The Run, Jump, Bump Book* by Robert Brooks, Theresa's problem can be inferred at first only from such sentences as "Theresa was a city girl," because outdoor spaces (a street on Beacon Hill in Boston and a New England country house) are featured in the first two openings. Such preemptive labeling by the narrator makes the child's place seem quite natural (and to her, on the surface, it is), when it is actually a function of the economic, physical, and social constraints of big-city life. Theresa is already "bound up" in language and, as it were, intentionally misconstrued. But the language of the title has already presented the reader with an alternative, her ultimate deliverance as a running, jumping, and bumping (into Daddy) little girl in the park along the Charles River. By the third opening we are drawn further into the constrained life the so-called city girl must lead in a fourth-floor apartment. Numerous possibilities for expression seem to be excluded by this confining space: "When she was inside her apartment at the top of all those stairs she could not say, 'I think I will just step outside.' She could not just step outside." Nor, according to her mother's strictures, should she be making "outdoor noise" inside. At the middle of the book, the double-page spread of Theresa lying on her bed, her face partially reflected in a round mirror, epitomizes her predicament when the text tells us that "the floor and the bed and the little night table in Theresa's room filled up quickly. By the time she had taken out the things that she needed, there was no place left for her to move without knocking them over." The need for an opening, for deliverance, for the enactment of another kind of behavior is clear. Her room is too full. The bedroom window, in which Theresa next appears, hints at her impending re-presentation as a "nature child," as she brushes the pigeons off the sill, a noisy behavior her mother will correct.

Both her mother and father are involved in her confinement, but it is with her father that she is "reborn," against whose body she "bumps," in the Charles River park scenes near the end. David McPhail's illustrations emphasize the dreamlike quality of this experience of deliverance at the hands of the father by placing father and daughter together in bubbles (26–27) captioned by capitalized or italicized words that fit a rhyming pattern: "RUN"; "and JUMP"; "and BUMP and swing and slide and ride. . . ." And in order to remind the reader of the link through the father between the natural and cultural worlds, the narrator tells us in the penultimate opening that "Theresa and her father walked slowly toward home over the bridge. It looked as if all the stars in the sky had come down [page turn] to live in the city." In the final opening, Theresa's cat, shown earlier on her bed and on a living-room table, sits in the bedroom window, gazing out at the city lights. From the old world, ruled as it seems by her mother, in which Theresa's longings are curbed, Theresa is led to the new world by her father, where she can give expression to the urge for movement and for a kind of poetry. The father's and daughter's mutual understanding of origins is acknowledged in the image of city lights come down from heaven, an image to which the cat, an ancient fixture, bears silent witness.

A similar kind of split between old and new worlds is dramatized in *The Snowman*. In this wordless picture "album," a boy, anonymous to the reader, wakes up to the new world of snow outside. The boy's mother acts as limiting authority in the old world, which, as we soon discover in the third opening, is cyclical, marked by periods of wakening and sleep. In the new world, however, life proceeds diachronically and irreversibly; there he creates the only named part of his world, the "snowman," out of parts of his old world (hat, coals, scarf) and parts of the new. The snowman—like Theresa's father, a mediator between the two, or a "transitional object"[10]— can take him deeper into both worlds than he can take himself. With the snowman, the boy tours his own house (the site of winter confinement), demonstrates the use of television set and lamp, shows off the kitchen, then leads the snowman upstairs and into his parents' bedroom (fig. 6). There, while his parents sleep, the snowman dons the boy's father's spectacles, trousers with suspenders, and tie as well as his mother's hat. With the snowman, the boy can explore the parental bedroom, test the family car, and even try out the freezer as a bed for the snowman. With the snowman the boy can fly into a remote world of blue-green mosques, to the minarets of which are affixed crosses. Like the boy's own old world of family, this one, too, seems nameless; if it enjoys a name, the boy (and readers, too) may not know how to pronounce it. The snowman returns the boy to his old world, descending to earth like Superman. After twelve frames of slumber, the boy again seeks the snowman, who in accordance with new world rules has "passed on." Through the split between old world and new, negotiated through the bedroom, we encounter the materialization of a second self, a composite of mother and father, an origin in the blanked-out world of snow rather than the cluttered world of house, and a provisional destiny (an experimental self melts away) in the dismantled image of the snowman, presented in a small square of color (like a snapshot) on a large blank page. The snowman "goes without saying"; his life stays secret from the parents, just as their life remains enig-

Fig 6. A silent scene in the parents' bedroom. Illustrations from *The Snowman* by Raymond Briggs. Copyright 1978 by Raymond Briggs. By permission of Random House, Inc.

matic to the boy, unspeakable. The snowman "shows the way," even
to places that don't have words: what is begotten in the old world
of the parents' bedroom (the boy as observer) is reborn in the new
world of snow (boy as visionary). The boy and snowman together
afford each other new ways of looking at familiar objects such as a
freezer (bed for snowmen), ice cubes (food for snowmen), lamps,
radiators, and even Van Gogh's sunflowers (warmth that annihilates
snowmen) as well as new ways of looking at the vast snow-covered
world below. In this picture album lies not only the imaged history
of a boy's imaginative experience but its repetition in the potential versions (wordless, unspeakable, defamiliarized) of individual
readers.

   The bedroom scene, then, lends itself to the remakings and production of new meanings. In Catherine Brighton's *The Picture* or
Susi Bohdal's *The Magic Honey Jar*, illness is represented as confinement in bed. "Confinement," as we have seen, is a feature of their
old, current world. Neither heroine chooses to be sick—that is, a
captive of her old world. Once again, a framed view—a painting in
The Picture and a picture-book version of a tale from the Arabian
Nights in *The Magic Honey Jar*—offers a portal into the new. In *The
Something* by Natalie Babbitt, a hero is afraid of "something." He
has been put in a bedroom where he does not quite belong, where
he feels deeply uncomfortable. His mother persuades him to sculpt
the something that he fears, to objectify the unnameable, and thus
provides him with an outlet into a new world without fear. "Mean-
ingless clutter" is another feature of the old world in which the
hero is held captive. In Max Bolliger's *The Lonely Prince*, the hero
has been "given everything that he wanted," most of it stored in
his room, but "everything" is not enough. His darkened bedroom
is full of substitutes for what would mean most, a companion or
friend. Successive returns to the bedroom do not yield friends but
more toys and possessions, more frustration, a fullness that is empty
of meaning. Through a window of the castle he spots what he is
looking for. In his final return to an "enlightened" bedroom, he
can smile and laugh for the first time. All the bedroom activities
mentioned here constitute attempts at re-creation which lead to an
alteration of perspective, a new look.

   The bedroom may also be a place to account for the new look of
objects beyond its walls. Dinah, in *How My Library Grew by Dinah*, by
Martha Alexander, tells us the story of a library's construction and

of her writing for it. Dinah is both author and subject, from the first opening, in which she looks out the window from her bed and asks, "I wonder what all that noise is?" to the last, in which she lies in bed with a book, saying, "Listen carefully, Teddy. I'm going to read you a bedtime story. It's a special book about a Teddy Bear. . . ." It is she who presents the new library with a book called "How My Library Grew," for which she has done the pictures and her mother the text, and it is also she who shows us, as does Beckett's Molloy, how personal experience and its written documentation co-exist.

The "new look" of things in the bedroom may appear at first downright intimidating. Lester in Kay Chorao's *Lester's Overnight* and Ira in *Ira Sleeps Over* both encounter in the bedroom feelings of estrangement and lost confidence through wild images occasioned by the utterance of suggestive words. When Lester's aunt lovingly suggests that after dinner he will meet her new tiger cat, Lester declines. What he imagines and the reader sees in the illustration is a large tiger with big teeth; Lester seeks a place to hide. In *Ira Sleeps Over*, after playing "office" with Reggie, exercising his power over language with Reggie's rubber stamp collection, Ira hears Reggie's ghost story: "And every night this ghost would walk around this house and make all kinds of clunky, creaky sounds. *Aroomp! Aroomp!* Like that." The cure for the alienation and insecurity that ensues lies in the recovery of the familiar and tangible in both word and image. Realizing that Reggie has to take his teddy bear to bed gives Ira the courage to run home to "get something." His own "Tah Tah" remains nameless and invisible to Reggie, who has already fallen asleep by the time Ira returns. "Tah Tah," as his name suggests, is part of what Ira comes from, of sound patterns attempted by a preverbal child, full of personal and private meanings, now, in Reggie's bedroom, ready to go public.

Let me attempt a brief review. The main character is somehow "sent,"[11] brought before us as an actor or mime for whom the bedroom is theater. But something is wrong with this first appearance. Max is sent to bed as "the most wild thing of all"; the "city girl" is in the wrong place; Corduroy has been delivered to the store with a button missing. Some are sick in bed; some are disturbed in the night. Who put them there to be "city girl" or a "most wild thing of all"? Frequently, this sending seems like a mistake, a verbal one, a misnomer, and the fault of something in the "old world." Hostages to values not their own, trapped in circumstances they did not create, the characters, like the reader, must recover their freedom. But how? The character's mission, like Bastian's in *The Neverending Story*, is to take over the role of sender, to become an author, to rephrase, revise, or review what is given. Some of us may recall the testimonials in James Janeway's *Token for Children*: followed quickly to their deathbeds, children as young as three and four utter their last words as good news; like Mrs. Sarah Hawley (aged eight to nine), they are "full of Divine Sentences" (86). For them, confinement is the beginning of deliverance. For the picture-book character, to be in the bedroom is to be "mediated," halfway between images and words, between "nameless things" and "thingless names," between images worded and reworded, interpreted and reinterpreted, played one way and then another. In the bedroom scene the picture book celebrates origins, whether of being or naming, and a destiny of continual re-presentation.

Notes

1. Bader favors this expression (1, 359 [credited to Remy Charlip], 532). Terms or expressions like "melodrama," "dramatic flow," "sidewalk comedy," and "star of the group, its virtuoso performer" provide clues to her orientation as a reader.

2. In a remarkable memoir, Sontag records the bliss of a bedroom of her own: "If I didn't mope or sulk, it was not because I thought complaining wouldn't do any good. It was because the flip side of my discontent—what, indeed, throughout my childhood had made me so discontented—was rapture. Rapture I couldn't share. And whose volume was increasing steadily: since this last move I was having nearnightly bouts of jubilation. For in the eight houses and apartments of my life before this one I had never had a bedroom to myself. Now I had it, and without asking. A door of my own. Now I could read for hours by flashlight after being sent to bed and told to turn off the light, not inside a tent of bedclothes but outside the covers" (38).

Picture books, except for fairy-tale adaptations, about homeless children (those without a bed or bedroom of their own) are indeed scarce; the industry is hard put to accommodate characters without beds unless they are disguised as animals. If a picture book has to be taken home to be fully experienced, what is its status in the world of readers without homes? The answer lies beyond the scope of this essay, but the question places the issue of "bedroom as reading sanctuary" before us as a political and historical construct. The Children's Literature Association, recognizing the critical connection between literacy and "home," addressed the issue of homelessness in a petition drafted at its annual meeting in May 1988.

3. Bed and bedroom as "notepad" for subjective "impressions" has an impressive literary history of its own, from Jacob's pillow and Penelope's rooted rest to Freud's couch. The metonym of sheet (for bed, for writing pad) is converted to metaphor in "The Blank Page" of Isak Dinesen; likewise, "l'oreiller" as pillow and as "ear-er" takes on metaphorical significance in the opening scene of *A la recherche du temps perdu*. The snow-in-the-window convalescence and the ironing-of-the-linens-by-his-mother scenes in *Sons and Lovers* make similar gestures in this direction.

4. Or, we might say, bedroom "sweet." In Balian, the child acquires the power to transform each element of the bedroom into a sweet. This makes for a sticky repose.

5. For further discussion of line and angle in picture books, see my "Introduction to Picturebook Codes." My thanks to Jackie Eastman for her insights into the function of framing.

6. Avery cites a story remembered by Annie Keary: "Called *The Warning Clock*, it began with a picture of a little girl asleep in bed, a clock on the wall of her room, and an old nurse drawing aside the bed curtain. The child wakes and says, 'Call me again, nurse, in an hour's time, then I will get up.' Thus it goes on all day, till midnight comes. Then there was a picture of the clock pointing to twelve, in the doorway a man with a veiled face, of whom the story said that 'he would brook no delay,' and the child sitting up in bed at last, but with an expression of agony on her face" (104).

7. Eco's summary of Jakobson on the aesthetic use of language can be cited here: "For an aesthetic message to come into being, it is not enough to establish ambiguity at the level of the *content-form;* here, inside the formal symmetry of metonymic relationships, metaphorical replacements are operated, enforcing a fresh conception of the semantic system and the universe of meanings coordinated by it. But, to create an aesthetic message, there must also be alterations in the form in which it is expressed, and these alterations must be significant enough to require the addressee of the message, though aware of a change in the *content-form,* to refer back to the message itself as a physical entity. This will allow him to detect alterations in the form of expression, for there is a kind of solidarity binding together the alteration in content with any change in its mode of expression. This is the sense in which an aesthetic message becomes self-focusing; it also conveys information about its own physical make-up, and this justifies the proposition that in all art there is inseparability of form and content" (90).

8. Chukovsky reports a version of prenatal experience by Volik Schmidt at age five: "'There was a partition there . . . between her back and her tummy. . . .' 'What kind of partition?' 'The kind with a door. The door was very tiny. Yes, yes—I saw it myself when I was in your insides. And there is also a tiny, tiny room there. A little uncle lived in it when I was in your tummy'" (38).

9. Rose 74–75. Rose mistakenly attributes the anecdote to Applebee himself rather than to Dorothy White.

10. See Winnicott, especially "Playing: Creative Activity and the Search for the Self" (53–64) and "Creativity and Its Origins" (65–85).

11. For further discussion of this "actantial" function, see Greimas 129–34, 177f.

Works Cited

Alexander, Martha. *How My Library Grew by Dinah.* New York: H. W. Wilson, 1983.

Applebee, Arthur N. *The Child's Concept of Story.* Chicago: University of Chicago Press, 1978.

Avery, Gillian. *Childhood's Pattern: A Study of the Heroes and Heroines of Children's Fiction, 1770–1950.* London: Hodder and Stoughton, 1975.

Babbitt, Natalie. *The Something.* New York: Farrar, Straus & Giroux, 1970.

Bachelard, Gaston. *The Poetics of Reverie.* Trans. Daniel Russell. French original, 1960. Boston: Beacon, 1971.

Bader, Barbara. *American Picturebooks: From Noah's Ark to the Beast Within.* New York: Macmillan, 1976.

Baker, Alan. *Benjamin and the Box.* Philadelphia: J. B. Lippincott, 1977.

Balian, Lorna. *The Sweet Touch.* Nashville: Abingdon, 1976.

Bemelmans, Ludwig. *Madeline.* New York: Viking, 1937.

Bohdal, Susi. *The Magic Honey Jar.* Trans. Anthea Bell. Faellanden, Switz.: North-South, 1987.

Bolliger, Max. *The Fireflies*. Trans., adapt. Roseanna Hoover. Illus. Jiri Trnka. New York: Atheneum, 1969.

———. *The Lonely Prince*. Illus. Jürg Obrist. New York: Atheneum, 1982.

Bottner, Barbara. *There Was Nobody There*. New York: Macmillan, 1978.

Briggs, Raymond. *The Snowman*. New York: Random House, 1978.

Brighton, Catherine. *The Picture*. London: Faber & Faber, 1985.

Brooks, Robert. *The Run, Jump, Bump Book*. Illus. David McPhail. Boston: Little, Brown & Co., 1971.

Brown, Margaret Wise. *Good Night Moon*. Illus. Clement Hurd. New York: Harper and Row, 1947.

Bunting, Eve. *Barney the Beard*. Illus. Imero Gobbato. New York: Parents' Magazine Press, 1975.

Charlip, Remy, and Burton Supree. *Harlequin and the Gift of Many Colors*. New York: Parents' Magazine Press, 1973.

Chorao, Kay. *Lester's Overnight*. New York: E. P. Dutton, 1977.

Chukovsky, Kornei. *From Two to Five*. Trans. Miriam Morton. Berkeley: University of California Press, 1963.

Eco, Umberto. *The Role of the Reader*. Bloomington: Indiana University Press, 1979.

Freeman, Don. *Corduroy*. New York: Viking, 1968.

Greimas, A. J. *Sémantique structurale: Recherche de méthode*. Paris: Larousse, 1966.

Janeway, James. *A Token for Children, 1671–1672*. In *Masterworks of Children's Literature*, ed. Jonathan Cott and Francelia Butler. New York: Stonehill / Chelsea House, 1983.

Lobel, Arnold. "The List." In *Frog and Toad Together*. New York: Harper and Row, 1971.

Moebius, William. "Introduction to Picturebook Codes." *Word & Image* 2:2 (April–June 1986): 141–58.

Munsch, Robert. *50 Below Zero*. Illus. Michael Martschenko. Toronto: Annick Press, 1986.

Piaget, Jean. *The Child's Conception of the World*. 1929 in English. Trans. Joan and Andrew Tomlinson. Totowa, N.J.: Littlefield, Adams, 1960.

Poupart, Jean-Marie. *Nuits Magiques*. Illus. Suzanne Duranceau. Montreal: La courte échelle, 1982.

Rose, Jacqueline. *The Case of Peter Pan or the Impossibility of Children's Fiction*. London: Macmillan, 1984.

Sendak, Maurice. *Where the Wild Things Are*. New York: Harper and Row, 1963.

Sontag, Susan. "Pilgrimage." *The New Yorker*, 21 Dec. 1987.

Waber, Bernard. *Ira Sleeps Over*. Boston: Houghton Mifflin, 1972.

White, Dorothy. *Books before Five*. New York: Oxford University Press (for New Zealand Council for Education Research), 1954.

Winnicott, D. W. *Playing and Reality*. London: Tavistock, 1971.

Aesthetic Distancing in Ludwig Bemelmans'
Madeline

Jacqueline F. Eastman

Ludwig Bemelmans' *Madeline* (1939), a Caldecott Honor Book in the third year the award was given, has remained on the shelves for over half a century, continuing to garner new readers every year. Two years ago, Viking Penguin celebrated the book's fiftieth anniversary by issuing yet another edition, grouping a small format of *Madeline* with two of the sequels in a cardboard *Madeline's House*. Certainly the publisher's vigorous promotion of *Madeline* has contributed to the book's success, yet the pleasures of the work itself are the real justification for such marketing.[1] For a young reader, one of the most satisfying of these delights is a pervasive sense of controlled danger—a tantalizing tension between the anarchical naughtiness of a supremely vulnerable heroine on the one hand, and, on the other hand, the order and sense of aesthetic distance implicit in such elements as rhymed couplets and the recurring image of "twelve little girls in two straight lines." Madeline's central crisis is as compelling as that of many fairy tales; the climactic rush to the hospital for an emergency appendectomy embodies two of childhood's most painful and frightening possibilities—separation from loved ones and a brush with death. Furthermore, Madeline, unlike other famous picture-book protagonists, such as Peter Rabbit, and her contemporaries, Ping and Ferdinand, has no biological parent close at hand. To alleviate the anxiety of such danger and emotional isolation, to make the story comfortably exciting rather than overwhelming, Bemelmans employs a variety of visual and verbal techniques to create a subtle yet pervasive consciousness of aesthetic distance.

As Bemelmans revealed in his 1954 Caldecott acceptance speech for *Madeline's Rescue*, *Madeline's* setting, characters, and plot have roots in his personal experience. Certainly his own and his mother's familiarity with boarding schools enhanced his understanding of

Children's Literature 19, ed. Francelia Butler, Barbara Rosen, and Jean Marsden (Yale University Press, © 1991 by The Children's Literature Foundation, Inc.).

his heroine and inspired the story's most famous motif, the "two straight lines":

> [Madeline's] beginnings can be traced to stories my mother told me of her life as a little girl in the convent of Altoetting in Bavaria. I visited this convent with her and saw the little beds in straight rows, and the long table with the washbasins at which the girls had brushed their teeth. I myself, as a small boy, had been sent to a boarding school in Rothenburg. We walked through that ancient town in two straight lines. I was the smallest one, but our arrangement was reversed. I walked ahead in the first row, not on the hand of Mademoiselle Clavel at the end of the column. [256][2]

In 1938, only one year before *Madeline's* publication, during a summer sojourn on the Île d'Yeu, a chance encounter during a hospital stay after a cycling accident inspired the fuller development of both heroine and plot: "In the room across the hall was a little girl who had had an appendix operation, and, standing up in bed, with great pride she showed her scar to me" (257).[3]

In *Madeline*, Bemelmans' assimilation of Modernist aesthetic principles ultimately accounts for the highly personal, strongly patterned art generated by these personal experiences.[4] The post-Impressionist movements leading to the early-twentieth-century experiments of Picasso, the Cubists, and the Fauves turned away from mimesis and toward autonomy. The work of art now insisted upon its independence from reality, upon the validity of its own formal structures, its own patterns of shapes and colors, and its manipulation of these as a means of expressing the artist's feelings about his subject. An anecdote about Matisse sums up the attitude: "When a lady visiting his studio said, 'But surely, the arm of this woman is much too long,' the artist replied politely, 'Madame, you are mistaken. This is not a woman, this is a picture'" (quoted in Gombrich 115). A corollary of this insistence upon the separateness of art soon emerged in examinations of the ontology of reality and illusion. For instance, in the years 1912–1914, Picasso explored this issue using a variety of techniques, including collage (thereby introducing into the picture actual fragments of the "real" world) and dramatically framed pictures within pictures (Rudenstine).

Bemelmans' absorption of the lessons of Picasso's framed pictures within pictures is nowhere more apparent than in *Madeline's*

endpapers (fig. 1). Here, in fact, he inverts the traditional function
of frames, which, according to Patricia Dooley, have long been used
in children's book illustration as a means of enhancing the reality
of the book's illusions: "The pictorial tradition, that ambition to
make a window in the book, derives from the Western tradition of
the framed easel painting as a 'window in the wall.' One of the most
useful conventions for sustaining the illusion of the window in the
book, then, is that of a frame surrounding the illustration, because
it tends to associate the illustration with painting's representational
efficacy" (109). Breaking with tradition, Bemelmans no longer uses
the frame in the endpapers to reinforce the reader's belief in the
book as a "window" to reality. Instead, he uses it from the outset
to force upon the reader a consciousness of the book as illusion,
thereby establishing aesthetic distance.

Madeline's endpaper illustration presents a picture of a group of
convent-school girls and their attendant nun passing by the Place
de la Concorde; surrounding the picture is a large, slightly cock-
eyed wooden frame, which in turn is surrounded by a solid pattern
of green leaves and white doves. The imperfection of the frame,
as well as the hand-lettered, museumlike identification tag, draws
attention to the illusory nature both of the frame itself and of the
picture within. Furthermore, the green leafy margin with Chagall-
like doves suggests that the page, too, is "art"—not a real wall on
which a picture is hung, not the real world defined by its contrast
with what is within the frame. The real—the world outside of the
frame—is art; the art—the world inside of the frame—is also art.
Peggy Whalen-Levitt points to more recent artists, such as Tomi
Ungerer and Richard Egielski, who "keep us poised on the threshold between an internal and an external point of view: who draw
our attention to the act of framing itself. . . . It is as though they
want their beholders to be at least half aware of the fact that they are
having an illusion" (100). As early as 1939, Bemelmans teased the
reader with the same double vision, at once distancing us—because
it draws attention to our separation from the world of the book—
and reassuring us—because it reveals the author-illustrator's control.

The flexible symmetry which organizes this illustration of the
Place de la Concorde is the major formal principle of *Madeline*,
one important indicator that the work is illusion and not reality.
Furthermore, not only does the frequent repetition of symmetrical

Fig 1. "Place de la Concorde." Full-color wash with ink. Endpapers from *Madelin*
by Ludwig Bemelmans. Copyright © 1939 by Ludwig Bemelmans, renewed 1967 b
Madeline Bemelmans and Barbara Bemelmans Marciano. Reprinted by permissio
of the publisher, Viking Penguin, a division of Penguin Books USA Inc.

structures create the security of aesthetic distance; in and of itself the symmetry gives a controlling sense of order. In an article entitled "On the Problem of Symmetry in Art," Dagobert Frey writes that "symmetry signifies rest and binding, asymmetry motion and loosening, the one order and law, the other arbitrariness and accident, the one formal rigidity and constraint, the other life, play and freedom" (quoted in Weyl 16). Although Bemelmans presents the Place de la Concorde asymmetrically, the dominant impression before us is symmetrical. Within a large frame centering the illustration on the page, majestic buildings mirror each other on either side of the square. Centered between them, one block in the distance, is a famous church of classical symmetry, l'église de la Madeleine (whose name is the French equivalent of Madeline). Yet Bemelmans' asymmetrical treetop perspective places the central Obélisque just slightly to the right of the book's spine and shows less of the building on the right than of its mirror image on the left. Not only would a perfectly symmetrical perspective have obscured our view of the Madeleine behind the Obélisque; it would also have lacked the dynamic tension of Bemelmans' illustration.

This opposition between symmetry and asymmetry, between order and anarchy, civilization and nature energizes all of *Madeline*, at the same time that the dominance of the forces of order affords us a sense of security. The mightily glowing sun—a powerful locus of yellow which our black-and-white reproduction cannot adequately depict—suggests the unharnessed force of nature. On the other hand, the massive buildings, the perfect double-line formation of children, and the placement of trees symmetrically suggest the restraints of civilization. Furthermore, the nun, the *gendarme,* and even the tamed waters of the fountains iconographically signal the same forces of order. The word *concorde* printed on the frame's name tag subtly reminds us of peace, as do the doves in the surrounding greenery.

As he does in the endpapers, so on the opening page of *Madeline* Bemelmans creates an atmosphere of security with a centered illustration of a large, predominantly symmetrical building. Here, before formally introducing any of the characters, he presents the comfortable, harboring structure in which they dwell.[5] Five windows on the first and second floors are more or less evenly spaced from right to left, so that window number three is more or less centered; a fence of nearly equal length flanks the house on right and left. The front door, which is slightly to the right of center, almost balances a gable which is slightly to the left. Bemelmans uses the most obvious break with symmetry—a flag post and a large lamp hanging off the right side—to suggest movement in this direction—specifically, the page turn, which is further hastened by the unfinished sentence: "In an old house in Paris / that was covered with vines. . . ." The vines themselves have been planted symmetrically between the windows of the first floor but show their natural resistance to man's efforts by producing different amounts of foliage on the right and left sides. Most strikingly, the roof line and the bottom of the house do not parallel each other; the same is true of the right and left walls. Thus, the whole building, studied carefully, appears as if it might cave in or out, providing a perfect example of one *Design* critic's observation of Bemelmans' architectural illustrations: "His buildings would undoubtedly collapse if unseen carpenters weren't frantically scurrying around behind them, nailing away like mad" ("Art, as Bemelmans Sees It" 106). Bemelmans outlines the house in a light gray stroke, using curly lines for the gate and chimney smoke, shaggy lines for the vine leaves. The dominant impression is one of solidity and symmetry, but accomplished with haste, softness, and a certain precarious balance.

Bemelmans' verbal text reveals the same trademark of tension between regularity and irregularity as does his illustrative style. From the first page on, he sets up a pattern of regular verse, a symmetrical verbal structure in which one line repeats the formal aspects of the preceding line—the rhythm, the number of feet, and the vowel and final consonant of the last word. Yet he departs immediately from rhythmic regularity. Although the first two lines are predominantly anapestic,—"In an old house in Paris / that was covered with vines"—after a page turn, the sentence is completed in a line of mixed meters: "lived twelve little girls in two straight lines." Indeed, much of the fun of *Madeline* comes from the surprise of Bemelmans' ingenious rhymes and variations of rhythm. For instance, at the moment of crisis in *Madeline*, when Doctor Cohn calls the hospital, the verse jolts: "And he dialed: DANton-ten-six—'Nurse,' he said, 'it's an appendix!' " (In the Caldecott acceptance speech, Bemelmans playfully asserts that he "looked up telephone numbers to rhyme with appendix" [257]). Thus, the verse, which dictates the completion of a thought within a certain number of syllables, is both an ordering and a dynamic element. The continuous breaking of perfect metric regularity reveals the illusion, re-establishing aesthetic distance.

At the point of entering Madeline's "old house in Paris," Bemelmans again makes his readers "at least half aware of the fact that they are having an illusion" (Whalen-Levitt 100). Only this time, he neither hints that the illusion is illusion, as he did with the end-papers showing the Place de la Concorde, nor does he suggest, more traditionally, that the illusion is real. Instead, for a flicker of consciousness, he renders the real world illusory. Turning the page to find out what goes on inside "an old house in Paris," as the in-complete verse requires us to do, becomes equated with opening the front door; in other words, a book (a "real" object) becomes the "house" (an artful illusion). This momentary equation of the book with the house—solid and symmetrical but somewhat precariously balanced—in itself makes the adventure of going into the book safe, though not so safe as to be boring.

Turning the page, we find the first formal identification of the book's most often repeated image of symmetrical security: "twelve little girls in two straight lines." The image reveals twelve identi-cally dressed girls, six on each side directly opposite each other, neatly embodying the two equal halves suggested by the caesura after "girls" in the verse itself. At the outset and close of *Madeline*, Bemelmans emphasizes the double-line formation as a means of establishing order; it is the norm which contains disorder. Appear-ing first on the front cover, the endpapers, and then on page two, where the text provides the first formal introduction, the image dominates the lower two-thirds of the next three pages, accompa-nying the words which describe the end-of-the-day activities: "In two straight lines they broke their bread / and brushed their teeth / and went to bed." We find it again, reduced in size, on pages six through eleven, as this phalanx of *jeunes filles*—this *crocodile*—walks around Paris. Thus, the formation represents the security of rou-tine activities, the protection of numbers, and, like the house itself, a point both of departure and of return.

Obviously, the cost of the conformity implicit in the image of twelve nearly identical children is the repression of individuality, an individuality which peeps through asymmetrically in minor dif-ferences of hair color and style from girl to girl. As he introduces the group of unnamed children, Bemelmans comically exaggerates this stifling of personality: like a miniature Greek chorus, the twelve figures even smile, frown, and look sad in unison. Finally, how-ever, after appearing anonymously on the ten opening pages, our heroine can stand it no more. All by herself, Madeline fairly bursts forth, proudly standing on a chair—and not in a uniform, but in her underwear. Even though her relationship to the group gives her an identity ("the smallest one was Madeline") and a special place at the back of the line, her self-delight, curiosity, and energy—the anarchy of her nature—will always resist the conformity exacted by the double-line formation.

To the extent that she breaks away from the security of the "two straight lines," Madeline is at risk. On the fifth page devoted to establishing her character, she leaves the ranks and runs ahead of the other girls and Miss Clavel, who watches in horror as her charge totters on the railing of a bridge: "And nobody knew so well / how to frighten Miss Clavel." The image is remarkably like that of a Tarot deck Fool gaily walking on the edge of a precipice, suggesting Bemelmans' tapping of a universal symbol for inexperience on the verge of becoming experience. On the right-hand side of this double-page spread, following a narrative break which moves us quickly away from this dangerous sight, Miss Clavel sits up in bed, knowing that "'something is not right!'" Even though there is no causal link between Madeline's adventure on the bridge and her attack of appendicitis, the visual logic suggests that Madeline is the source of the problem: it must be she who has "fallen." On the very next page, Madeline again disrupts the symmetry of twelve little girls in two straight rows of dormitory beds by wailing in pain while the other eleven look alarmed. Uncontrolled, out of order, nature now rears a threat to Madeline's very life.

Whereas Madeline represents a tangent—a pull away from symmetry—and an energy which must be controlled, the trusted nun, Miss Clavel, embodies the predominant force of cohesiveness and centrality. Virtually omnipresent, she appears in thirty-five out of fifty-one illustrations, while Madeline herself appears only twenty-three times, eleven of them anonymously. Frequently Miss Clavel stands in the center at the back of the line or in the approximate middle of a cluster of girls, indicating by her position that she is the unifying force. Furthermore, Bemelmans' cartooned illustration for her figure heightens her resemblance to a number of symmetrical symbols of strength and security. A beneficent reminder of peace on earth, in those pictures where her short veil forms one line with her robes, her shape recalls that of the Madonna. Often—for instance, on the front cover, where she and the girls approach the Eiffel Tower, or in the endpapers, where they pass by the

Obélisque—she suggests a pillar (one is tempted to say a "pillar of strength") towering over her charges much like the Eiffel Tower or the Obélisque. On the final page, with her line-arms outstretched on either side as she prepares to draw closed the dormitory's double doors, her stance approximates the image of the cross on the wall above her head (fig. 2). Centered on the page, Miss Clavel's image suggests that, despite Madeline's disruptive absence, peace will be restored.

Inasmuch as the tension between order and anarchy persists up until the final page of the book, Miss Clavel's power to instill peace, to quell danger, cannot be absolute. Bemelmans uses her appearance as a barometer to the well-being of her charges. On the two occasions when she sits up in bed, head uncovered and wearing a white nightgown, her dramatically altered appearance indicates an unexpected vulnerability. And in the sequence of four pictures illustrating the words "And afraid of a disaster / Miss Clavel ran fast / and faster," she brings to mind a toppling tower, as in each successive picture the angle of her body to the floor narrows, signaling an imminent catastrophe.

As Bemelmans presents the drama of pain and separation which forms the emotional core of the book, his insistence on the illusion of his art holds his young reader at a safe distance. Madeline's departure in an ambulance from the safety of her house forms the story's climax: "In a car with a red light / they drove out into the night." The resolution follows immediately on the right-hand side of this same double-page spread: "Madeline woke up two hours / later, in a room with flowers." The choppiness of this verse momentarily arrests our attention, subtly drawing us away from the story. Bemelmans' sudden switch to full color in this spread after the yellow wash of the immediately preceding pages not only signals the arbitrariness of his means of representation but also reassures us of a positive resolution even before we read the words; for we see at once that from left to right the setting changes dramatically from night to day, from dark to light. The asymmetrical composition of the Eiffel Tower and other buildings on the left signals the danger of the moment, whereas the near-perfect centering of a pot of flowers on the right suggests the restoration of safety and order. The illustrations for both climax and resolution are markedly non-mimetic: the surface of the picture on the left is covered with urgent scratch lines having no atmospheric explanation; the flowers on the

"Good night, little girls!
Thank the lord you are well!
And now go to sleep!"
said Miss Clavel.

And she turned out the light—
and closed the door—
and that's all there is—
there isn't any more.

Fig 2. "'Good night, little girls!'" Yellow wash with ink. From *Madeline* by Ludwig Bemelmans.

right appear to be half in and half out of a window. Finally, Bemelmans' sudden shift from the relatively distant perspective of an ambulance riding through the streets of Paris to Madeline's close-up view of the flowers at her bedside makes us forget that we have been spared the frightening sight of the appendectomy.

Madeline's hospital stay disrupts the near-perfect symmetry of the story's structure, for, while the story itself returns to the "old house in Paris," our heroine does not. By her very absence, Madeline manages to cause a second crisis as well; for this time, the words "They went home and broke their bread / brushed their teeth / and went to bed" are ironically accompanied by pictures in which eleven jealous little girls, though in their assigned spots at the table, at the washbasins, and in the dormitory, glumly refuse to eat, brush their teeth, or go to sleep.[6] The asymmetry caused by the missing child in the previously established image of "twelve little girls in two straight lines" indicates the problem: anarchy is contagious when it brings not only a remarkable scar, but also "toys and candy / and the dollhouse from Papa." Bemelmans' repetition of his bouncy formula— "They went home and broke their bread / brushed their teeth / and went to bed"—even though the little girls are patently *not* performing their routine activities, causes us to attend to the verbal text, seeing it all the more clearly as a rhythmic pattern of words rather than the language of "real" speech.

The same mixing of illusion and reality, of house and book, which marks the opening of *Madeline* recurs as the story closes. Here, the words read "'Good night, little girls! / Thank the lord you are well! / And now go to sleep!' / said Miss Clavel. / And she turned out the light— / and closed the door— / and that's all there is— / there isn't any more." The illustration shows Miss Clavel standing in the doorway, hands outstretched and ready to bring the double doors shut behind her as soon as she finishes speaking. At this point, the action of closing the door suggests that of closing the book; by extension, the child reader, like the eleven little girls, is encouraged to go to sleep. The author's voice visibly disappears as the print size diminishes through each of the last four lines, momentarily drawing our attention to the arbitrary and malleable nature of this means of representation. Assuring us that "there isn't any more," the narrator emphasizes that Madeline's world has been, after all, only a story.

Although the sense of security provided by the symmetrical structures and by the playfully asserted aesthetic distance cannot provide the warm closeness we associate with the more traditional family setting, they nevertheless provide a safety net for our boarding school heroine. The "dollhouse from Papa" provides our only tantalizing glimpse of a biological father—and embodies a value that permeates the book: the structure stands for the absent parent.[7] The controlled encounter *Madeline* offers a child reader with real fears—separation and death—is one compelling explanation for the book's continuing popularity. In an era when a plethora of "how not to be afraid of the hospital" books flood the market, *Madeline* offers the real thing—a fictional experience with danger through which the young reader can successfully overcome the obstacles while maintaining her distance.

Notes

1. After the war, Bemelmans resumed the *Madeline* series in 1953 with *Madeline's Rescue*, which won the 1954 Caldecott Award. This was followed quickly by *Madeline and the Bad Hat* in 1956, *Madeline and the Gypsies* in 1959, and *Madeline in London* in 1961. Viking published the *Madeline* sequels, and in 1958 bought the rights from Simon & Schuster to the original *Madeline*. *Madeline's Christmas*, which Viking Penguin brought out in 1985, was originally a small self-covered book insert in the 1956 *McCall's* Christmas issue, and was rewritten and redesigned for the 1985 publication. Viking Penguin also brought out the *Madeline* Pop-Up in 1987 and *Madeline's House* in 1989. For Neiman-Marcus, Bemelmans did *Madeline's Christmas in Texas*, another small format book, in 1955. The work, consisting of a single signature fold with a stiff paper cover, was probably a department store giveaway; the inside front cover reads, "This book is a christmas [sic] gift to you from Neiman-Marcus."

2. Although he makes no mention of the fact in his Caldecott acceptance speech, *Madeline* is not the first children's book in which Bemelmans introduced a redheaded "Madeleine" (French spelling) while depicting convent school life. In one chapter of *The Golden Basket* (1936), his Newbery Honor Award winner, Bemelmans permits us a brief glimpse of the students of the Sacred Heart in Bruges. Just as Madeline lives in "an old house in Paris," these students live in a "great square white house" (53) at the edge of the canal. Twelve of them walk about the city in pairs with their "lovely, tall, and never severe Madame Severine" (51)—the fictional predecessor of Miss Clavel. And at the back of the line walks Madeline's prototype: "The name of the smallest girl is Madeleine. Her hair is copper-red" (51).

3. Curiously, May Massee of Viking Press, who "discovered" Bemelmans and published his first four books, beginning with *Hansi* in 1934, turned *Madeline* down. Perhaps this was the kernel of truth in Bemelmans' own exaggerated statement about the length of time it took him to get *Madeline* published. At the time of his death, *Newsweek* quoted Bemelmans as declaring, "'Nobody wanted to publish it. . . . They said it was too sophisticated for children. . . . But finally Simon and Schuster took it, after it had been sitting in a drawer for five years'" ("Madeline's Master"). The five-year delay, which has been published in the *Dictionary of Literary Biography* as factual (and which I have cited elsewhere), is doubtless what Mrs. Bemelmans has called in a letter to me a "gross exaggeration" (July 1988). In the same letter,

Madeline Bemelmans writes, "After May Massee of the Viking Press . . . turned down *Madeline*, he took it to Simon and Schuster, where it was promptly accepted." In a more recent letter (Jan. 1990), Mrs. Bemelmans' positive statement that "the sojourn on the Île d'Yeu was *definitely* during the *summer of 1938*" further corroborates her earlier assertion, inasmuch as Bemelmans' hospital stay occurred during this sojourn and *Madeline* was published only the next year, in 1939. Bemelmans' habit of blending "fact and fiction," as Mrs. Bemelmans has stated, "not for purposes of deception but to make a good story" (letter, July 1988), makes one cautious in asserting biographical certainties.

4. Bemelmans' formal art instruction was limited. At some time during the first two years after he had emigrated to America, he studied in Greenwich Village with someone whom he identifies as "Thaddeus." Although the experience taught him "to see," he could not commit his vision to paper: "The moment I started to draw, a paralysis overcame me." Thaddeus, understanding Bemelmans' fear, assured him that confidence would come in time: "'I can't help you much, nobody can. The colors, the design, the line, are all your own, you yourself must get them out'" ("Art Class" 66). Of this experience, Madeleine Bemelmans observes: "The time spent with Thaddeus could not be considered formal art training, since Ludwig merely studied the model but did not draw" (letter, July 1988). In the same letter, in response to my question, "Did he express particular admiration for any post-Impressionists or Modernists?", Madeleine Bemelmans observes that her husband "admired Paul Klee, Georges Braque, Vlaminck, and many other artists." In Klee, Bemelmans doubtless appreciated a kindred whimsical spirit. The influence of Cubism, of which Braque was a principal practitioner is apparent in *Madeline* in Bemelmans' use of multiple perspectives, a technique which is particularly evident in the scenes of "two straight lines" at the table, at the washbasins, and in the dormitory. Finally, as Lyn Ellen Lacy has pointed out in *Art and Design in Children's Picture Books*, one sees the influence of Vlaminck and Derain, both Expressionists, in Bemelmans' use of intense color in such scenes as the near-drowning sequence in *Madeline's Rescue* (99). Despite these similarities between Bemelmans' work and that of each of these artists, his color washes, exuberant calligraphic line and overall decorative quality in the *Madeline* books are most reminiscent of the style of Raoul Dufy (1877–1953). Bemelmans apparently admired Dufy, for in May 1962 (not long before Bemelmans' death), *Time* magazine noted that he had a work by this artist in his bedroom. The same writer referred to Bemelmans' "distinctively daffy-Dufy style" in his recently published work for adults, *On Board Noah's Ark*. ("Buoyant Return"). For all the Modernists, of course, a fundamental aesthetic principle is a belief in art's validity without reference to the "perfection" of its mimesis.

5. Bemelmans assigns a high comfort value to houses in all his fiction. In his first book, *Hansi* (1934), the endpapers present a large-scale schematic cutaway of each room of the house of Hansi's uncle Herman, and Bemelmans names his next three works after the structures in which they primarily take place: *The Golden Basket* (1936), a hotel in Bruges; *The Castle Number Nine* (1937), a castle with this fanciful address; and *The Quito Express* (1938), a train which is baby Pedro's moving home until he returns to his family. *Sunshine: A Story about the City of New York* (1950), deals with a New York housing shortage, and *The High World* (1954) concerns the threats to the home of a Tyrolean mountaineer. *Welcome Home!* (1960), after a poem by Beverley Bogert, delights in the return of clever daddy fox to his cozy hut, where a loving wife and children pamper him after the annual hunt.

6. In the image accompanying "They went home and broke their bread" at the end of *Madeline*, Bemelmans does not count correctly. There should be only eleven little girls in this picture, Madeline being in the hospital, but Bemelmans has drawn twelve. In a recent French edition, a twelfth little girl has been removed, although

apparently technical considerations prevented the removal of the one who stands in Madeline's place. (Paris: *lutin poche de l'école des loisirs*, 1985, 40).

7. In two of the books preceding *Madeline*, Bemelmans focuses on the child outside of the traditional two-parent family. Hansi lives with his mother alone, while Celeste and Melisande of *The Golden Basket* travel with their father. In both cases, the absence of the other parent is never explained. Perhaps this reflects Bemelmans' own upbringing: his father ran away with his governess, and young Ludwig was raised by his mother and his maternal grandfather. After doing badly in more than one scholastic setting, he was sent to work with an uncle in the hotel business. Finally, in 1914, at age sixteen, he emigrated to America.

Works Cited

"Art, as Bemelmans Sees It." *Design* (Jan.–Feb. 1962): 106–08.

Bemelmans, Ludwig. "And So Madeline Was Born." 1954 Caldecott Award Acceptance Paper. In *Caldecott Medal Books, 1938–1957, with the Artist's Acceptance Papers and Related Material Chiefly from the Horn Book Magazine*, Horn Book Papers, vol. 2, ed. Bertha Mahony Miller and Elinor Whitney Field. Boston: Horn Book, 1957. 254–65.

———. "Art Class." In *Tell Them It Was Wonderful: Selected Writings by Ludwig Bemelmans*, ed. and intro. Madeleine Bemelmans; foreword Norman Cousins. New York: Viking, 1985.

———. *The Golden Basket*. New York: Viking, 1936.

———. *Hansi*. 1934. Reprint. New York: Viking, 1962.

———. *Madeleine*. Paris: *lutin poche de l'école des loisirs*, 1985.

———. *Madeline*. 1939. Reprint. New York: New Viking Ed., 1960.

Bemelmans, Madeleine. Letter to the author. 31 July 1988.

———. Letter to the author. 26 Jan. 1990.

"Buoyant Return." *Time*, 21 May 1962: 98.

Dooley, Patricia. "The Window in the Book: Conventions in the Illustration of Children's Books." *Wilson Library Bulletin* 55:2 (Oct. 1980): 108–12.

Gombrich, E. H. *Art and Illusion: A Study in the Psychology of Pictorial Representation*. 2d rev. ed. 1961. Princeton: Princeton University Press, 1961.

Lacy, Lyn Ellen. *Art and Design in Children's Picture Books: An Analysis of Caldecott Award-Winning Illustrations*. Chicago: American Library Association, 1986.

"Madeline's Master." *Newsweek*, 15 Oct. 1962: 115.

Rudenstine, Angelica Zander, with contributions by Emily Rauh Pulitzer and Joseph Pulitzer, Jr. "Pablo Ruiz Picasso: *Verre et bouteille de Bass*." Vol. 4 of *Modern Painting, Drawing and Sculpture Collected by Emily and Joseph Pulitzer, Jr*. Cambridge: Harvard University Art Museums, 1988. 809–15.

Weyl, Hermann. *Symmetry*. Princeton: Princeton University Press, 1952.

Whalen-Levitt, Peggy. "Breaking Frame: Bordering on Illusion." *School Library Journal* 32:7 (March 1986): 100–03.

The Illustrator as Interpreter: N. C. Wyeth's Illustrations for the Adventure Novels of Robert Louis Stevenson

Susan R. Gannon

Castles, sailing ships, a pirate cave; tall, big-boned figures caught in mid-gesture; and all the swords, boots, swirling cloaks, and flintlock pistols a romantic could wish—dramatically lit and freely painted. The illustrations for Stevenson's adventure novels in Scribner's Illustrated Classics series are obviously N. C. Wyeth's. But though all Wyeth's pictures share a family resemblance, each sequence of illustrations also renders a markedly personal reading of a single novel and has its own mood, tone, palette, and recurrent images. Wyeth's pictures, like all good illustrations, create for each novel a rich and rhetorically powerful narrative sequence well able to modify a reader's experience in significant ways; for, if narrativity is "the process by which a perceiver actively constructs a story from the fictional data provided by any narrative medium," it is clear that the reader's own active narrativity is susceptible to the powerful impact of an illustrator's vision as he or she works on the cues provided in the discourse "to complete the process that will achieve a story" (Scholes 60).

Stevenson himself appreciated this, commenting approvingly of a set of illustrations that its "designer also has lain down and dreamed a dream, as literal, as quaint, and almost as apposite as . . . [the author's]; and text and picture make but the two sides of the same homespun but impassioned story" ("Bagster's Pilgrim's Progress" 296). And Stevenson's discussion of those illustrations goes on to trace the interactions between text and picture as they might be experienced by a perceptive reader. Following Stevenson's lead, I would like to examine some of the choices Wyeth made in illustrating Stevenson's novels—choices which can shape a reader's experience of a novel in significant ways—and then to offer a reading of the way Wyeth's illustrations for *Treasure Island* (arguably his best) work together in sequence to interpret that text.

Children's Literature 19, ed. Francelia Butler, Barbara Rosen, and Jean Marsden (Yale University Press, © 1991 by The Children's Literature Foundation, Inc.).

N. C. Wyeth illustrated four of Stevenson's adventure novels for Scribner's Illustrated Classics Series: *Treasure Island* (1911), *Kidnapped* (1913), *The Black Arrow: A Tale of the Two Roses* (1916), and *David Balfour* (1941). Wyeth's illustrations for each of these novels set up an immediate field of reference for the reader, enacting and embodying the story like a play or a film in specific visual terms. When the details of a verbal description are turned into visual images they become more precise and limited. A hat or coat must be cut a certain way; a human figure must be of a certain height and build; a house must have specific architectural features. Each choice which "places" details for the reader both limits and—paradoxically—offers a potential enrichment of the reading experience as the illustrator puts his own complex experience of the text at the reader's service.

One of the most important choices an illustrator can make is the selection of scenes to be shown. All of Wyeth's pictures accent thematic and structural development in the novels, but in the design of an illustrated book there are some illustrations which hold positions of special rhetorical force. In illustrating Stevenson's novels for the Illustrated Classics Series, Wyeth used cover, endpapers, and title page to make a strong thematic statement and set the tone for his whole interpretive reading of each novel. The cover of *Kidnapped* shows young David Balfour apparently stranded on the "island" of Earraid, unaware that he will be able to walk to freedom when the tide goes out. The cover of *David Balfour*, Stevenson's sequel to *Kidnapped*, dramatizes an important thematic difference between the novels. Highlighting the older David's inability to make any decisive moves for himself, it shows him bound hand and foot and carefully guarded, a real prisoner on a real island.

Wyeth also used endpapers to sum up the conflict in a book. In *Treasure Island* and in *The Black Arrow*, novels filled with violent contention for power and wealth, brutal pirates and members of an outlaw band stride purposefully across these pages, whereas the endpapers in *David Balfour* depict the Bass—the rocky islet on which David is helplessly imprisoned during much of the action. The title page sketches for both of the David Balfour novels metaphorically express the central concerns of the books. In each case the figure of David is more clearly realized and substantial than the shadowy and rather fantastic background, suggesting that the picture really shows what is on his mind. On the title page of *Kid-*

napped a thoughtful David contemplates a dreamlike rendition of the House of Shaws; in the title sketch for *David Balfour*, a shadowy gibbet with its swinging noose looms over the frightened boy. Wyeth draws attention to the terrible dilemmas David faces. In the first book he must risk enslavement and death in order to claim his inheritance; in the second, if he offers the testimony needed to clear an innocent man of murder, he risks the gallows himself. Wyeth's cover and endpapers for *David Balfour* pinpoint at once the conflict between freedom and bondage, between action and passive acceptance of the status quo, which will dominate the story.

The illustrations for a book, by epitomizing the plot, can often serve as a sort of trailer for it, much like the "previews of coming attractions" familiar to us from the movies. Wyeth thought "a person should be able to walk into the book store and just thumb through a book and get the idea of the story by the drama of the illustrations—very quickly" (*An American Vision* 80). His pictures represent carefully chosen moments more or less evenly spaced throughout the story and so arranged as to provide not only a sense of the story's continuity, its drama and emotional force, but to complement each other aesthetically, offering contrast and comparison in subject matter, coloring, and design.

Andrew Wyeth has described his father's way of setting about deciding which moments in a novel to foreground for the reader: "after initially reading the story, especially if it was a good yarn, Pa would reread it carefully and underline the passages that he felt were the essence of the story" (*An American Vision* 80). When he looked for moments which would show "the essence" of a story, Wyeth sometimes chose obvious moments of crisis or decision—Jim Hawkins's confrontation of Israel Hands in *Treasure Island* is a good example. But sometimes he chose a moment which would capture his idea of a character (Ebenezer Balfour in *Kidnapped* crouched over his porridge, plotting murder) or a relationship (Silver in *Treasure Island* leading Jim Hawkins on a leash) or a situation (Dick Shelton and Joan Sedley in *The Black Arrow* at bay in the forest). In Stevenson, Wyeth was working with a writer who had a marvelous ability to paint vivid and succinct word pictures of people and places, an artist with a knack for setting up important scenes in a very dramatic way. Yet often Wyeth would avoid the very scenes Stevenson made most striking. In explaining to his son why he chose to illustrate a scene an author had not described very fully, Wyeth once said: "'Why take a dramatic episode that is described in every detail and redo it? Instead I create something that will *add* to the story'" (*An American Vision* 80).

That something is often a symbol of the whole as much as a simple image of one small part. Wyeth ignores the famous scene from *Kidnapped* in which David climbs the unfinished staircase at Shaws only to find himself poised on the brink of an abyss; instead, he settles on a less obvious scene which serves as an even better visual emblem of the entire situation in which David has been caught. The illustrator shows the boy stranded on a rock in the middle of a dangerous current, unable to move forward or backward until Alan Breck forces him to take a blind leap to safety. Wyeth focuses attention here on a moment of choice involving that combination of trust and daring which will be vital to David's ultimate salvation.

Highlighting two scenes which might easily have been passed over by the reader of *Treasure Island*, Wyeth uses them to symbolize the complex relationship between Jim Hawkins and Long John Silver. The first picture of the two together shows Silver as an amiable substitute father; the second reveals him to be a cruel bully. And the self-defeating confusion which prevents Dick Shelton in *The Black Arrow* from knowing who his real friends are is brilliantly captured in Wyeth's picture of him knee-deep in an icy sea, fighting his own potential ally Lord Foxham on so dark and snowy a night that neither of them can really see the other.

In most cases when Wyeth departs from Stevenson's text, it is because he is deliberately adding or omitting details for artistic and interpretive reasons of his own. Often Wyeth extends Stevenson's narrative, picking up some symbolic touch and giving it a clear visual reference which Stevenson never supplied. He captures very well Stevenson's intent to supply his hero with a series of "doubles" in *The Black Arrow*, older men who represent in various ways the kind of person Dick Shelton might grow up to be. Dick is given a vividly recognizable appearance. He is a tall, well-built boy with dark hair, an oval face, a strong profile, and straight brows that meet across his nose. As Dick Shelton and the outlaw appropriately named Lawless prowl stealthily through the snow toward Lawless's lair, they look almost like identical twins. The young Richard III who appears in the book seems older in the illustrations than he is said to be, resembling more the traditional image from historical portraits, but there is a speaking family resemblance between the infamous king and Dick—the same straight browline and profile; in his effort to create this effect, Wyeth even minimizes Richard's "crookback" so that it is hardly noticeable. Further, in the final illustration, depicting the last scene in the book, the scowling and dour Ellis Duckworth (the Robin Hood figure in the novel) who bids farewell to Dick is dressed exactly like him and could be the boy's older brother.

Wyeth uses his own recognition of an elaborately coded world to place the details of each Stevenson story firmly in a social and historical context. His use of physical types which have come to be associated in our culture with certain values is an important part of his rhetorical strategy. The brutal, battered-looking pirates who stride across the endpapers of *Treasure Island* announce their ruthlessness in their very physical presence. The wiry, lithe Alan Breck who fights best when cornered has a distinctly rodent-like grin as he battles the invaders of the roundhouse in *David Balfour*. His face tells you something of his mindset. Wyeth makes David Balfour a handsome, brawny boy, whose burly shoulders and well-developed, muscular arms and legs seem too powerful for his sensitive and almost girlish face. The artist adds a certain charm to this character, conveying David's boyish clumsiness as he sits awkwardly in a delicate Queen Anne chair in a fussy and crowded lawyer's office. The posture of the boy suggests strongly his sense of being not only a dirty and ragged stranger in this respectable place but also something of a young bull in the china shop.

If bodies have a language, then so do the shadows they cast; indeed, the human shadow has a rich and highly conventionalized set of meanings in art and literature, and Wyeth often uses it to symbolize a character's inner nature. Thus, Ebenezer Balfour's shadow looms ominously on the wall behind him as he eats his porridge and plots to murder his nephew, and Alan Breck's dances, twice his size, on the walls and ceiling of the roundhouse as he gamely fights off a pack of sailors aboard *The Covenant*. Sometimes a person's shadow is thrown before him, portending the ill effects of his actions, as in the case of the pirate Billy Bones on the cliffside, and sometimes a figure is surrounded by shadows which suggest an atmosphere of all-encompassing evil, as in the treasure cave scene in *Treasure Island*.

Wyeth gives his Stevenson characters eloquent body language, often presenting them in the act of making slightly exaggerated gestures which "mime" their intent. This slight exaggeration draws attention to the gesture and creates a certain fictionality about it—puts it in quotation marks, so to speak. Figures gesturing like this rely for some of their impact on arousing a kinesthetic response in the viewer like that evoked by Marcel Marceau "walking against the wind." Thus Dick Shelton and his henchman, Lawless, prowl through a snowy forest, bent forward intently, miming "stealth" with every muscle. Wyeth prided himself on his ability to convey this sort of effect, claiming that his early work on a farm had given him an "acute sense of the muscle strain . . . the feel . . . the protective bend of head and squint of eye that each pose involves." In fact he complained that "after painting action scenes I have ached for hours because of having put myself in the other fellow's shoes as I realized him on canvas" (quoted in Wyeth 6). That Stevenson shared Wyeth's appreciation of this particular effect is evidenced in his admiration for an illustrator's depiction of Bunyan's "Christian, posting through the plain, terror and speed in every muscle" and Mercy eager to go her journey with "every line" of her "figure yearning" ("Bagster's Pilgrim's Progress" 300).

There is, of course, a veritable lexicon of body language which can be called upon in drama, fiction, and illustration, so sometimes Wyeth need only quote from an already coded social text to make his point. A bereft mother in *Treasure Island* hides her face in her apron, and a conventionalized message is conveyed immediately about her social class, her powerlessness, her maternal feeling. When one of the Black Arrow's band climbs a tree to get the lay of the land his costume makes a silent allusion to Howard Pyle's illustrations for Robin Hood, while his brow-shading hand evokes "sailor searching the horizon" in a gesture at once conventional and mimelike.

Stevenson is famous for his use not only of gesture but of costumes and props to suggest aspects of character, and Wyeth follows him closely here. "Character," Stevenson once said, "to the boy is a sealed book; for him, a pirate is a beard, a pair of wide trousers, and a liberal complement of pistols" (*Essays* 261). He signals the outlaw status and desperate situation of Alan and Davie in *Kidnapped* by the increasingly wretched state of their clothes. Wyeth carefully shows the two declining into raggedness, picture by picture, until David suddenly springs forth in the final illustration in a fine brown suit, carrying a fashionable cane (not mentioned by

Stevenson). The differing lots of the young gentleman and the man with a price on his head are brilliantly summed up by the contrast in their appearance in this last picture.

One of Wyeth's trademarks as an illustrator is his fondness for depicting actions caught in mid-movement. Catriona's skirts billow out around her as she leaps from one ship to another; an inn sign just nicked by a sword blow swings violently from the impact; a sturdy inn table is shown tipping over and spilling its burden of pewterware. Though he is working in a static medium, Wyeth creates the illusion that each scene represents part of a rapid, almost headlong sequence of action. In doing so, he well reflects the speed and action of Stevenson's narrative, and he captures an effect Stevenson himself admired in another illustrator whose pictures he felt captured an author's "breathing hurry and momentary inspiration" ("Bagster's Pilgrim's Progress" 304).

It is not just choice of subject that determines Wyeth's interpretation of a particular novel but also choices of color, design, light, and shade. Wyeth's artistic choices operate as an effective visual rhetoric, creating pictures the viewer can "read." Each of his sets of illustrations has its own palette. The Balfour novels are set in a world of soft blues, greens, and silver-grays. The pictures for *The Black Arrow* suggest medieval illuminations in their clear colors and decorative detail, though a number of the scenes are dark and somber in tone: two young people drink from a forest pool under the stars; armed men struggle desperately in snowy battle scenes; a wounded spearman returns home just before dawn. Wyeth's *Treasure Island* is a place of harsh tropical sun and dark shadows, highly theatrical in the posing and lighting of the major scenes. The sunlight is dazzling as Jim leaves his seaside home for a shadowy world where good and evil will be strangely mixed. The shocking difference between two ways of life is symbolized by the arresting blocks of sharp and uncompromising light and shade in this picture. The same effect is repeated in one of the last pictures for the novel as Jim is marched from the bright cliffside into blue shadows by John Silver. In another picture, harsh yellow light from an oil lamp pours down on the cabin where the brutal Israel Hands struggles with his shipmate O'Brien, turning everything in the room flat brown and gold. And as Jim looks through a loophole in the stockade wall he sees a group of pirates crouched in a semicircle lit luridly from below by torchlight. In the final scene, a masterpiece of artistic restraint, Jim kneels in a fairy-tale cavern all in sepia tones, where the only bright spots are the glittering gold coins that seem dimly to illuminate the cave.

For Stevenson it is "the triumph of romantic storytelling" when the reader consciously plays at being the hero: "Then we forget the characters; then we push the hero aside; then we plunge into the tale in our own person and bathe in fresh experience; and then, and then only do we say we have been reading a romance" (*Essays* 231). Wyeth's use of perspective cleverly conveys the feel of Stevenson's narrative method. Over-the-shoulder views in which we see "with" the protagonist, who is placed in the foreground as an observer of action rather than a participant, are common in the pictures for those novels which are narrated in the first person. When David Balfour bids farewell to his old teacher, his back is to the viewer, and over his shoulder we see the old man and the landscape David must leave. Another device for emphasizing the first-person perspective is the presentation of a scene from an unusual angle distinctively identified with the narrator in the text. When David lies in bed, looking up at Alan and Cluny playing cards, the illustrator shows us the scene from a low angle, as David would have seen it; and when Jim Hawkins peeps through a cabin window or a chink in the stockade wall, we see what he sees.

The structural design of Wyeth's illustrations often underscores their meaning. When Catriona leaps dramatically from boat to boat in a rough sea, she falls right into David Balfour's outstretched arms. In this picture, his arms and her billowing petticoats form a small but attention-getting circle in a picture full of strong, thrusting diagonals. The completion of the circle also works well to suggest that David and Catriona, who in many ways represent different but necessary aspects of a single personality, belong together and cannot be "whole" unless each has what the other can give.

Color, lighting, and design are all used by Wyeth to convey his own reading of a scene in his portrait of Lord Prestongrange in *David Balfour*. The picture illustrating David's confrontation by the powerful Lord Advocate of Scotland shows them meeting in a darkened room. The tall figure of Prestongrange, looming in the darkness, dominates the scene. The shape of his elongated figure is echoed in the two candles he has lit—which give off a dazzling light—and in the wine decanter, glass, and candle snuffer on the table before him. One fist is on the table, knuckles down; and in the other hand, the taper he used to light the candle points down and toward the viewer. There is a dark shadowy area to the right of him, and the paneling behind him forms a large cross—suggesting again the gibbet, but also, perhaps, David's willingness to sacrifice himself for his friends. The picture dramatizes forcefully the emotional effect of interrogation by a judge whose power to condemn or free his prisoner is absolute, and Wyeth cleverly puts the viewer in the position of the prisoner.

Each set of illustrations Wyeth did for a Stevenson novel constitutes a highly personal reading of the written text, often accenting the undertones of tragic conflict which appealed to the artist. His pictures for *The Black Arrow* capture Stevenson's lightly satiric treatment of knighthood but also stress a darker suggestion that, in the corrupt world of this novel at least, the possibility of heroic action is no longer available.

Those of Stevenson's stories which are told in the first person by a mature narrator who explains both how he felt at the time of his adventures and what they mean to him now offer a special challenge to the illustrator. The ironic perspective the mature David Balfour can give to the story he relates in *Kidnapped* is rarely felt in the illustrations, which show us David as victim or—at best—survivor rather than as the foolish, stubborn prig the narrator feels himself to have been. Wyeth's pictures emphasize external events, dominated by the figures of energy and menace which seem so often to threaten David. But the essence of Stevenson's story, David's awkward, moment-to-moment struggle to appreciate and assimilate the virtues of his alter ego, Alan Breck, in order to become a more complete human being, cannot effectively be dramatized in fourteen pictures, though it is emblematized in several of them. Similarly, the pictures for the sequel, *David Balfour*, project effectively David's inability to act and the consequent aura of guilt which hangs about him, but the social comedy of Stevenson's story and the pained irony of the narrative voice are again missing.

Wyeth's pictures for *Treasure Island*, on the other hand, convey wonderfully well the intriguing doubleness of that novel, which from one perspective seems like a stirring adventure story; from another, something of a tragedy. Without ever picturing Stevenson's mature narrator, Wyeth has managed to create a parallel narrative to Stevenson's which stresses the difference between the way the story was experienced by its focal character and the way the teller understands it, now that he is older and wiser. But only a more detailed examination can do justice to the way Wyeth manages, in a brilliantly structured sequence of pictures, continually to remind the reader of the shadow side of young Jim Hawkins's blindness to the future without downplaying in the least the glamor and sheer romantic appeal of his adventures.

Wyeth's choice of moments to illustrate in *Treasure Island* is as carefully calculated as Stevenson's own choice of scenes to narrate in detail. His pictures are deliberately arranged so that the meaning of each picture is related both to the pictures that surround it and to the text in which it is set. The cover illustration showing three pirates raising the Jolly Roger does not correspond to any particular scene in the novel but offers a generic reference to that grim moment in any pirate saga when the buccaneers run up their colors in preparation for an attack. Thus the pirates appear to prepare an attack on the cover, sweep down the beach on the endpapers, and pause guiltily on the title page, reflecting on the price they are likely to pay for their crimes as they bury their treasure.

Stevenson divided his story into significant parts, each of which is carefully subtitled and develops a particular phase of the action. Wyeth takes advantage of the way Stevenson sets his story up, arranging his illustrations so that those grouped together play off one another effectively. In the pictures for the opening sequence of the story, called "The Old Buccaneer," Bill Bones stands lookout in the first illustration and lunges out of a darkened doorway in the second; then Blind Pew moves menacingly toward the viewer in the third, tapping his way with a stick that sweeps dangerously across the road. These images, full of energy and menace, suggest strongly that the springs of action in this story lie with the pirates.

The details Wyeth has added to Stevenson's narrative at every turn magnify the impressiveness of the pirates. In the first illustration, Bones is posed like a monumental statue on a cliff, seen from below. His stance, his billowing cloak, and his telescope held like a weapon make him at once the archetypal seaman on the lookout and a commanding figure—much more imposing than the sick old pirate of Stevenson's story. The figure of Blind Pew is never very clearly described by Stevenson, but Wyeth has given him the face of a death's head, with broken teeth. And the fingers of his outstretched hand, which claw at the air in a threatening gesture, are echoed in the thrusting tree branches of the wintry scene and especially in the shadows of those branches which lie across Pew's path. The effect is thoroughly chilling.

The pictures for the second segment of Stevenson's story, "The Sea Cook," are more static, more emblematic. In the first, Jim Hawkins says goodbye "to Mother and the cove" (57). In the next, Jim enjoys a quiet moment in the galley of the Hispaniola with the friendly sea cook, Long John Silver. Taken together, this pair of pictures is designed to emphasize the contrast between the safety of the cove and the dangerous and deceptive world into which Jim is moving.

In his depiction of the first scene Wyeth employs color, composition, and original added detail to give the reader a feeling for the complex emotional tone of the moment. The composition of the picture is quite striking. Dazzling sunlight illuminates the left side of the picture, where a sturdy woman stands weeping, her face buried in her apron. Jim is turned away from her, advancing toward the viewer and into the dark shadows cast by the house, which somewhat obscure his face. He is seen in outline, like Bones and Pew; and, like the blind Pew, he carries a stick which extends before him. The picture presents the moment of choice as Jim leaves home to pursue the pirate treasure, and he is shown pausing "on the sill of shade." There is a certain poignancy in the situation which is not grasped by the Jim Hawkins who, as Stevenson describes him in this moment, thinks only of the captain and the treasure. Stevenson's Jim has no weeping mother to make his leavetaking difficult; indeed, the reader is specifically told that Mrs. Hawkins was in good spirits as her son left, and for Stevenson's Jim it proves surprisingly easy to turn the corner and put "home out of sight" (57). Wyeth's picture, however, picks up the faint undertones of tragic retrospect which appear in the narrative of his own adventures by an older and wiser Jim Hawkins, a Jim who can describe his own boyish daydreams of adventure this way: "Sometimes the isle was thick with savages, with whom we fought; sometimes full of dangerous animals that hunted us; but in all my fancies nothing occurred to me so strange and tragic as our actual adventures" (53). Stevenson's reminder here of the fallibility of the young focal character lends a certain plausibility to Wyeth's suggestion in his illustration that Jim might not have "seen" his mother's tears.

Wyeth makes the seamen of the "faithful party" (164) square-shouldered, clear-eyed, resolute, and unmarked by a brutal past.

They have no broken teeth, sabre scars, sinister tattoos, or appalling deformities. Among the pirates, Pew is blind, Bones scarred, Black Dog has lost two fingers, and, of course, Silver has lost a leg. The very idea of the pirate with one leg haunts Jim's nightmares in the beginning of the story; and yet when he meets Silver the boy is struck by his pleasantness and his normality. Wyeth dramatizes this by taking care, in his picture of Jim and Silver in the galley, to disguise Silver's handicap. As Jim stands (in the same pose as Billy Bones atop the cliff), hands on hips, leaning backward to compensate for the roll of the ship, a thoughtful Long John regards him quietly, head bent, face in shadow, his tell-tale leg concealed from view.

The third part of the story, "My Shore Adventure," features two illustrations. In one, the leaders of the "faithful party" hand out loaded pistols "to all the sure men" (101); in the other, a feral Ben Gunn leaps "with great rapidity behind the trunk of a pine" (111). Wyeth stresses here the ironic twist of fate which awaits the treasure hunters: the weapons of these strong men will guarantee neither their survival nor their triumph—these will depend instead on the sly, childlike castaway. Wyeth's portrait of Ben Gunn is a clever visual allusion to the traditional "resourceful" image of Robinson Crusoe, and readers reminded of it may be encouraged to accept a little more readily the perhaps excessively convenient activities of Stevenson's deus ex machina later in the story.

The section Stevenson calls "The Stockade" has two pictures which clarify the differences between the "faithful party" and the pirates. In the first, the dutiful Captain Smollett defies the pirates, running up the Union Jack on the roof of the blockhouse with his own hands. This scene offers a vivid contrast to the similar scene on the book jacket in which the pirates hoist the Jolly Roger. Wyeth gives Captain Smollett snowy linen, a carefully powdered wig, and a most dignified bearing. All these proclaim him to be an eighteenth-century gentleman, above manual labor. When he climbs to the roof of the rude blockhouse and removes his coat to run up the Union Jack, the significance of the moment is clearly asserted by the details supplied by the artist. Stevenson's hints concerning body language, gesture, clothing, architecture, and iconic symbols like the flag are translated into visual specifics by Wyeth, who shares with the inexperienced reader his own knowledge of the elaborately coded symbolic systems human beings have contrived to convey information about themselves. In the second picture for this section, in contrast to the world of order and dignity suggested by Smollett's gesture in raising the flag, the savage pirate crew, armed to the teeth, swarm "over the fence like monkeys" (161). Like Stevenson, Wyeth tends to show the reader the moment just before a bloody confrontation— but the pirates look strong and menacing as they move into the foreground, almost seeming to threaten the viewer, and their bestial appearance contrasts effectively with Captain Smollett's elegant rectitude.

To the innocent eye of a reader concerned mainly with action and adventure, Jim Hawkins's great triumph in the story must seem to be the sequence in which he single-handedly steals the Hispaniola from the villains. But a close reading of Stevenson reveals that here, when he seems most free, Jim is caught up in circumstances beyond his control, and this paradoxical situation is well imaged in the pair of pictures Wyeth provides for the next section of the story. When Hawkins relates the next section of the story, "My Sea Adventure," Wyeth shows the reader what Jim sees through the window of the ship's cabin where two of the pirates, Hands and O'Brien, are "locked together in deadly wrestle"; this is followed by a picture of Jim's confrontation with Hands. The first of these pictures in effect shows a murder, and the second depicts the split second before a fatal accident: Hands is about to hurl the dagger which will cause Jim's pistols to discharge and so, in effect, bring about his own death. In the first picture, Wyeth shows Hands and O'Brien struggling for a knife (not mentioned in the text) and the reader is free to conjecture that this is when Hands acquires the weapon which he will throw at Jim in the next picture. In the fight scene, Wyeth adds a discarded jacket, an overturned chair, and a bottle rolling about the floor among scattered cards, as if to indicate what "drink and the devil" have done to the combatants.

In these pictures Wyeth capitalizes on the unsettling effect produced by the roll of the ship. In the scene with Hands and O'Brien, the lines of the wall and floor indicate that the ship is rolling badly, and the effect is even more striking in the next picture, where the steady line of the sea on the horizon and a bit of land visible in the corner of the picture suggest that the ship, which has gone aground on a sandbar, is canted at a forty-five degree angle. The lines of the mast and the rigging lead upward and converge on the figure of Jim, who clings to the mast, pointing two pistols down at Hands, who holds the knife he is about to throw. Jim's face is an important focal point here. It is close to the viewer and only in light shadow; but, inexplicably, it is so badly blurred that the expression cannot be read. The pitch of the ship suggests the uncertainty of the world in which Jim is moving, and Wyeth's blurring of Jim's face is perhaps an attempt to convey visually that what is about to happen will do so without Jim's volition. Like Stevenson, Wyeth wishes to attenuate Jim's responsibility for the killing of Hands, which becomes nothing but a reflex action. Jim, whose firing of the pistols is neither conscious nor deliberate, is well imaged in the featureless automaton of Wyeth's illustration.

Wyeth concludes his set of illustrations with three magnificent pictures for the section Stevenson called "Captain Silver." The first shows what Jim saw through a loophole in the Stockade wall: a semi-circle of pirates cutting the Bible so that they can pass Silver the "Black Spot." Wyeth contrasts the Bible-cutting of the superstitious and self-defeating sailors, posed and lit like some kind of satanic ritual, with a picture of Long John swinging along on his crutch, a purposeful figure of demonic energy who easily pulls the helpless Jim along on a rope "like a dancing bear" (244). This illustration serves as an emblem of the real relationship between Jim and Silver. The figure of the boy struggling at a rope's end evokes the image of the doomed, hanged man Wyeth devised for the title page and may remind the reader of how often Wyeth has chosen to show the young Jim echoing in stance and gesture the pirates with whom he will eventually recognize a fearful kinship.

The title-page illustration for *Treasure Island*, as is usual with Wyeth, had suggested the nature of the essential conflict in the story (see fig. 1). In it the pirates look furtively about as they bury their loot, projecting fear and guilt in every gesture. One crouches in despair with his head in his hands, while another is in the act of drawing his sword to protect himself against invisible enemies. These figures are painted brilliantly in realistic detail, but about them and above them swirl billowing, dreamy clouds, and in the sky overhead Wyeth has lightly sketched the huge, translucent image of a hanged man. Part of the horror of this figure is its helplessness as it dangles, arms bound, head bowed, above them. The hanged man symbolizes their fate, their future, their deepest fear. Yet, significantly, they do not seem to see him. They are armed to face a more immediate enemy and are blind to what looms above them. This

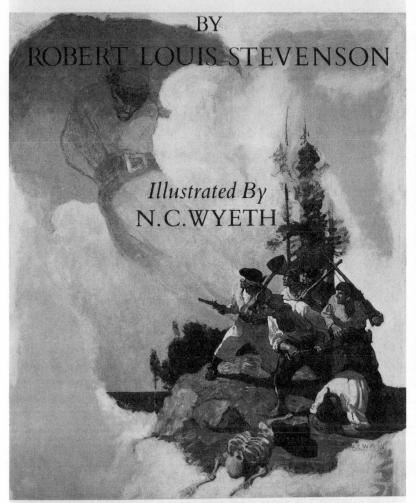

TREASURE ISLAND

BY

ROBERT LOUIS STEVENSON

Illustrated By
N.C.WYETH

CHARLES SCRIBNER'S SONS

NEW YORK

Fig 1. Illustration by N. C. Wyeth for the title page of *Treasure Island* by Robert Louis Stevenson, reprinted with permission of Charles Scribner's Sons, an imprint of Macmillan Publishing Company. Illustration copyright 1911 by Charles Scribner's Sons; copyright renewed. Photo: Rolf Krauss Graphics, Mt. Kisco, N.Y.

picture strikes the keynote of Wyeth's version of the story, stressing the themes of helplessness and tragic blindness that in Stevenson's narrative are conveyed by the voice of the older Jim as he reflects on the exciting treasure hunt which initiated him into the ways of a corrupt world.

The final picture of a series, like the opening picture, occupies a powerful rhetorical position. If Wyeth had used his title-page illustration to suggest the atmosphere of guilty fear which pervades the book and to hint at the tragic blindness with which its protagonist stumbles through his adventures, here he had to convey the hollowness of Jim's triumph at the end of the story and the boy's dim recognition both that the treasure had been fatally tainted by all the crimes committed for it and that he and Silver have more in common than he would like to admit. In his final illustration, Wyeth shows us the treasure cave at last. He catches the disillusioned tone of Jim's description of the treasure that had been the occasion of so much "blood and sorrow," such "shame and lies and cruelty" (265) by choosing to make the cave not the "large, airy place, with a little spring and a pool of clear water, overhung with ferns" of Stevenson's description (275) but a dark brown cavern with a great curved roof, like the inside of a giant mouth. In this deeply shadowed final picture Wyeth suggests the rueful self-knowledge of the older Jim by showing the blind, unthinking boy who had left on his quest with such bright dreams as a faceless creature hunched over his treasure hoard, letting the glittering coins slide down his fingers into storage bags like some fairy-tale gnome or like a sad allegorical embodiment of greed.

An illustrator's vision, as I have suggested, can have a powerful impact on the way a reader experiences a text, and Wyeth's pictures embody the story in a very different way from, say, the fluent drawings of Louis Rhead or the mordant sketches of Mervyn Peake. Stevenson as author and Wyeth as illustrator seem unusually well-matched. Wyeth's pictures for *Treasure Island* translate the ironic doubleness at the heart of the written narrative into effective visual terms and open up alternative aspects of character and unexpected thematic and structural nuances for the reader's consideration. Perhaps they are especially effective in projecting the darker strain in Stevenson; Wyeth once confided to his mother that "for some reason or other *Anything* that I appreciate keenly and profoundly is always sad to the point of being tragic" (quoted in *An American*

Vision 4). But, as many a dazzled reader can attest, they also do full justice to the romance, the glamor, the purely aesthetic appeal the pirate myth held for them both. Stevenson's and Wyeth's characters may do the darkest of deeds, but the pictures presenting them are invariably beautiful.

Works Cited

An American Vision: Three Generations of Wyeth Art: N. C. Wyeth, Andrew Wyeth, James Wyeth. Essays by James H. Duff, Andrew Wyeth, Thomas Hoving, and Lincoln Kirstein. Boston: Little, Brown & Co., 1987.

Scholes, Robert. *Semiotics and Interpretation.* New Haven: Yale University Press, 1982.

Stevenson, Robert Louis. "Bagster's Pilgrim's Progress." In *Familiar Studies of Men and Books: Criticisms*, vol. 5 of *The Works of Robert Louis Stevenson.* South Seas Edition (32 vols.). New York: Charles Scribner's Sons, 1923.

———. *The Black Arrow: A Tale of the Two Roses.* New York: Charles Scribner's Sons, 1916.

———. *David Balfour.* New York: Charles Scribner's Sons, 1941.

———. *Essays.* 1892. Reprinted with an introduction by William Lyon Phelps. The Modern Student's Library. New York: Charles Scribner's Sons, 1918.

———. *Kidnapped.* New York: Charles Scribner's Sons, 1913.

———. *Treasure Island.* New York: Charles Scribner's Sons, 1911.

Wyeth, Betsy James, ed. *The Wyeths: The Letters of N. C. Wyeth, 1901–1945.* Boston: Gambit, 1971.

Satoshi Kitamura: Aesthetic Dimensions

Jane Doonan

Satoshi Kitamura, a Japanese artist now living in London, won the 1982 Mother Goose Award, given annually to the most exciting newcomer to British children's book illustration. His subsequent picture books have fulfilled this promise. They show a striking originality of vision, a criterion Maurice Sendak considers paramount for the judgment of picture books. Sendak suggests that we should look for "someone who says something, even something very commonplace, in a totally original and fresh way. We shouldn't look for pyrotechnics but a person who thinks freshly" (quoted in Lanes 125). Kitamura's work is notable as well for the artist's material skills and for his distinctive relationship to the pictorial tradition of Japan. Consideration of all three aspects—vision, material skills, and tradition—is a way of traveling toward a sympathetic understanding of Kitamura's accomplishment.

Kitamura's first three picture books—the prize-winning *Angry Arthur*, *Ned and the Joybaloo*, and *In the Attic*—were produced in collaboration with Hiawyn Oram, who wrote the texts. Each is an extended metaphor for one of three very different states of being. *Angry Arthur* exemplifies the destructive rage of a thwarted small boy who does not want to go to bed, *Ned and the Joybaloo* gives form to the human frailty of wishing to control and perpetuate happiness, and *In the Attic* celebrates the imagination as a source of nameless and profound satisfactions. Each story sends its central character traveling out to the farthest reaches of the physical universe, deep into the psyche, and away to the wildest stretches of childhood's imaginings. The barriers between inner and outer lives are removed.

These collaborative works were followed by educational picture books for which Kitamura was wholly responsible: *What's Inside? The Alphabet Book* and *When Sheep Cannot Sleep: The Counting Book*. The former, virtually textless, involves the beholder in a guess-

Children's Literature 19, ed. Francelia Butler, Barbara Rosen, and Jean Marsden (Yale University Press, © 1991 by The Children's Literature Foundation, Inc.).

ing game and in opportunities for do-it-yourself story making; the
latter has a memorable hero, Woolly the Sheep, with all the appeal
of a Snoopy, whose adventures are well worth watching whether
or not one counts as the pages turn. Both books go far beyond increasing literacy and numeracy; each has an inventive approach to
a traditional form. Other picture books have followed which are
charged with honest humor.

The values Kitamura promotes are aspects of an independent
and creative nature: curiosity, resourcefulness, self-sufficiency, and
the need for self-expression. One suspects that if he had his way,
artists' materials and the means of making and listening to music
would be every child's right. Arthur has a gramophone and piano;
Ned, when not occupied with the Joybaloo, practices his recorder
and relaxes to the sounds of Erik Satie and Charlie Parker. The
child who explores the attic owns an accordian and a trumpet, and
mathematician Woolly tunes in to the radio. H for Hippo playing his G for guitar has enough musical instruments in his sound-
proofed studio to service a symphony orchestra, a jazz band, jungle
drummers, gypsy fiddlers, pipers Aegean and Scottish, harpers
Jewish and Welsh. Sharpened pens, paints, sketchblocks and easels
also are at hand. The omnipresence of musical and artistic instruments reveals Kitamura's focus upon the inner life, as well as
providing intertextual reference to the artist's own creativity, and
indicates a source for the self-reliance and independence of his
characters.

With the exception of the alphabet book, each story features a
single character accompanied, if at all, only by an animal, though
friendly relatives are never far away. These independent youngsters are able to resolve most of the difficulties they encounter
from strengths within themselves. Kitamura's task is to find graphic
equivalences for both their outer and their inner worlds that are
sufficiently seamless and convincing to provide his reader with opportunities for identification. He brings out the abstract qualities
of both worlds. Through particular emphases in depictive style he
captures on the page the effects of physical objects as we experience
them; the imaginary inner life, "past everyday night and everynight
dreams" (a quotation from *Ned* which applies to most of the picture books) often is visualized through innovative organization of
the spatial and temporal framework of his compositions and by an
evocative use of color.

Kitamura uses simple materials, pen and watercolor, to construct compositions of extraordinary subtlety. In this as in other characteristics of his style, his indebtedness to the pictorial traditions of Japan and such artists as Utamaro, Hiroshige, and Hokusai is evident. When faced with a graphic problem, his instinctive response is to find a compositional solution which has its origins in the Japanese print or scroll. Such solutions in conjunction with Western imagery give his style a strong individual identity.

The quality of Kitamura's line is one of the distinctive aspects of his artwork, though it can hardly be separated from other such vital elements as his use of color. There is no underdrawing, so the line goes down once and for all, with no margin for error, no chance to reconsider. The line is fine, unbroken, and exhibits a slight tremor which charges the drawing with energy. It is as if the concentration required to limn the line is still present in the record of the movement of the artist's hand.

To define objects Kitamura uses a closed contour line precisely filled with color. A closed contour contains an object and separates it from its surroundings. This mode of drawing separate attention to an object suits Kitamura's purpose well, since many of his images have symbolic or narrative value and thus reward close looking, and since he often is concerned to promote a surreal effect by juxtaposing unlikely objects to suggest his characters' inner lives.

If he used the continuous line and local color alone, Kitamura would have no way of softening the passage from the shape of one object to another, no way of suggesting the relativity of existence or the connections between objects. To some extent he resolves this problem by plain water or water paint washes. In places, the precise definition of the line is modulated by a wash which causes a slight bleeding (either blue-black or sepia, according to the type of ink chosen for a particular set of illustrations). These passages, with their cunning shifts and drifts of color and tone, have a unifying effect on the composition as a whole. Often they refer to background motifs or textures—bricks, tiles, foliage—against which the objects with closed contours are thrown into sharp contrast. The tension between the tightly controlled line and the escaping watery staining gives the picture much of its sense of movement and vitality.

Kitamura is always a sophisticated colorist; he uses white areas skillfully in conjunction with subtle combinations of hues like cinnabar and ocher opposed by intense inky violet. Pale milky tints and chalky grays are contrasted in hue and tone with full grape red, with hyacinth and Prussian blues. Color modifies the directness of his forms as well as having a vital expressive function.

The emotional use of color is in accord with the artist's style of drawing. Kitamura draws intuitively rather than from life, a quality foremost in Japanese and Chinese art, as Frederick Gore suggests (66). The shapes of Kitamura's forms are sculptural, simplified, and tend toward the angular, with scant concern for anatomy or the rules of projective realism. He is after the essence of things rather than their (mere) appearance. Kitamura emphasizes the clumpfootedness of a child wearing training shoes, the snaking hazards of electrical cords, the comforting possibility of delving deeply into a stew pot, the cheery stir-it-all-about directness of the frying pan. He often gives two viewpoints on individual objects; we may look at something—say a jar—at eye level, the better to read its label and observe how solidly it sits upon a surface, but in addition we may look down on it from above, the better to enjoy its contents. The effect of the second viewpoint is to tilt the upper surface toward us and to make the total form more accessible. This is how we "know" a jar, as we handle it and glance at it from different angles.

Kitamura's use of perspective is eclectic. He readily juggles between the Western Renaissance convention, which dictates that parallel lines should converge in the distance, and a system of perspective widely used in China and Japan which may be related to the concept of the "traveling eye." The beholder is assumed to be scanning the painting in different directions rather than maintaining one fixed viewpoint and is not looking at a scene so much as wandering about in it. Kitamura also favors inverted perspective—diverging rather than converging parallels—on furniture like sturdy wooden beds, tables, and chairs; inverted perspective maintains symmetry as a whole and exposes both sides of an object to the spectator. As well as offering much more access to and information about an object, inverted perspective gives it an air of stability. This quality acts as a comforting counterbalance to the unsettling, sometimes intemperate, and often mysterious happenings in the stories themselves.

Through such stylization Kitamura offers an interpretation of life as we experience it emotionally; his paintings strike a chord of recognition. Nothing could be more down-to-cement than his depiction of a busy and cluttered urban domestic environment with many things to mind and tasks to do. Toys must be tidied away, musical instruments have to be practiced, house plants wilt for want of water, dishes wait to be dried, dust bins overflow. Every viewer, whether child or adult, recognizes this world firsthand and easily identifies with it. Taken together, the unbroken tremulous contour, the simplified shapes, and the multiple viewpoints cause objects to impinge upon the consciousness of the picture-book beholder, just as the maintenance and manipulation of objects impinge in reality. Thus Kitamura draws us into the lives of his protagonists.

Within his compositions every element is unerringly spaced and placed. This depends in part upon the importance of negative space, the acceptance of which is of comparatively recent origin in our culture, though not so in the arts of the Far East. Gore points out that the eloquence of drawings and paintings of Japanese and Chinese artists often lies in the contrasted and beautifully shaped and proportioned areas of plain background (69). In Kitamura's paintings, however many objects are disposed upon the picture plane, the impression is never one of overbusiness; he ensures that there are unworked passages upon which to refresh the scanning eye. The last four words imply that effort is required on the part of the reader-beholder, as indeed it is. Whether through images or the organization of any other of the abstract elements, Kitamura's work stimulates an aesthetic attitude which, in Nelson Goodman's words, is "restless, searching, testing—less attitude than action: creation and re-creation" (*Languages* 242). Encouraging creativity in his readers is arguably Kitamura's greatest gift.

In discussing each of the picture books already mentioned, I should like to focus on two aspects in particular: first, on structural elements which contribute to the expressive content of the composite text and second, on the special qualities of each particular picture book, which the adult mediator might find valuable and useful to share with a child reader.

Angry Arthur is the portrait of a rage. Arthur wants to stay up to watch a Western on the television but is told that it is time for him to go to bed. " 'I'll get angry,' said Arthur. 'Get angry,' said his mother." And he does. Arthur goes on to indulge in the terrible and secret urge of the impotent child to annihilate everyone and everything which oppose him. Hiawyn Oram's text is flat, unadorned matter of fact, with the interjection, " 'That's enough,' But it wasn't" repeated at spaced intervals, as each member of the family in turn attempts to pacify the child. His response is to notch up the force of his tantrum which becomes a stormcloud, a hurricane, a typhoon, an earth tremor, a universequake in which all perish except the protagonist and his pet. Two elements make a major contribution to the mood of intensive emotional energy of this picture book. One is the color, which includes the open face of white, and the other is the sparseness and intricacy of the forms and the quality of space surrounding them, which sets up waves of visual rhythms.

On the very first opening, Kitamura uses color and white to carry a carefully constructed emotional charge. To the left, Arthur is placed on a white unworked page, watching a Western on the television in a relaxed pose, while the kettle puffs cheerfully on the stove and the cat snoozes contentedly. The strong vertical emphasis of the stove pipe and the flattened perspective of the television set give stability to this scene of the child absorbed in what is, at present, a secondhand experience of conflict. Arthur is viewed from above, on a reduced scale, as if to emphasize the physical insignificance of the small being from whom the mighty drama is soon to spring. The pure white space surrounding him signifies his total concentration. Nothing but the film exists for Arthur, and little else but Arthur exists for the beholder. The composition is a pleasing adaptation of a visual technique used for representing interior scenes in Japan since the mid-seventeenth century. Its essence— simple but forcible and flexible—is the omission of any background except for a few indicators left as clues.

Opposing this comfortable scene is a full plate in somber grayish hues of ocher, violet, and Vandyke brown. Still small in scale and viewed from above, Arthur is now placed against a painted background which represents a darkened room. The outside world intrudes. A block of light falls across the planked floor by way of the open door. Arthur's mother is on the threshold. Her figure throws a huge diagonal shadow across the floor and across the picture plane. We see only her feet, but her presence is unavoidable. Arthur's form and those of his cat, the television set, and his toys are all aligned with the direction in which the floorboards run. These present a series of rising diagonals (thus mirroring the child's rage) across which the mother's shadow is cast. Arthur and his mother are visually, verbally, and metaphorically on a collision course.

Kitamura fractures the picture plane on the next opening as Arthur's rage is unleashed (fig. 1). From the evening sky outside the window it strikes, Jove-like, ricocheting off the walls, smashing the furniture, and concentrating in an explosive flash at the lower edge of the picture plane. The surface of the flash acts as a label for the brief text, making a perfect example of the integration of typographical word and plastic image. Furniture and household objects are flung across space. The hues which so ominously echoed Arthur's mood in the previous painting have now lightened in tone as this therapeutic rage rises and erupts.

Over the next four page openings the proportion of details in each painting crescendos to a climax as Arthur systematically destroys his room, his garden, his house, his street, his town, and his country. Terraces tilt, horizons heave, trivia and treasures tumble.

As Arthur goes on to attack the surface of the earth as if he were a giant cracking eggs, so the details fall away. Galactic acrobatics soothe the child. He and his pet—depicted in small scale—twist and turn, rise and descend in a starry continuum. Material means match the emotional tenor: the fluid brushstrokes stain the paper with floating, weightless, incandescent color. As the last pages turn, aerial tissues of luminous gold and violet give way to dusky blue, then return, and finally fade away altogether. Arthur's bed on its fragment of Mars drifts above a generous area of unworked white open space, symbolizing a return to normality, blessed sleep. The storm has blown itself out. A musical analogy suggests itself. This final sequence is like a coda which returns us through a series of cadences to a tranquil conclusion. The ebb and flow of images, the balance of saturated and unsaturated hues and of light and dark tones form a visual counterpart to a musical rhythm which is at one with the impulse of the text.

Any work of art creates its own universe, which is a whole, built upon a space-time framework. Kitamura's aesthetic arrangement of this framework is one of the most innovative features of his next collaboration, *Ned and the Joybaloo*. Space (what's inside and what's outside) and time (how the speed of its passage varies according to circumstance) are central to the story and its themes. Ned quests for happiness and finds it in the form of a big and beautiful creature, resembling a seaside inflatable toy. A cross between a dog and a seal, the Joybaloo has "a funny leathery nose and its breath full of paper roses." Every Friday the Joybaloo takes Ned to its playgrounds, where they squeeze "the last drop of mischief" out of the night. But this is not enough for Ned. He wants every night to be a

Fig 1. *Angry Arthur*, by Hiawyn Oram, illustrated by Satoshi Kitamura. Text copyright 1982, Hiawyn Oram. Illustration copyright 1982, Satoshi Kitamura. Reprinted by permission of Andersen Press.

So he did. Very, very angry.
He got so angry that his anger became a stormcloud
exploding thunder and lightning and hailstones.

Joybaloo night. Through his insatiable greed and selfishness he exhausts the Joybaloo. And after that he has no choice but to set about making his own happiness, which is not so difficult after all, given his creative nature. The picture book concludes with Ned dreaming happily of the Joybaloo, knowing that one day it will return, in its own good time. Happiness cannot be commanded.

Here is the classic tale of the rise and fall and coming to wisdom of the hero, shaped for a child. It shows that happiness, especially when entirely dependent upon outside factors, is elusive and ephemeral; we may enjoy moments of unlooked-for happiness, but may equally well take pleasure in more modest forms which we create for ourselves. As befits the nature of childhood, Joybaloo-happiness is linked to extreme physical gratification: dancing, bouncing, laughing, flying, playing sensuously in mud and water, and "running wild." On the other hand, there is contentment to be gained from music, toys, and delighting others, as when Ned picks some flowers for his mother. Summarized as baldly as this; *Ned and the Joybaloo* sounds fiercely didactic. The good humor which pervades the visual narrative ensures that the total experience offered by the picture book is thoroughly enjoyable, as well as morally sound.

In six of twelve page openings in this book, Kitamura uses what Joseph Schwarcz (chapter 3) calls a "continuous narrative" technique which emphasizes the space and time spans of the story. In each of these illustrations, either Ned alone or Ned and the Joybaloo appears several times at different places, while the background remains broadly the same. A similar device is common both to Western late medieval narrative painting and to the scroll of the Far East, whereby a progression through time is suggested by a repetition of the figure of the protagonist. Such compositions not only incorporate in their structure a strong sense of time; they also ask for time from the beholder.

The continuous narrative needs to be read in a certain order—that is, the one which indicates progress in space and time of the recurring figure(s). Therefore the beholder is obliged to spend a period of dynamic contemplation—a time in which to do visual thinking and attend to inner speech—in order to make meaning. Both the story's participants and the beholder are taking up more time than is perhaps generally the case in a single picture in a children's picture book. Studying the illustrations, one cannot help but

be impressed by the different ways Kitamura structures his continuous narrative composition, thus demonstrating that the same
technique can serve a variety of effects. Each composition presents
a fresh challenge for a young viewer, who, like Ned, must consciously spend time and effort in his search for pleasure. The search
becomes the pleasure, through effort.

The continuous narrative is introduced first to show the search
for the Joybaloo, a protracted and daunting task (fig. 2). A rising
diagonal, from lower left to approximately top right, divides the
two-page spread into halves. The resulting smaller upper inverted
triangle, which carries the text upon the open face of white, provides a restful contrast to the lower, larger, near-triangular shape,
which is colored, dark in tone, and seething with images. A stretch
of brown background reads as carpet or garden, depending on
whether Ned's activity suggests that he is indoors or outside. To the
right is a section of a house facade, complete with an open back
door we can see through.

Disposed over the picture plane of this lower shape, nine little
Neds look in, under, through, and behind the likely and unlikely
places for finding a Joybaloo: in the cellar, vase, flower pot, boot,
vacuum cleaner bag, washing machine, dog kennel, under the
couch, and (very sensibly, Ned has donned a rubber apron for this)
in the dustbin. In the upper right of the picture plane we see a
tenth Ned, backview in pajamas—see how time has flown—peering
into the dark depths of the airing cupboard. A huge pair of eyes
stares back. The triangular wedge of color and activity created by
the rising diagonal is a fitting visual metaphor in itself for Ned's
uphill struggle, finally to be crowned by success. His changes of costume, the scattered tools he has used for dismantling and smashing
objects, the opened doors and disturbed drawers signify the long
passage of time in which Ned has been engaged upon his search.
Every element in the busy composition contributes to exemplifying the keyed-up intensity of Ned's feelings, his determination and
single-mindedness. And while Ned has been looking for the Joybaloo, the viewer has been looking equally hard, making a logical
sequence out of a chaos of instances.

Kitamura's inventiveness allows him another arrangement when,
in a collection of little separate episodes, he depicts Ned, hell-bent
on making everyone's life as miserable as his own, as he waits from
one Joybaloo night to the next. Ned is remarkably busy (fig. 3).

Not that meeting a Joybaloo had been easy for Ned.

He'd looked in everything, under everything, through everything, behind everything. He'd even looked in places he knew a Joybaloo could not possibly be.

Fig 2. *Ned and the Joybaloo*, by Hiawyn Oram, illustrated by Satoshi Kitamura. Text copyright 1983, Hiawyn Oram. Illustration copyright 1983, Satoshi Kitamura. Reprinted by permission of Andersen Press.

So how did next Friday begin to seem like never?
Ned didn't know but it did. He began to want more.
He began to want lots. He began to want every night to
be Joybaloo night.

Fig 3. *Ned and the Joybaloo*, by Hiawyn Oram, illustrated by Satoshi Kitamura. Text copyright 1983, Hiawyn Oram. Illustration copyright 1983, Satoshi Kitamura. Reprinted by permission of Andersen Press.

To fill in the time between one Friday and the next he
ame impossible.
He wouldn't eat. He wouldn't practise his recorder. He
w on every wall and put tacks in people's shoes.

This time the composition is based on a fan-shaped arrangement of forms with oblique or vertical emphases that suggest spokes. Just as a fan opens by separate movements of the spokes, so, by association, here they evoke the temporal breaks Ned experiences in the course of the week. Once again, there is no distinction made between the inside and outside of the house. Roof and walls have been taken away. In both the illustrations discussed, Kitamura has adapted and extended the convention known as "taking off the roof," as seen in early Japanese prints, which allows the beholder to dive in and out of doors and follow the action from one room to the other. It makes a particularly effective way of letting the picture-book viewer into Ned's life. Very different in feeling and appearance, the painting of the playground of the Joybaloo is structured in four curving horizontal bands, which suggest that we are looking at a section of something like a huge roundel composed of ceaseless pleasurable physical experiences. The figures of Ned and the Joybaloo are seen four times, in four different locations, experiencing four different sensations; the transitions from one to the other are seamless, as in dreams. Overleaf Kitamura temporarily abandons continuous narrative, and, in a typically Japanese way of making space, he gives his reader a ride on the Joybaloo.

This memorable composition depicts Ned in his aviator's goggles hanging onto the Joybaloo's ears as they dive diagonally across the picture plane, exemplifying an excess of daring, buoyancy, exhilaration. The saturated violet night sky concedes to the approaching dawn with its open face of white (white also being used for the pure-joy-Joybaloo). Multiple viewpoints of the landscape are from above. Kitamura creates the impression of circling and soaring by curling the horizon, metaphorically transferring loops from the motion of flight to the Joybaloo landscape. It is as if there is no beginning or end to the picture, as in a Japanese hand scroll which can be unrolled either way, and what is space spreads out in all directions. The beholder might well start by looking at the illustration with the book held upside down and gradually turn it, enacting the flight, sharing the view with Ned.

The illustrations for *In the Attic* display a more cerebral and reflective mood. A small boy, the narrator, sits bored in a sea of toys, the forms of which incidentally contain apt visual allusions to works by Tatlin and Brancusi, artists who extended the boundaries of sculpture. Climbing up the ladder of his toy fire engine and going into the attic is a metaphoric trip extending the boundary of the narrator's mind.

Kitamura depicts the young narrator's changes of thoughts in successive openings by changes of settings and of pictorial style. The text is virtually superfluous until the penultimate illustration, when the child goes to tell his mother about where he's been. " 'But we don't have an attic,' she said." He smiles.

As each page turns we watch his thoughts traveling far and wide. His building blocks become immense cavernous architectural edifices which hint at the structures of Piranesi. Then toy mice take on life and organize heroic games with everyday objects, such as a toothbrush and a corkscrew. Further on, the child rests and reflects in the middle of a colony of Klee-like insects, which hum and buzz with the music of whirring wings. Next he meets a spider and joins it in making a web, the pair of them thus matching the extraordinary engineering feat of the pyramids pictured below them. The connection between web and mausoleum is waiting to be made in terms of the materials, construction methods, aims, survival span, and symbolism, according to the "reading" skills and experience of the beholder. Later the boy opens surreal windows in space and traveling on, meets and makes a friend—a tiger—with whom he can share his wonders. And, best of all, the two of them find a "game that could go on for ever because it kept changing."

In the Attic has one quality I would like to single out above others. Some of the illustrations do not offer much scope for making a literal story from what they denote, though they display qualities which encourage active contemplation and response of a nonverbal kind. Too often children see pictures as just more words in a different form, not a different symbol system with its own language. As John Dewey points out (chapter 3), reading pictures is thinking directly in terms of colors, tones, images, and their disposition on the picture plane and in imagined space. Pictures have values and meanings which cannot be expressed in words without loss in translation, and this applies to pictures in picture books as well as those on walls.

The needs of our daily life have given superior practical importance to speech, and picture books are used for language development, teaching children how to point and say, read, and generally generate talk. As parents and teachers we foster the impression that pictures are for talking about. But pictorial art is specifically made for looking at; a feature of seeing and looking is silence, though it may be accompanied by what Dewey calls "inner speech." Galleries are full of people reading the attribution labels and exhibition catalogs, listening to lecturers, talking about what paintings denote, and sparing little time for reading the painting itself. Nonrepresentational art gets the shortest shrift; since it appears to be about nothing, what is there to say? It is as if we are at a loss to know how to approach visual art without the written or spoken word in attendance.

Among the many reasons why we should have become so dependent upon words, one could well be the outcome of our earliest experiences with pictures—the picture book. In a paper exploring the apparent compulsion, as well as the difficulties and dangers, of translating visual experiences into language, Ciaran Benson examines the role images play in teaching literacy, the narrative traditions of picture-book illustration, and the research on aesthetic responses of young children to the visual arts (111–23). He argues that if children grow up thinking visual art is only to be talked about, as well they might, then the effect of such a theory on their relation with the visual arts will be positively procrustean.

In the Attic is the perfect book for exploring what properties the pictures display as well as denote, because the text has minimal narrative thrust, and the layout is organized in a series of self-contained, separate plates; measured rhythms encourage a reflective stance. For example, Kitamura's illustration of the "game that could go on for ever" cannot adequately be translated into words (fig. 4). The game is depicted in Kandinsky-like free form and geometric symbols because it is too wonderful for words. Children might be encouraged to contemplate such a picture, or the one in the insect colony, confident that to feel something and say nothing is still a valid response.

As well as an illuminator of the texts of others, Kitamura is a picture-book maker. His alphabet and counting books bring to his youngest audiences delightful instruction and instructive delight. *What's Inside? The Alphabet Book* poses just that very question: we look inside assorted containers including a carton, dustbin, crate, cases, tubes, and even a spine-chilling coffin lying in the snow. The most innovative technically of the books for which he has had sole responsibility, the layout and dynamics are complex, though regular in pattern, and exert a strong influence on the rhythms of reading the pictures. On each page opening, a puzzle is posed on the right half of the picture, cued by a pair of initials on or by a container; the solution appears overleaf on the left, where the hidden objects are revealed and labeled by words. In addition to the strong linear thrust from one page opening to the next, generated by the curiosity to discover "what's inside," the focus of the picture also alternates rhythmically between large-scale close-ups and small-scale wide-angled views, as selected details on one page become the main subject matter on the next. Furthermore, the spectator's viewpoint shifts between inside and outside localities. This picture book, like others by Kitamura, exhibits a strong kinship to musical form. Here he extemporizes with the letters of the alphabet as in jazz, where the rhythmic framework allows for tremendous energy and freedom.

A reading of figures 5 and 6 illustrates some of the book's dynamics. Beginning with the former, from a viewpoint inside the corner of a bathroom the beholder looks out of the window to the left and sees a small boy who has just retrieved a lost kite. Marginal details from the previous double spread—a kite-tail fluttering from the crown of a distant tree and a mere glimpse of a ladder—are now the framed focus of attention. On the right half of the opening, a flotilla of toy boats floating in the washbasin offers a bold visual play between a large monochrome sculptural form and intriguing, colorful little objects. On the shelf above, paired initials are sited on tubes of toothpaste, one boxed in light blue and the other in dark blue. Guessing begins here. Overleaf (fig. 6), as if the beholder has stepped back, more of the bathroom comes into view, and the boy is now inside, wearing pajamas and expressing more than amazement. Squeezing the toothpaste tubes, he releases twin jets of "morning" and "night" which, gathering volume and momentum, spiral and swell into a climactic cosmic conjunction of lightness, darkness, sun, moon, and stars. A fresh set of initials and partial forms on the extreme right beckons to the reader.

One of the strengths of this picture book lies in the different ways it can be used, for it is capable of sustaining many pictorial re-readings long after the puzzles have been solved and the alphabet sequence mastered, by virtue of the detail in the compositions. By "detail" I mean some part of a picture which meets two conditions as identified by Richard Wolheim (13–16). In the artist's perspective, detail makes a distinctive contribution to the whole

My friend and I found a game that could

Fig 4. *In the Attic*, by Hiawyn Oram, illustrated by Satoshi Kitamura. Text copyri
1984, Hiawyn Oram. Illustration copyright 1984, Satoshi Kitamura. Reprinted
permission of Andersen Press.

go on forever because it kept changing.

Fig 5. *What's Inside? The Alphabet Book*, by Satoshi Kitamura. Copyright 1985, Satoshi Kitamura. Reprinted by permission of A. & C. Black and Farrar, Straus & Giroux

Fig 6. *What's Inside? The Alphabet Book,* by Satoshi Kitamura. Copyright 1985, Satoshi Kitamura. Reprinted by permission of A. & C. Black and Farrar, Straus & Giroux.

while, in the spectator's perspective, it elicits and rewards focused perception. Traditionally, detail has been the locus both of personal imprint and of heightened pleasure; however, too often in picture-book illustration it fails to meet either condition. Not so in Kitamura's case. The detailed compositions in *What's Inside?* invite the viewer to read visually all over the picture plane, to search, observe, discover, test, ponder upon, make connections, and construct subplots from this idiosyncratic assembly of characters, objects, and settings.

In *What's Inside?* we see musical and writing instruments, ladders, black bats, striped clothing, empty streets, the friendly tiger—all recurring motifs in Kitamura's work, linking them to a larger whole. Observant young viewers, spying a detail in one picture, may well greet its relocation in another picture or picture book with a sense of delighted recognition. Particularly intriguing are glimpses of characters like two small boys and a tiger, who have made the journey from other works to *What's Inside?* and appear to be waiting to be given new roles in stories from the viewer's imagination. These compositions have the same kind of flexibility and story-making potential as the game which the little attic explorer found that "can go on for ever, because it keeps changing."

And so to bed. *When Sheep Cannot Sleep*, or small children either, what better than to start counting? The nature of a counting book generally works against coherence and flow, normally essential elements of the picture-book experience; not so with Kitamura's, which eschews stereotype. One rare feature is the absence of explicit instruction. The verbal text, apart from one instance, is free from any mention of number, though there are clues by name or sound as to what might be counted. Nor are there any depicted numerals; it is as if the pictures just happen to display increasing numbers of interesting objects within them.

The story addresses itself to the child with unforced humor. Woolly the Sheep goes on his insomniac rambles under dramatic night skies. He observes first a butterfly and then a pair of ladybirds, plays hide-and-seek in long grass with fireflies, and so on until, finally exhausted by his adventures, he falls asleep counting his relatives. The layout is simple. Nothing distracts from the orderly sequence of three-quarter plates, beneath each of which is set a brief portion of text. There is an airiness about the generous proportion of open face of white which frames the narratives, providing an area of contrast to the richly colored plates. The compositions are masterly, with flawless clarity of communication.

Woolly is an endearing creature with a sagacious look, a thoroughly credible being. Anthropomorphized by expression and pose, he is to be seen more often on two legs than on four. Though he looks very funny he is never a figure of fun; Kitamura no more trivializes Woolly than John Tenniel trivializes the White Rabbit, nor is there a trace of sentimentality.

One touching portrait shows Woolly alone in an unoccupied house and engaged in what everyone does—telling stories to himself about himself in order to make sense of what is happening. Being a Kitamura hero, Woolly does this storytelling by drawing (fig. 7). Serene hues of light rose and light ocher dominate a composition which exemplifies Woolly's happy, childlike absorption, and the results of his labors are to be seen overleaf (fig. 8). Woolly has painted fifteen pictures, one for each of his night's encounters, which he now hangs upon the wall and stands back to admire. Kitamura is playing a game with continuous narrative technique of a very special kind, in which everything counts for Woolly as well as for his beholder. The latter has the chance to tally the score and also benefit from a pictorial summary of the story so far; Woolly's memory of time past gives him a sense of identity in time present—a comforting feeling for an isolated being to have in an unfamiliar setting, and a sophisticated comment on the nature of the text itself.

In common with all the other books, there are little running jokes, meaningful details, faultlessly placed and spaced elements; but the most outstanding feature is Kitamura's use of color and tone. I have been suggesting throughout that the distinctiveness of Kitamura's picture books can best be understood by situating them within his own culture; particularly in Woolly's tale, the artist's preference for rich and often somber color characteristic of Japanese traditions finds its expression in his painting.

The narratively oriented English picture-book tradition has an emphasis on the quality of the line rather than of color. Much of the time the line varies in pressure and plays a large part in modeling and texturing; often it is deceptively sketchy and displays an insouciant liveliness. The pen sets up such a spanking pace that the brush barely manages to catch up, it seems, and contour and color hit and miss. I am thinking now of such artists as Quentin Blake,

In one of the rooms, he found some
coloured pencils. "Good," said Woolly.
"I'll do some drawing."

Fig 7. *When Sheep Cannot Sleep: The Counting Book*, by Satoshi Kitamura. Copyright
1986, Satoshi Kitamura. Reprinted by permission of A. & C. Black and Farrar, Straus
& Giroux.

He was so pleased with his pictures
that he hung them on the wall.

Fig 8. *When Sheep Cannot Sleep: The Counting Book*, by Satoshi Kitamura. Copyright 1986, Satoshi Kitamura. Reprinted by permission of A. & C. Black and Farrar, Straus & Giroux.

John Burningham, Tony Ross, and Tracey Campbell Pearson. Such
illustrators are the descendants of Thomas Rowlandson, master of
a "romping, bouncing calligraphy" as Brian Alderson describes him
(49). Kitamura's way of drawing is quite different, the energy less
overtly physical. Color plays a more important role in Kitamura's
work than in the classic English tradition and is satisfying enough
to dwell upon for its abstract qualities alone.

There is a Japanese text of the year one thousand to which Kitamura is very close in spirit in the way in which he puts colours
together (Lemière). The writer is describing a journey in winter
by cart.

> Our carriage has no inner curtains and as the blinds above
> were drawn right back, the moon's light reached quite down to
> the bottom. So one could see a lady who wore seven or eight
> garments, light violet, plum red, white . . . and over all a dark
> violet cloak whose striking brightness shone beneath the moon.
> Beside this delightful being there was a courtier. He wore laced
> trousers of brocaded cloth of vine colour, and several white
> garments. Stuffs of golden yellow and some of scarlet hung
> from his sleeves. . . .

Light violet, plum red, white, dark violet, vine color, golden yellow, scarlet: if we add the strong unfading Prussian blue so favored
by Hokusai, we could be reading about the hues of Woolly's noctur-
nal wanderings nearly a thousand years later.

In Kitamura's picture books color offers sensuous delight, reflects
the tone of the text, and heightens the drama. Just by looking at the
portraits of Woolly at work and of Woolly tucked up in bed under
his feather-white coverlet, in his room with its walls in many tints of
gray, its terra-cotta curtains, deep vine red carpet, and beech brown
bed, a child is exposed to the possibility of appreciating differences
in hue and tone, contrasts and similarities in relationships. Color,
the child discovers, tells its own kind of tale.

In less than a decade Kitamura has made, and continues to make,
a distinctive contribution to the art of the children's picture book.
The fresh way of saying "even something very commonplace" is
evident in all he does.

Works Cited

Alderson, Brian. *Sing A Song for Sixpence*. Cambridge University Press, 1986.

Benson, Ciaran. "Art and Language in Middle Childhood: A Question of Translation." *Word & Image* 2:2 (April–June 1986): 123–40.

Dewey, John. *Art as Experience*. New York: Doubleday, 1958.

Goodman, John. *Languages of Art*. Indianapolis: Hackett, 1976.

Gore, Frederick. *Painting: Some Basic Principles*. London: Studio Vista, 1965.

Kitamura, Satoshi. *What's Inside? The Alphabet Book*. London: A. & C. Black, 1985.

———. *When Sheep Cannot Sleep: The Counting Book*. London: A. & C. Black, 1986.

Lanes, Selma. *The Art of Maurice Sendak*. New York: Abrams, 1980.

Lemière, Alan. *Japanese Art Handscrolls*. London: Methuen, 1958.

Oram, Hiawyn. *Angry Arthur*. Illus. Satoshi Kitamura. London: Andersen, 1982.

———. *Ned and the Joybaloo*. Illus. Satoshi Kitamura. London: Andersen, 1983.

———. *In the Attic*. Illus. Satoshi Kitamura. London: Andersen, 1984.

Schwarcz, Joseph H. *Ways of the Illustrator*. Chicago: American Library Association, 1982.

Smith, Lawrence, ed. *Ukiyoe, Images of Unknown Japan*. London: British Museums Publications, 1988.

Wolheim, Richard. "Hans Hofmann: The Final Years." *Modern Painters* 1:2 (Summer 1988): 13–16.

Writing the Empty Cup:
Rhythm and Sound as Content

George Shannon

No one questions that the picture book, like film, is a blending of word and image, yet most discussions of the genre approach the picture book as if it were a silent movie—virtually wordless and without any sound. A typical perspective is that expressed by Mary Agnes Taylor in *Horn Book*: "Although an aural experience usually accompanies the picture book, the fact remains that the young child must depend more on what he sees than on what he reads or hears if he is to comprehend the full meaning of a picture story" (634). In thus disengaging the visual from the aural, Taylor divests the text of its crucial role in the process of creating a picture book—a process that is experienced anew with each reader and reading. She also completely ignores the text's sounds and rhythms, which contribute to the reader's comprehension as surely as do the book's pictures.

Ongoing improvements in printing have brought the picture book to the same level of technical expertise, appreciation, and imbalance that writer-director David Mamet sees in film. Writing of current trends, Mamet discusses the frequent dialogue: "Q. 'How'd you like the movie?' A. 'Fantastic cinematography.' Yeah [states Mamet], but so what? Hitler had fantastic cinematography. The question we have ceased to ask is, 'What was the fantastic cinematography in *aid* of?'" (16). Was there any story, any substance, any breath behind the beautiful images? How do the images relate to one another and to the viewer?

Even if one believes that the text serves as little more than a series of road signs through the scenery or visual story, the removal of the words from most picture books changes the journey and, in turn, a reader's comprehension of it. Without Arthur Yorinks's words in *Louis the Fish* (Farrar, 1980) Richard Egielski's images tell not the story of a man becoming a fish, via flashbacks, but the story of a man becoming a fish becoming a child becoming a man becoming a

Children's Literature 19, ed. Francelia Butler, Barbara Rosen, and Jean Marsden (Yale University Press, © 1991 by The Children's Literature Foundation, Inc.).

fish. If, that is, the young reader's mind even connects the man and fish and child as being the same character. Remove Munro Leaf's words from Robert Lawson's illustrations in *The Story of Ferdinand* (Viking, 1938) and the conflict—the heart of the story—is completely lost. Alone, Lawson's images tell a quiet and all-but-plotless story of idyllic growth rather than a story of individualism versus expected behavior. Without words the reader has no comprehension of Ferdinand's differences, of his mother's concern over those differences, or of the absurdity of his being selected to fight in the ring.

Good texts, however, are far more than just road signs. As texts move from transactional to expressive to poetic, the sounds of words and the rhythm of their linking become as expressive as their definitions and what they describe. Perry Nodelman has pointed out that the manner in which a picture shares information changes the information: "The style changes the substance enough to become the substance" (21). The same is true of the writer's contribution through the sounds, rhythm, and shape of a text. "As soon as we start talking about alternative possibilities of form," writes Robert Hass, "we find ourselves talking about alternative contents. . . . The search for meaning in the content and shape in the rhythm are simultaneous, equivalent" (126).

Characters, setting, and plot are vital elements of the narrative text, but it is the writer's use of sound and image that makes the difference between sharing information and sharing the emotional experience—the art—of the story. The writer evokes the experiential world of his characters through image *and* sound. Just as the rhythm, pace, volume, and pitch of unidentified footsteps evoke a particular experience within the listener, the same elements in a text evoke the particular emotional experience of that story.

In novels, short stories, and narrative poetry the images and sounds which bring the work to life within the reader's mind are under the writer's individual control. In picture books, however, image and sound are shared (not divided) between writer and illustrator.

Master illustrator-writers Maurice Sendak and Arnold Lobel have stated respectively that the best picture-book texts are "ambiguous" (135) and underwritten (12), but they certainly did not mean bland or weakly written. A well-written picture book is sure of its voice and emotions (what it wants to share and how) yet retains a richness of space which stimulates the illustrator to create his individual images in response to his experience of the text.

An excellent example of this and of silence as evocative sound can be found in Anne Turner's *Dakota Dugout* (Macmillan, 1985). After two pages—two sentences—of relating how the narrator's husband built their first home, the turn of the page brings Ronald Himler's stark and simple image of a sod house. Turner's text is minimal, isolated on the double-spread page: "I cried when I saw it." There is no need to say why. The reader has already felt it. When key images or details are set up by the writer and completed by the illustrator, readers discover for themselves the connection between text and image and thus more deeply absorb the scene.

The text not only clarifies the interrelationship of images; its sounds and rhythms create the book's supporting emotional content. These sounds and rhythms become the book's underlying structure, the cup which holds the book's images. A brief look at three different picture books provides solid examples.

Cynthia Rylant's opening lines of *The Relatives Came* (Bradbury, 1985) are relaxed and anecdotal. "It was in the summer of the year when the relatives came. They came up from Virginia." Already she has created an aural sense of cycle through words with "the summer of the year," the repetition of "came," *and* the dialogue tone of her sentences. She also creates in the next line ("They left when their grapes were nearly purple enough to pick, but not quite") an informal jauntiness which extends the story's tone—the joyful cycle of breaking smaller daily cycles to enter the larger one of when the relatives come. Rylant's vernacular phrasings and cadence also help locate the story in geography. Her relatives don't just come to visit; they "come up from Virginia." A lesser writer might have written, "Our relatives who live in Virginia always came to visit in the summer." The rhythm, the music (and, as a result, much of the content by way of altered form) would have been missing.

Stephen Gammell's images are as easygoing, as filled with breath, and as jaunty as Rylant's text. His people are at home, slouching in comfort. Clothes, hair, and objects are in mild disarray, all part of the emotional reverie and freedom of the holiday. His attentiveness to the text extends in all directions, creating, like Rylant's sound, information that is absorbed without being pronounced. One example in this tale of travel is the broken truck tucked in the lower right-hand edge of an early illustration. When the relatives later fix "any broken thing they could find" that truck is the dominant image.

Imagine *The Relatives Came* illustrated by Barbara Cooney and the scruffy informality disappears. Cooney's dominant style is far too still, hushed, and settled to have matched the informal and rumpled playfulness of Rylant's sounds and rhythms. Cooney created a wonderful balance, however, for Donald Hall's *Ox Cart Man* (Viking, 1979) which would not have been as well complemented by Gammell's style and the palette used in *The Relatives Came*.

Hall's text, originally published as a shorter poem for adults in *Kicking the Leaves* (Harper, 1978), is another excellent example of evoking the heart of a story through rhythm and sound. *Ox Cart Man* is the distillation of an early New Englander's yearly cycle:

> In October he backed his ox into his cart
> and he and his family filled it up
> with everything they made or grew all year long
> that was left over.

"He backed" is echoed again and again in "He packed," as the ox-cart man loads all the items. Once in town the rhythm begins again with "He sold . . . he sold . . . he sold. . . ." All this is heightened by Hall's use of stanzas and line breaks as punctuation to emphasize words and sound as surely as an illustrator's use of shadow and light emphasizes visual shapes. Everything is fully distilled—making, selling, buying, leaving home, and returning home to begin the cycle again. There is a deep calmness to Hall's words, a sense that no matter what else transpires, this family's cycle will exist as the primary current in their lives like breathing and the seasons. There are no sudden stops or turns or breaks in this text. Each line flows into the next like the rhythm of the family's year.

Barbara Cooney's images extend this emotional tone of *Ox Cart Man* through her style and color as much as through content. There is a reminiscence of early American painting to her illustrations—a flatness of perspective and color that evokes the innocent approach of a time past. Horizontal brushstrokes predominate throughout the book, quietly underlining the story's sense of perpetual movement. An example of her harmonic extension of the text is her second large image. As Hall's content and rhythm evoke the activity of packing the character's prized creations, Cooney shows them proudly holding the same items. Husband and wife have stopped for a second to show the reader their work. Their daughter remains more interested in the mittens, both pleased with her craftsmanship and perhaps not quite sure if she is ready to sell them. Whereas Gammell's characters are pure kinesis, Cooney's are as measured and focused as their cycle and Hall's lines. Rather than the movement coming from within them, they join—are in tune—with the movement of the year.

Louis the Fish by Arthur Yorinks and Richard Egielski has a completely different rhythm and emotional core. Yorinks's opening lines are absurd in content and matter-of-fact in delivery, creating a sense of bold comic nonsense. "One day last spring, Louis, a butcher, turned into a fish. Silvery scales. Big lips. A tail. A salmon." Egielski matches Yorinks's tone by also giving "nothing but the facts" and extends the nonsense. Images are framed and presented like evidence in a police case. His cool, dusty palette gives the book a central warmth and quietness that, by juxtaposition with the wry sling-shot text (for example, " 'Someday this will all be yours,' his father would say. And it was. His parents died suddenly and Louis took over the butcher shop"), evokes the contradictions between Louis the butcher's inner and outer selves.

Few illustrators have been as attentive to the unique rhythms of individual texts or more successful in visualizing their overall patterns than Arnold Lobel. "In a book," stated Lobel in 1984, "you are using pictures in a narrative way and the turning of the page is like a cut in a movie. If a movie is well done and you're caught up in it, even if you know the plot backwards and forwards, you're still pulled along by a rhythm. Alfred Hitchcock movies are a good example. And in children's books, the pictures have a rhythm, from large to small, for instance. And sometimes really sequential pictures work, but I wouldn't force that on something I didn't think called for it" (195). Lobel's illustrative extensions of *The Comic Adventures of Old Mother Hubbard* (Bradbury, 1968), *Hildilid's Night* by Chili R. Duran (Macmillan, 1971), and *As Right as Right Can Be* by Anne Rose (Dial, 1976), to choose just three, are vibrantly successful in visualizing the sounds and rhythm of the text and its emotions.

For the burlesque on again-off again rhythm of *Old Mother Hubbard*, Lobel's design is consistent page after page as if each page were a new act on a theater stage. The rhythm is full, even and steady. In *Hildilid's Night* Lobel varies the size of his images in relation to page size and neighboring images to reflect both the rhythm and the emotional content of events. The quickening fury of Hildilid's attempts to conquer the night, for example, is illustrated in smaller and smaller framed images with several per page. When she gives up—relaxes—Lobel's images relax and stretch across the pages, reflecting the slowed pace. These larger images are the equivalent of a film camera's pulling back for a more panoramic shot, which again evokes Hildilid's feeling of being overwhelmed by the night. Throughout, it is one of Lobel's most cinematic books. Rose's text for *As Right as Right Can Be* pivots on a strong see-saw rhythm of wish-wish fulfillment. Lobel again contrasts the size of his framed images with the page size to establish rhythm and time. The wider the image, the longer its length of time (like a cut in film) within the story's pattern and the quieter its emotional pace.

With writers and illustrators equally aware and respectful of their individual collaborative elements in the language of story, personal encounters between the two artists are not entirely necessary. Yet, as one who has written ten published picture books, I've found that most people assume that writer and illustrator create their picture book in tandem over coffee and danish. When I tell people that I make few specific contributions, if any, to the illustrations, they become defensive *for* me. When I try to explain that because the illustrator was not peering over my shoulder as I wrote nor telling me what to write I have little business peering over his shoulder dictating images, my questioners remain incredulous. "But how can you just let them?" they ask.

Once they are convinced that I do not have much overt control over the images and that perhaps I don't even want specific control, their next question is inevitable. "How do you like what they did with your story?" Or, to use Mamet's phrase, "How do you like their cinematography?" Their question assumes that the writer always knows what is best for each illustration. One could just as easily and perhaps more wisely ask: "If the writer has the ability to see and know exactly what images are best for a text then why hasn't he already drawn them himself?" If the writer has embodied his content and meaning in rhythm and sound, he knows he has given the illustrator the best possible direction for his visual extension of that meaning through color and line. With such direction from the writer, the illustrator has something with which he can truly blend, and it is less likely that readers will experience or remember only fantastic cinematography.

A vital element in this blending of sound and image is the picture-book editor, who must function in the role of a film producer or matchmaker. The best editors (at the same time as they are dealing with the solid mathematics of business) dwell in continual creative possibilities. Few texts even by the same writer will be identical in sound and rhythm, and there is an ever-expanding range of illustrators who might be selected to extend each text. The editor is the first to truly "hear"—and, as a result, "see"—what the picture-book author has written. Often seeing more than the writer himself initially sees, it is the editor who gathers the right ingredients to create a whole greater than its parts.

Depending on the personalities of the author, illustrator, and editor and on geographic realities, the writer and illustrator may never talk, may talk briefly, may correspond about background information, or may, on occasion, work in dialogue. But whichever level of "cooperation" transpires, the primary visual concern of the picture-book writer—the writer who trusts his own contribution—is based in sound and rhythm as emotion. If the tone, mood, timbre, atmosphere, and so on of the illustrations are not in harmony with what he feels in his texts, the specific content of the pictures becomes all but incidental.

Though at times those who ask, "How do you like what they did with your story?" have disagreed with me (a curious experience in itself), I feel my texts have always been well served by both editors and illustrators. I have, at times, been surprised, but never angry.

In one situation, Barbara Lalicki's praise of a new illustrator's ability to depict and evoke subtle movement helped me complete a manuscript that had been stalled for years. My awareness of Jacqueline Rogers's use of line was the catalyst for completing *Dancing the Breeze* (Bradbury, 1991). Concentrating on evoking the sense of a slight breeze which evolves into a moment of dancing reverie and then back to a stillness that I wanted her to feel and draw, I was able to write more richly. It was my chance to lead her as surely and as gently as if dancing a real dance.

> Rocking and waiting
> to see the moon
> both of us suddenly
> turn and smile.

> Both of us hear it—
> in soft notes of leaves
> twisting green-silver-green. . . .

As the father and child begin dancing the breeze, the rhythm evolves, and so does the mood of Rogers's images.

> Long steps with lupines
> and short ones with phlox,
> the breeze leads us gently
> around the front yard.

> Big steps with allium,
> small steps with chives. . . .

While not as overt or "tappable" as in *Dancing the Breeze*, *Sea Gifts* (Godine, 1989) has a sure aural sense and inner rhythm that is felt by the reader. Audrey Bryant wisely selected woodcut artist Mary Azarian to visualize not only my content, but my sounds as well. Beyond the surface connection of a text about a woodcarver being illustrated with wood, Azarian's images hold and evoke *Sea Gifts*'s sense of quiet pattern in the woodcarver's life and the warmth and hallowedness that a simple object acquires when viewed with loving eyes.

> Of an empty shell
> he wonders how any could leave
> such a handsome home.

> And quietly says,
> "Come join the village
> on my shelf."

In direct contrast to both *Sea Gifts* and *Dancing the Breeze* are the illustrations by Jose Aruego and Ariane Dewey for *Lizard's Song* (1981), *Dance Away* (1982), and *The Surprise* (1983—all Greenwillow). No one could have created images that more thoroughly translate the sounds and resulting emotions of the texts. Nor could any editor have made a wiser and more intuitive decision that Susan Hirschman in selecting them. While Azarian beautifully extended the quiet beckoning of *Sea Gifts*, Aruego and Dewey's work *is* the infectious joie de vivre I had hoped to convey in these three earlier texts. All three stories are quickly paced and comic in tone. Aruego's

lively line and cartoon facial expressions immediately evoke a sense
of zest and playfulness. Adding to this are Dewey's party colors that
jump out to greet the reader.

A good illustrator with an attentive ear may well be able to recognize and reveal aspects of the writer's text that the writer himself has yet to see. This has happened to me on several occasions,
the most dramatic being Peter Sis's wonderful images for *Bean Boy*
(Greenwillow, 1984).

The story has a strong folk flavor and an overt pattern of repetition. As a way of reinforcing this tone and rhythm I had suggested such illustrators as Anita Lobel and Margot Zemach, who
are known for both their peasant characters and their comic sense.
Though I had begun to imagine my text in such tones, I was excited
when my editor, Susan Hirschman, selected Peter Sis, who was at
the time a new illustrator in this country.

The first example I saw, however, of "what he did with my story"
made me panic. My folk-type Bean Boy was standing smack-dab in
the middle of a big city. Once I got to see the entire book a week
later I was not only relieved but enthralled. Sis had not so much
added a new level to my text as unearthed one of my favorite tale
types (The Treasure at Home, Aarne no. 1646) that I had not yet
realized was there. By beginning *Bean Boy* in the city, then going
to the country for help, and returning home to the city, Sis not
only extended the sense of cumulative action, but was able to add a
greater sense of inner journey and the circular motion which is the
heart of the story. His illustrations remain a special gift to me—a
prismed looking glass.

More than any other experience, *Bean Boy* taught me that, rather
than taking the role of protective mother hen, the most rewarding
approach to take as a picture-book writer is that of the Zen student
in the tale "A Cup of Tea." The Zen master fills the student's tea
cup to overflowing, then says: "Like this cup you are full of your
own opinions and speculations. How can I show you Zen [more]
unless you first empty your cup?" (5). Creating through collaboration more of my initial idea than I can create on my own is one of
the joys of writing picture books.

Works Cited

Aarne, Antti. *The Types of the Folk-Tale*. 1928. Trans. Stith Thompson. New York:
    Burt Franklin, 1971.

"A Cup of Tea." In *Zen Flesh, Zen Bones: A Collection of Zen and Pre-Zen Writings*, compiled by Paul Reps. Garden City: Doubleday, 1961.

Hass, Robert. "Listening and Making." In *Twentieth Century Pleasures: Prose on Poetry*. New York: Ecco Press, 1984.

Lobel, Arnold. Quoted in "Authors and Editors." *Publishers' Weekly*, 17 May 1971: 11–13.

———. Quoted in Rollin, Lucy, "The Astonished Witness Disclosed: An Interview with Arnold Lobel." *Children's Literature in Education* 15 (1984): 192–97.

Mamet, David. "Radio Drama." In *Writing in Restaurants*. New York: Viking, 1986.

Nodelman, Perry. "How Picture Books Work." In *Festschrift: A Ten Year Retrospective*, edited by Perry Nodelman and Jill P. May. West Lafayette, Ind.: Children's Literature Association Publications, 1983.

Sendak, Maurice. Quoted in Lorraine, Walter, "An Interview with Maurice Sendak." *Wilson Library Bulletin* 52 (1977): 152–57.

Taylor, Mary Agnes. "In Defense of the Wild Things." *Horn Book* 58 (1970): 642–46.

Varia

Tove Jansson and Her Readers: No One Excluded

Nancy Huse

Tove Jansson has not written a Moomintroll novel since 1970, when *Moominvalley in November* left the Moomins somewhere at sea, with only the youngest member of their extended household, Toft, awaiting their return. Those who know the Moomins are alive, however, include the large number of Jansson readers whose twelve cartons of letters, drawings, and artifacts (such as a pebble found by a four-year-old in Sweden, a purse for Moominmamma's handbag from a Japanese woman, a condensed thesis from a British psychologist) are stored in the Åbo Akademi library in Åbo (Turku), Finland. While many writers receive such mail, few engage in extensive correspondence with their readers, and fewer still seem to depend on such correspondence as a way of keeping intact a hardwon psychological stance intrinsic to ongoing work as an artist. For three decades, Jansson answered personally the approximately two thousand letters she received each year. An examination of this reader-writer interaction provides insight into Jansson's particular history. It also suggests some of the implications of the adult-child connection in literature, when the adult draws from her socialization as a daughter to create art and the child perceives the adult woman's ambivalence about the act of writing truthfully. Furthermore, it underscores the importance of children's responses in the literary system.

The daughter of two visual artists, the sculptor Viktor Jansson and the illustrator-engraver Signe Hamer Jansson, and a member of Finland's Swedish-speaking minority, Tove Jansson was educated as a painter. But the stories she constructed around her Moomin

Children's Literature 19, ed. Francelia Butler, Barbara Rosen, and Jean Marsden (Yale University Press, © 1991 by The Children's Literature Foundation, Inc.).

cartoons marked a transition to verbal art and to a life that continued her family's aesthetic tradition while delineating a new chan-
nel for it. Despite the difficulty of producing new fiction based on
her adult identity, Jansson maintains her ties to her birth family and
to her child readers via continuing contact with the Moomin family,
thereby demonstrating the complex female perspective discussed
by Nancy Chodorow (*The Reproduction of Mothering*) and Carol Gilligan (*In a Different Voice*).

Gilligan's work in developmental psychology indicates that
women mature into "the vision that everyone will be responded to
and included, that no one will be left alone or hurt" (63). According
to Gilligan, women are socialized to preserve relationships, achiev-
ing integrity by caring for others while defining their own needs.
Jansson, in a letter to a librarian, simply says, "One can't very well
leave the letter of a child unanswered." Unlike Michel Tournier,
however, who writes gleefully of his exchanges and visits with children but seems to view his young readers as clearly separate from
his own identity (183), Jansson's immersion in her correspondence
and visits with children seems directly related to her understanding of her moral selfhood. This is evident in some of her replies,
such as the thoughtful and lengthy letter she writes to an American
girl who wonders if the bombing of Hiroshima could in any way
be justified by the creator of the Happy Valley. Persistently in such
letters Jansson rejects an end-justifying-means ethic, yet she credits
her correspondents with forcing her to confront questions she has
avoided.

Such a perspective involves balancing rights and responsibilities, aggression and tenderness; it differs from twentieth-century
images of maturity as independence and separateness, and of art as
a unique product of isolation or alienation. Jansson acts the way a
writing mother is said to do, alternating between "'resentment and
tenderness, negation of the child and reaching out for the child'"
(Adrienne Rich in Suleiman, 366).

The first Moomin book, *Smaatrollen och den Stora Oversvamningen*
(*The Small Troll and the Big Flood*), appeared in 1942, when Jansson
was twenty-eight. From the episodic adventure structure of the first
few novels (there are nine novels and a collection of stories in the
series), the books evolved into complex psychological fantasy, with
accompanying shifts in illustration style from romantic to surreal
(Hollander). A story collection, published in Swedish as *Det Osynliga*

Barnet (*The Invisible Child*, 1963) and in English as *Tales from Moomin-valley*, was followed by two additional novels, *Moominpappa at Sea* (1965) and *Moominvalley in November* (1971), exploring adult-child relationships and the aging process. In 1966, Jansson received the Hans Christian Andersen medal. Over the next decade, she gradually separated her writing from her drawing, seeing fiction as a means of exploring adult themes and pictures as a way of providing children with humor and support. Continuing her children's literature involvement only with Moomin picture books, the writer has since produced a number of stories, novels, and autobiographical works for a sophisticated adult audience.

Across the manuscript of her first short story for adults, "The Listener" (1971), Jansson scrawled "*Inte for barn!*" (not for children); her theme in this and later fiction is the power of language, a "mind-game called Words That Kill—." Despite her wish to keep children at a distance from such themes, to avoid projecting her own needs onto them over a long process of accepting and articulating a lesbian identity (interview), many child readers have traced themes of alienation, doubt, artistic isolation, and maturation in the Moomin series books which precede Jansson's conscious attempt to write only for adults. The children's letters, and Jansson's replies to them, suggest how Jansson's creative process depends on the links to her own childhood that the Moomins represent. The correspondence also shows that—despite notions of children's radical difference from adults which lead such critics as Glyn Jones to assert that the later Moomin novels are not children's books at all, and that children "do not interpret"—young readers' responses are in fact rich strategies for explicating and extending the Moomin books as literary texts.

By some criteria Jansson's inability to prevent children from "reading" her own deepest concerns could signal the writer's lack of control of her craft. For example, Michael Egan has used the term "Double Address" to identify a convention of children's literature whereby writers explore their unconscious while seeming not to (46). Yet to call Jansson an unskilled writer would be preposterous. A better explanation for the responses her work evokes from children lies in the novels themselves, where adults and children have richly connected lives. Children who write comments like "Why don't you write a book of Moomin poems" or "on the laws of nature according to a whomper" or who show keen sensitivity in observing

that "the books are getting sadder and sadder" with advice such as
"You like *November* best. I'll read it again if you'll read *Midwinter* (my
favorite) again" demonstrate first-rate ability to interpret. Contrary
to some developmental theory (Piaget's, for example), such child-
readers can enter into the viewpoints of others, and they provide a
valuable, often whimsical ("Do snorks have pockets?") commentary
unavailable in reviews or formal criticism of the books. Their mode
of interpretation centers on producing new versions of the books
they read. Many write creatively in the persona of Snufkin or Sniff,
addressing their letters not to Jansson but to Moominmamma; and
new characters (such as "Smicker"), new forms (such as "Snufkin's
log book"), or new plot ideas (such as "Snufkin as Heraclitus")
abound. This process makes the children "collaborator(s) in the
polysemic life of the text" (Corti 44), disseminating Jansson's characters and ideas within the literary system, somewhat like directors
who both replicate and alter Shakespeare's texts. Perhaps because
of a general devaluing of metaphor and playful language, children's
discourse seems unrelated to interpretation or criticism. Yet in an
era when many critics have deliberately engaged in playful elabo-
rations of texts, it may be possible to recognize children's abilities
as interpreters.

Though Jansson's lesbian orientation has remained hidden from
them, child readers have recognized and empathized with her shift-
ing existential beliefs, the yearning of the artist for solitude and of
the person for affection, and the questioning of the nature of reality
and illusion. Frequently children exchanged letters with Jansson
over a period of years because her combined sense of responsibility
and pleasure in the correspondence prolonged it. "I can't resist the
little devils" is one bemused description of her letter-writing; she
also describes herself as "cornered" by these readers (interview).
Thus, she articulates in the letters to children her dual wish for rela-
tionality and solitude. To Japanese children who ask her what she
would do if she learned of her imminent death, she writes, "I would
walk along the sea with one I love best and not betray" (that is, not
cause pain). To a reader who loves Jansson's poet-philosopher Snufkin, she comments ruefully, "He is free to come and go as he wishes
and be silent without a bad conscience." More than once, Jansson has defended writers who, like Astrid Lindgren, send printed
messages to children who write to them. But the children who address her as "Dear Moominmamma" may have correctly interpreted

the centrality of that character's pre-oedipal, steady presence in the author's own personality—despite her admiration for the freer Snufkin.

An example of the creative tension in the correspondence is Jansson's habit of pasting an insightful letter on her studio wall or carrying one (as Moominmamma would) in her handbag, hoping to sustain inspiration and even to stimulate the allegedly impossible and undesirable return to writing Moomin books (interview). One such letter, from a boy in Sweden, detailed the way "The Invisible Child" (in *Tales from Moominvalley*) had brought peace to a classroom full of emotionally disturbed children on one especially desperate afternoon. The teacher (mother of the boy, Dan) had been unable to reach the children that day. But the account of how an unloved child becomes a rambunctious Moomin daughter, able to push Moominpappa into the sea without herself disappearing from fright, fulfilled a therapeutic function which the boy described eloquently. The children grew calm, intent on Ninny's gradual recovery from abuse. Jansson's reply to Dan explained how the famous story originated in her own family, with the adoption of a troubled child. This deeply personal and functional tale is one of Jansson's earliest attempts to probe her own subconscious and to experiment with language, and the letter shows how fully children understand it.

The children represented in the collection are, of course, often similar to Dan—and to Moomintroll himself—in being sensitive dreamers and already fluent writers. Yet letters from a range of ages and personalities indicate that various kinds of children make valid interpretations of even the later Moomin books. Many letters show the comic zest with which young readers enter into the wordplay and illogic of the early books; they send their own drawings of Moomins, hemulens, fillyjonks, and hattifatteners, characters which even in the first books embody odd moods and personality structures found in adults who live alone, become bureaucrats, or are caught in self-destructive moods of long duration. These children frequently move from playing with verbal and pictorial elements to a mode of interpretation in which they comment on how their own fears and delights have been reflected and made comprehensible in new ways through the stories. Child readers explicate such passages as the one in which Moomintroll is enchanted by the goblin's hat and recognized only by his mother, or they note that they were "achingly sorry for the hemulen, when no one would play with him." When readers say which character represents them, Little My, Sniff, Snufkin, and Toffle are cited nearly as often as the protagonist, Moomintroll, thus underscoring the multidimensional affective structure of the tales and their complex cumulative meanings. Child readers, not yet bound by the convention of identifying with a single main character, readily enter and describe Jansson's mythic world, where all child and adult creatures are welcome and necessary.

Some children then move from what James Britton would call the expressive and poetic modes to that which is more discursive and rational, the transactional. To one English child who wrote, "I enjoy the Moomins so much, because they are so unreal in form, and so real in person," Jansson replied, "I couldn't have got a finer compliment from a child." Nor, one might suspect, from an adult; the comment recognizes the psychological aspects of the fantasies. Noting the unique elements of the books, an American girl wrote, "They are wonderful, because they are different from any stories I've ever read"—a perceptive remark, since Jansson has been difficult for Anglo-American critics to describe and she herself stresses the personal (and Scandinavian) nature of the tales. Most such analytic comments appear in letters that individuals have chosen to write rather than in the school-generated packets Jansson despises and fears (because of her compulsion to answer even these letters).

More interesting, and probably more disturbing to Jansson's wish to be free of the demands childhood makes of her female moral self, is the outpouring of advice from young readers who recognize the doubt and anguish in *Moominpappa at Sea* and *Moominvalley in November*—books they name as favorites. Readers as young as nine, begging for a new Moomin book to follow the *November* text's focus on aging, suggest ways Jansson can write herself out of a corner, picking up with integrity the unwoven threads in her Moomin tapestry. Some of these letters, no doubt, have spent time on the studio wall or in Jansson's handbag as a help in her struggle and determination to retain creativity. Certain children (including Dan, the teacher's son) write to Jansson well into adulthood, further obscuring boundaries between "child" and "adult." A Norwegian boy, Einar, sent Jansson poems over a span of fifteen years. Another child, Tom, continued his habit of sending postcards signed "Sniff" from all over the world, writing of his adult search for love and work. Another, Richard, sent Jansson a copy of his novel, an achievement hardly surprising to a reader of the letters and stories he had written her in his boyhood. Simon Short, a frequent letter writer in boyhood, took a university degree in philosophy and as a young adult wrote again to discuss the existential themes of the books which fascinated him still.

A persistent theme of the child readers has been their wanting, like Holden Caulfield, to be with their favorite writer in actuality. In more than one instance, Japanese children have shown a particularly future-oriented response that Jansson thinks distinguishes them from more present-oriented American children. Some Japanese children have saved their money until they could make a pilgrimage to Helsinki to meet Jansson. Others have written to say that they want to come to Finland to live. One teenager realized that her childhood reading of the Moomin books had been a significant part of her development: "I found your books. I met your world. Always they make me a human." Another youth wrote to Jansson throughout his orphaned adolescence, receiving encouragement from her to become a teacher and find a place in Japanese society despite his yearning to be the writer's adopted son. While other writers or celebrities might have ignored the stream of letters from these young people, Jansson must follow up on the relationships her writing initiates, even though she says the role of "guru" is exhausting and debilitating (interview).

Unerringly sensitive to the needs of the individual child, the author explains her obsession—when amused rather than disgusted by it—with such comments as "They *tell* me things. They tell me about their cat. . . ." Fluent in English, Jansson has some mastery of German, French, and Finnish in addition to her first language. She gets help in reading messages in Russian, Polish, and Japanese. Nearly half the letters are in English, and she frequently replies in English. The children who "tell" her things range from the articulate and wealthy Pablo writing in German from Barcelona, at first at his mother's urging, to the Puerto Rican child in the East Bronx who copied out a long passage from *The Exploits of Moominpappa* on his own volition. The child's teacher sent a note explaining that the boy had never before done sustained reading or writing and needed the writer's encouragement. The children less needy than these, such as the American girl who sent her picture in a Moomin costume, or the schoolchildren who demand to know how Jansson gets ideas for books, receive witty replies. But the author explains at some length to Pablo, for instance, why he must first learn the thoughts of others in order to be truly original. Jansson writes that the Moomin texts are "memories of a happy childhood mixed with the comments of an adult," a distinction which helps her to view her newer work as "adult," linked not to her childhood directly but to experiences she has had as an adult woman artist whose almost cruel voice in her recent fiction represents a world she is determined to claim as her own.

The lengthy correspondence with individual children shows that Jansson is working through her sense of artistic vocation even as she takes care of the child she is writing to. Touched especially by the Japanese girl who signed herself "One of Your Children," Jansson seems willing to share with such young readers her most personal concerns—concerns she had hoped would be inaccessible to child readers of her Moomin books but which actually inspire letters to the author. For such readers, Jansson will allude to the "dry dust" of her mind; the potential for stories in her dreams and travel; her fears that the Moomin pictures will not be suitably recognized as art; her frequent regret that she created the Moomin comic strip in her youth and thus assured herself of "no peace ever since" to be an artist. In these letters, it is clear that the writer is willing to be mother, teacher, and mentor because these roles meet the artist's need for community. At the same time, the children's perspicuity has apparently made final Jansson's determination not to write anything but letters (and picture books) for child readers. Believing that children should not be burdened with adult concerns but given reassurance and cheerfulness by those who care for them, Jansson seems nevertheless to have accepted into her private circle those children who divine her secrets—and made up her mind to avoid future invitations to the young into her rich and hidden life. Thus, her canon—with its shift to an adult audience made explicit by a transition from fantasy to autobiography to surrealism—can be understood in developmental terms, especially in female developmental terms. Those letters to children who demand attention because they know Jansson's pain and sensitivity to others constitute an act of integration similar, as mentioned above, to the propitiation of crying children by mothers who are writers and whose continuing creativity is bound up in the continuing life of their children, even though this means interruption and diffusion of their thoughts.

Jansson's attachment to her own mother (who died at age eighty-eight) and wry affection for children are integral to both the Moomin books and the letters. Instead of separating from the all-good mother as Moomintroll does in his adolescence, the writer-daughter refuses to forget or abandon either the mother or the children who claim her attention through their letters and their insight into her books. In her autobiography, *Sculptor's Daughter* (1969), Jansson discusses an immediate source for the Moomin characters in "Snow," a chapter describing a few days sequestered with her mother in winter. For part of that time, she remembers, "Mummy didn't draw. We were bears with pine needles in our stomachs. . . . Only Mummy and I were left" (165).

Jansson's extensive, even obsessive letter-writing has taken away time and energy from other things. Yet the messages to and from Moomin readers sustain her creative powers as much as the process limits her. Unless she answers the letters, she can't work; yet the letter-writing keeps her from other writing (interview). It is apparent that Jansson's letters from and to child readers have neither simply encouraged her to write nor kept her from doing so; instead, they have caused her to write in certain ways, and her body of work has taken shape from the intensity of her involvement with children and her commitment to them as well as from her desire to be solitary and free of the demands of those who, in her judgment, need protection she cannot give.

One of Jansson's reasons for moving consciously into the writing of books directed toward adults was her fear that in her struggle to attain a clear sense of sexual identity, she would manipulate child readers. Aware of the artist's dependence on the unconscious, and fearing the psychoanalytic readings of such critics as Jacqueline Rose (*The Case of Peter Pan*), Tove Jansson has been wary of comparisons of her work to that of Andersen and Carroll, though in recent adult work, such as the 1982 *Den Erliga Bedraggeran* (*The Honest Deceiver*), she has been open about her lesbian partnership with Tuulikki Pietela, characterized as the helpful and spontaneous Too-Ticky in *Moominland Midwinter* (1957). Because Jansson's search for female artistic identity takes place in the context of her famous family (Viktor Jansson's sculptures dot Helsinki; Signe Hamer Jansson designed Finland's postage stamps) her personal life is always in markedly public view, thus heightening the sense of responsibility she feels and demonstrates toward her child audience.

Jansson turned to other art forms because, while continuing to keep the Moomins alive in pictures for children and for herself, she dared no longer allow the Moomin family to play out for children the terms of her psychosexual development. As she tells one reader, "it isn't a question of deciding. It comes to you or it doesn't. I am open for everything. But sometimes doors close and there is nothing to do about it" (1973 letter). Regardless of whether Jansson's later work endures—and such texts as *Sculptor's Daughter* (1969) and some stories in *The Doll's House* (1978) certainly have a resonance of their own—her Moomin novels and tales deserve more textual and historical criticism than they have received in English. Her integration of picture and narrative invites comparison with Sendak and Potter; her Moomin odyssey ought also to be addressed in the context of fantasy criticism. Above all, critics need to address the ways in which Jansson—like Anna Wulf, Doris Lessing's protagonist in *The Golden Notebook*—has discovered and dealt with the emotional difficulty of creating for oneself, for others, and for those others one must protect. These concerns make Jansson one of a relatively limited company of serious artists totally aware of a child audience.

Theories of projective poetics and reader response criticism come closest to explaining the relationship she has had with her child readers and its effect on her work. Georges Poulet, for example, emphasizes that in reading we are thinking the thoughts of another, experiencing the consciousness of another as if it were our own (44). Readers who write about the books they read, according to Wolfgang Iser, help to make conscious those aspects of the work which would otherwise remain in the subconscious (157). That readers and writers engage in "an intimate interaction . . . in and through which each defines for the other what s/he is about" is a familiar premise within much feminist criticism (Kolodny 244). In such a relationship, writers and readers create the works as well as each other's understanding of them. Such theories seem fully validated by this writer's continued involvement with her readers. The frequent and damaging assumptions that children cannot interpret, or that they are entirely victimized or controlled by the adults who produce children's books, are certainly called into deep question by the letters Jansson receives and answers.

Adults represented in the Åbo collection explicate some of the same themes as child readers do. But they make few demands on Jansson, supplying encouragement rather than requests or implicit pleas for attention. The adult readers typically write analytically, expressing their views by references to their other reading and learning rather than by sending story ideas or asking for the comfort they see as promised by the stories.

Although none of the letters has launched a return voyage for the Moomins, through them Jansson has engaged with readers in the quest for integration that remains primary to her. Aside from the therapeutic benefits of the correspondence, it has had the function of ordering her roles and values, allowing her to maintain an ethic of care while asserting an ethic of rights in her artistic and personal life. Like the hemulen who loved silence (*Tales*) but ultimately was unable to keep children out of the amusement park to which he had retired, Jansson has needed to live with the Moomins in the correspondence and in numerous exhibits and picture books concurrent with her adult books. In some ways, the correspondence may serve as pre-writing for these adult books, a moving in the letters through the stage of "innocence" to the "experience" of the surreal stories about art.

The child who told Jansson, "I hope you keep writing all your life," recognizing the terror of failed imagination in *Moominpappa at Sea* (1965), is one of several who have given Jansson their own hope. The connections between Jansson and her readers, a paradox of community and individuation, play out the dilemmas of the female writer which enable, even necessitate, the writer's growth and change. Jansson's example—children's writer turned adult author who still enters tangibly into the lives of children who understand her books—may not be followed by many other writers. Yet her wish to respect childhood as a period relatively free of adult pressures, her contradictory creation of fantasies which portray the full emotional range of human life, and, above all, her sense of responsibility for the effect of those fictions upon children suggest provocatively that the child readers of such authors may have a share in constructing not only their "own" literature but "adult" literature, too. *Tales from Moominvalley*, possibly Jansson's masterpiece, was produced at the height of the correspondence and generated some of the most insightful letters at Åbo, and perhaps "the voyage out" represented by the Moomin books which followed. For me, the protectiveness of Jansson toward her child readers is a reenactment of the stories she wrote for them, in which no one is excluded or hurt—not even a hemulen or a fillyjonk.

Notes

1. Solveig Widen, librarian at Åbo Akademi, helped to make the Jansson correspondence available for my visit. Petra Wrede, Marita Rajalin, and Tove Hollander
of the Åbo Akademi community provided a helpful context for interpreting the
materials.

2. I am indebted to Petra Wrede for this information about Jansson's recent novel,
Den Erliga Bedraggeran (The Honest Deceiver).

Works Cited

Britton, James. *Language and Learning*. London: Penguin, 1970.
Chodorow, Nancy. *The Reproduction of Mothering: Psychoanalysis and the Sociology of
    Gender*. Berkeley: University of California Press, 1978.
Corti, Maria. *An Introduction to Literary Semiotics*. Trans. Margherita Bogat and Allen
    Mendelbaum. Bloomington: University of Indiana Press, 1978.
Egan, Michael. "The Neverland of Id: Barrie, *Peter Pan*, and Freud." *Children's Lit-
    erature*, 10 (1982): 37–55.
Garner, Shirley Nelson, Claire Kahane, and Madelon Sprengnether, ed. *The (M)other
    Tongue: Essays in Feminist Psychoanalytic Interpretation*. Ithaca: Cornell University
    Press, 1985.
Gilligan, Carol. *In a Different Voice*. Cambridge: Harvard University Press, 1982.
Hollander, Tove. Interview with author in Åbo, 1983.
Huse, Nancy. "Tove Jansson's Moomintrolls: Equal to Life." *Proceedings of the Chil-
    dren's Literature Association* (1981): 44–49. Reprinted in *Webs and Wardrobes: Human-
    ist and Religious World Views in Children's Literature*, ed. Joseph O. Milner and Lucy
    Floyd Morcock Milner. Lanham, New York: University Press of America, 1987.
    136–46.
Iser, Wolfgang. *The Act of Reading: A Theory of Aesthetic Response*. Baltimore: The
    Johns Hopkins University Press, 1978.
Jansson, Tove. Interview with author in Helsinki, 1983.
———. *Comet in Moominland*. London 1951.
———. *Finn Family Moomintroll*. London 1951.
———. *The Exploits of Moominpappa*. London 1952.
———. *Moominsummer Madness*. London 1955.
———. *Moominland Midwinter*. London 1958.
———. *Tales from Moominvalley*. London 1963.
———. *Moominpappa at Sea*. London 1965.
———. *Sculptor's Daughter*. London 1969.
———. *Moominvalley in November*. London 1971.
———. *The Doll's House*. Helsinki 1978.
———. "The Monkey." Trans. W. Glyn Jones. *Books from Finland* 14 (1981): 62–63.
———. "Locomotive." Trans. W. Glyn Jones. *Books from Finland* 14 (1981): 64–71.
———. *Den Erliga Bedraggeran*. Helsinki 1982.
———. "The Listener." Trans. Nils J. Anderson in correspondence with author,
    1984.
Jones, W. Glyn. "Studies in Obsession: The New Art of Tove Jansson." *Books from
    Finland* 14 (1981): 60–71.
———. *Tove Jansson*. Twayne World Authors Series. Boston: G. K. Hall, 1985.
Kolodny, Annette. "A Map for Rereading; or, Gender in the Interpretation of Liter-
    ary Texts." In Garner et al., 241–59.
Poulet, Georges. "Criticism and the Experience of Interiority." In *Reader Response*

Criticism, ed. Jane P. Tompkins. Baltimore: The Johns Hopkins University Press, 1980, 41–49.

Rose, Jacqueline. *The Case of Peter Pan or The Impossibility of Children's Fiction.* London: Macmillan, 1984.

Suleiman, Susan Rubin. "Writing and Motherhood." In Garner et al., 352–77.

Tournier, Michael. "Writer Devoured by Children." *Children's Literature*, 13 (1985): 180–87.

Wrede, Petra. Conversation with author, 1983.

Not Every Giant Is a Winner:
A Contemporary Libyan Fable

Sylvia Patterson Iskander

Not Every Giant Is a Winner, a modern fable with political overtones, makes an impact through its illustrations, which are unusual
both in color and technique. The primitive style of the illustrations
is enhanced by an extraordinarily vivid use of color; the yellow
lion, for example, sports a blue nose, green eyes, orange under the
eyes, brown mane, and red toenails and has a pink, blue, green,
and white flower in his mouth. Backgrounds of the illustrations, at
first appearing in shades of blue and green, become warmer and
warmer as the action progresses to its climax, depicted in hot pink.
Flowers in a candelabra shape abound on every page; two or three
colors are used on a single flower, and different kinds of flowers
grow from various stems of the same plant.

Bubbles which normally enclose speech in cartoons have a variety
of functions here. They may indicate thought or emotion, as when
Bu Khodhaer, the green bird, puzzled over the disaster of his empty,
destroyed nest, is shown shedding a tear and a question mark appears in the bubble (fig. 1). Bubbles may depict a recollected scene,
as one does when Al Hamrayah, the red bird, relates to Bu Khodhaer that he saw the lion's cubs playing near the nest (fig. 2); they
may be blank, as one is when Bu Khodhaer calls his bird brothers
and listens for an answer (fig. 3); or they may contain dots expressing an emotion, as when Bu Khodhaer informs the lion about his
cubs' actions (fig. 4). The only bubble to contain "speech" appears
when little Bu Khodhaer arrives to confront the mighty lion, who is
asleep; the lion's bubble contains a repeated snoring sound (fig. 5).
What at first appear to be bubbles with dashes actually indicate
movement flowing from Al Hamrayah's tail (fig. 2), from Bu Khodhaer's tail (fig. 5), or from the lion's feet when he tries to flee from
the attacking birds (fig. 6).

Perhaps one reason for the speechless bubble is that the text in

Children's Literature 19, ed. Francelia Butler, Barbara Rosen, and Jean Marsden (Yale
University Press, © 1991 by The Children's Literature Foundation, Inc.).

Arabic would be too lengthy for inclusion in bubbles. Texts for young readers include both short and long vowels, whereas only long vowels are written out for advanced readers. In order for the letters to be large enough and "voweled" for beginning readers, the bubbles would have to be quite sizable. Other illustrated texts for young readers in Arabic that I am familiar with are voweled but do not contain bubbles. The bubbles appear to be a technique used by this illustrator to indicate speakers, express emotion, depict a recollected scene, or show movement.

The fable incorporates in its structure a number of Stith Thompson's motifs: Q211.6, killing an animal revenged (V: 201); B857, animal avenges injury (I: 481); and Q211.4, murder of children punished (V: 201). In addition to the element of revenge, a group in cooperation (in this case an alliance of birds) metes out the punishment. An analogue appears in Antti Aarne's 248A from India, "The Elephant and the Lark," a tale in which an elephant destroys the nest of a lark; the bird is aided in revenge by a frog, a crow, and a hive of bees, who ultimately kill the elephant (79). The motifs differ here insofar as (1) the avenging animals are all birds instead of a variety of animals and (2) the lion, whose cubs presumably attacked the bird's nest, is punished for the actions of his children, whereas the elephant receives punishment only for his own actions. However, the lion is spared when he requests mercy, unlike the elephant, who is killed. This element of forgiveness is "unusual" in folktales from the Middle East and may indicate a change made for the child audience (El-Shamy).

Both the lion and the elephant in African lore are frequently defeated by smaller animals, who usually outwit them rather than overpower them by uniting as a group (Jobes 999). In lieu of a trickster who is constantly the underdog and who seeks by his wits to acquire power over others, the little bird here seeks only to avenge a wrong and restore normal order. He does not require a life for a life, but he does want the lion to be humbled.

The source of this fable is "the popular oral text as narrated by Al Hag Mohammad Haqeeq." [1] According to Professor El-Shamy, however, this tale is probably a literary, not an authentic folk, narrative.[2] Though not unique to the Middle East, the concepts of granting mercy to one's enemies and of parental responsibility for children's actions are both admired and prevalent there. Political overtones, not unique to the Middle East, may be seen in the unwarranted

Fig 1. Bu Khodhaer is puzzled and saddened over the loss of his nest and his children; a tear falls from his eye. Illustrations from *Not Every Giant Is a Winner* by Al Labbad are reproduced with permission from the Public Company for Publishing Distribution and Advertising, Masarata, Libya.

عادَ طائِرُ «بو خُضَيْر» يوماً إلى عُشِّهِ ، فوَجَدَهُ مُخَرَّباً مُهَدَّماً ، ولَمْ يَجِدْ أيْضاً صِغارَهُ .

غَضِبَ «بو خُضَيْر» وبَدَأ يَبْحَثُ فى الأشْجارِ المُجاوِرَةِ فما وجَدَ شيئاً . وبَيْنَما هُوَ فى بَحْثِهِ وغَضَبِهِ ، قالَتْ لَهُ «الحَمْرايَةُ» ـ الّتى كانَتْ تَرْتَكِزُ على غُصْنِ الشَّجَرَةِ العالى :

« عَنْ ماذا تَبْحَثُ يا طائِرى الصَّغيرُ ؟ »

فقالَ : « أبْحَثُ عَنْ عُشِّى وعَنْ صِغارى . هَلْ جاءَ غَريبٌ إلى هُنا ؟ »

ى أنهمْ الْفَاعلونْ . فهمْ مَلاعينْ لا يُؤمنُ لهُمْ جَانبْ

Fig 2. The lion's children are arranged within the square in a manner depicting their frolicsome and rather wild nature. The tail of one cub extends beyond the boundary of the frame, perhaps indicating that the cubs have played too rough (gone outside the boundaries) in eating Bu Khodhaer's children.

أجابَتْ «الحَمْرَايَة» : «رَأَيْتُ أَوْلَادَ الأَسَدِ يَلْعَبُونَ قُرْبَ الـ
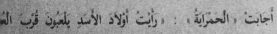

Fig 3. Bu Khodhaer calls his bird brothers to unite with him against the lion.

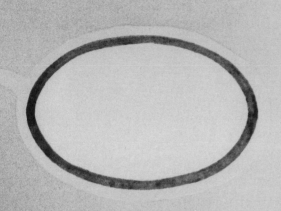

فوجِئَ « بو خُضَير » بكَلَامِ الأَسَدِ ، وحَزَّ فى نَفْسِهِ أَنْ يَسْمَعَ مِثْلَ هَذَا الكَلَامِ . فَقَالَ :

« سَتَرَى مَنْ مِنَّا لَيْسَ لَهُ اعْتِبَارُ ! » ، وَصَفَّقَ بِجَنَاحَيْهِ الصَّغِيرَيْنِ ، وطَارَ وَوَقَفَ على أَعْلَى غُصْنٍ فى أَطْوَلِ شَجَرَةٍ . وَنَادَى بِكُلِّ مَا يَمْلُكُ مِنْ قُوَّةٍ :

« يا إخْوَى ! يا طُيُورَ الغَابَةِ ! يا غِرْبَانَها ! يا عُقْبَانَها ! يا عَصَافِيرَها ! يا نُسُورَها ! يا صُقُورَها ! أخُوكُمُ الصَّغِيرُ (بو خُضَير) هَدَمَ أَوْلَادُ الأَسَدِ بَيْتَهُ . وَقَتَلُوا أَطْفَالَهُ . مَنْ يَأْخُذُ بِثَارِى مِنَ الأَسَدِ غَيْرُكُمْ ؟ مَنْ يَمْسَحُ العَارَ عَنِّى غَيْرُكُمْ ؟ يا إخْوَى عَلَى كُلِّ غُصْنٍ وَفِى كُلِّ وَكْرٍ ، الأَسَدُ غَرَّتْهُ قُوَّتُهُ ، فَاحْتَقَرَ كُلَّ ضَعِيفٍ » .

« يا طُيُورُ ! أَنَا أخُوكُمْ (بو خُضَير) أَسْتَنْجِدُ بِكُمْ . فَلَا تَخْذُلُونِى ! »

Fig 4. Bu Khodhaer standing on the lion's head enables the reader to compare the little bird's size with that of the great lion.

قَالَ « بُو خُضير » مُخَاطِباً الأَسَدَ :

« أَوْلَادُكَ هَجَمُوا عَلَى عُشِّي وَهَدَمُوهُ ، وَأَخَذُوا أَطْفَالِي . أَيْنَ هُمْ ؟ »

وَلِأَنَّ طَائِرَ « بُو خُضير » فِى حَجْمِ وَرَقَةِ الزَّيْتُونِ ، فَإِنَّ الأَسَدَ سَمِعَ صَوْتاً وَلَكِنَّهُ لَمْ يَرَ شَيْئاً . فَعَادَ إِلَى نَوْمِهِ . إِلَّا أَنَّ طَائِرَ « بُو خُضير » حَوَّمَ

قَلِيلاً ، وَوَقَفَ عَلَى رَأْسِ الأَسَدِ وَقَالَ :

« أَنَا أَقِفُ الآنَ عَلَى رَأْسِكَ وَلِذَلِكَ لَنْ تَرَانِي ، وَلَكِنَّكَ تَسْتَطِيعُ أَنْ تَسْمَعَنِي جَيِّداً . أَوْلَادُكَ هَدَمُوا بَيْتِي وَأَخَذُوا أَطْفَالِي »

قَالَ الأَسَدُ :

« أَنْتَ أَيُّهَا الطَّائِرُ الحَقِيرُ الَّذِى لَيْسَ لَهُ اعْتِبَارٌ بَيْنَ الطُّيُورِ ، تَقُولُ هَذَا الكَلَامَ ؟ أُغْرُبْ عَنْ وَجْهِى وَإِلَّا قَتَلْتُكَ بِضَرْبَةٍ مِنْ ذَيْلِى »

Fig 5. The lion is asleep and snoring when Bu Khodhaer flies to confront the mighty beast.

قال طائِرٌ «بو خُضَيرٍ» :

«أنا أصغَرُ الطُّيورِ ، وحَجمِي فِي حَجمِ وَرَقَةِ الزَّيتونِ ، لَكِنِّي سَأَذهَبُ إلى الأسدِ فِي عَرِينِه» .

قالتِ «الحَمرايةُ» :

«أنتَ ؟ كَيفَ تَتَحَدَّى الأسدَ وأنتَ فِي حَجمِ وَرَقَةِ الزَّيتونِ ؟» .

لم يَلتَفِتْ إليها الطّائرُ الحَزِينُ . وانطَلَقَ إلى عَرِينِ الأسدِ ، حَيثُ وَجَدَه نائمًا تَحتَ شجرةٍ كبيرةِ الأغصانِ ، وارِفةِ الظِّلالِ .

Fig 6. The motifs of the butterfly and the flower seem to lessen the impact of the lion actually being hurt, for he appears to cry more from fear than from pain. Bu Khodhaer appears at the end of the lion's tail.

اندَفَعَتِ الصُّقُورُ والنُّسُورُ والغِرْبانُ ، ومِنْ وَرائِها باقي الطُّيورِ ،
وهجمَتْ على الأَسَدِ . وأَوْجَعَتْهُ ضَرْباً بِمَناقِيرِها . عِنْدَها أَخَذَ يَبْكِي
ويَطْلُبُ مِنَ الطُّيورِ السَّماحَ والغُفْرانَ ، فغَفَرُوا لَهُ .

ومِنْ ذلكَ اليَوْمِ . والأَسَدُ لا يَخْشَى أَحَداً مِثْلَما يَخْشَى طَائِرَ
«بُوخُضَيْرٍ» !

attack on the nest, which must be avenged, and the necessity of allies for success against so large an enemy.

To a Western audience, however, the fable poses several problems. No absolute evidence ever emerges that the cubs ate the baby birds; only circumstantial evidence is given by Al Hamrayah that he had earlier seen the cubs playing around the nest. The lion's children, never called cubs, stand accused and presumed guilty, yet they remain unpunished;[3] the parent lion bears complete responsibility and the resultant punishment for them. The rather obvious moral depicts a humbled lion who recognizes strength in unity even when his opponents are individually weak. Yet, despite these logical problems, the book's illustrative techniques make the story both unusual and memorable.

Not Every Giant Is a Winner: Libyan Stories for Children

One day Bu Khodhaer [green bird] returning to his nest found it destroyed and his young babies missing.

Bu Khodhaer was angry and began looking in the surrounding trees, but he could not find anything. While he was searching and still angry, Al Hamrayah [red bird], who was standing on a high branch of a tree, addressed him:

"What are you looking for, my little bird?"

He replied, "I am looking for my nest and my young. Did any stranger come here?"

Al Hamrayah answered, "I saw the children of the lion playing near the nest, and I believe they are the ones who destroyed your nest. They are very bad children and cannot be trusted."

Bu Khodhaer said, "I am the smallest among all birds; even though I am about the size of an olive leaf, I will face the lion in its den."

Al Hamrayah replied, "You? How can you challenge the lion when you are the size of an olive leaf?"

The grieving bird did not turn to her, but flew to the lion's den, where he found the lion sleeping under a tree with large branches and shady leaves.

Bu Khodhaer addressed the lion: "Your children attacked my nest, demolished it, and took my children. Where are they?"

Because Bu Khodhaer was the size of an olive leaf, the lion, hearing a voice but not seeing anything, went back to sleep. But Bu

Khodhaer circled overhead, landed on the lion's head, and said, "I am now standing on your head and that is why you cannot see me, but you can hear me very well. Your children demolished my house and took my children."

The lion replied, "You little pipsqueak bird whom no one respects, how dare you talk to me like that? Get away from me, or else I will kill you with a flick of my tail."

Bu Khodhaer was surprised by what the lion said and saddened to hear it. He answered, "You will see which one of us is not respected!"

Then he clapped his little wings, flew to the highest branch in the tallest tree, and shouted with all his might: "My brothers! Birds of the forest! Crows! Swallows! Eagles! Falcons! Your little brother Bu Khodhaer is without a house. The lion's children demolished my house and killed my children. Who but you is going to avenge me on the lion? Who but you is going to wipe away my shame? My brothers on every branch, the lion is proud of his power and despises everything weak.

"Birds! I, your brother Bu Khodhaer, am imploring your help; do not let me down!"

Then the falcons, the eagles, and the crows all flew into the air, followed by the rest of the birds; they attacked the lion, and thrashed him with their beaks until he cried for mercy and asked forgiveness from them. Then they forgave him.

From that day on, the lion was more fearful of the little bird Bu Khodhaer than of any one else.

Notes

1. This comment, quoted from the unnumbered last page of the book, also indicates that the tale may have political overtones.

2. Professor Hassan El-Shamy, Indiana University Folklore Institute, has gathered some ten thousand texts from Middle Eastern and African tales for a book on motifs from these tales.

3. The word used for the cubs, *seghar*, usually refers to children in general.

Works Cited

Aarne, Antti. *The Types of the Folktale: A Classification and Bibliography*. Trans. and enl. Stith Thompson. 2d rev. ed. Helsinki: Suomalainen Tiedeakatemia, 1961.

Al Sharif, Youssif. *Not Every Giant Is a Winner: Libyan Stories for Children*. Illus. Al-Labbad. Cairo: The Public Company for Publishing Distribution and Advertising, People's Socialist Arabic Republic of Libya, with the artistic and technical cooperation of the House of Alif One for Children's Publications, n.d.

El-Shamy, Hassan. Telephone interview, 15 November 1989.

Jobes, Gertrude. *Dictionary of Mythology Folklore and Symbols*. 3 vols. New York: Scarecrow, 1962.

Thompson, Stith. *Motif-Index of Folk-Literature: A Classification of Narrative Elements in Folktales, Ballads, Myths, Fables, Mediaeval Romances, Exempla, Fabliaux, Jest-Books and Local Legends*. Rev. and enl. 6 vols. Bloomington: Indiana University Press, 1955–58.

Reviews

Pictures and Picture Books on the Wall
John Cech

Edward Lear, 1812–1888, by Vivien Noakes. New York: Harry N. Abrams, 1986.

Beatrix Potter, 1866–1943: The Artist and Her World, by Judy Taylor, Joyce Irene Whalley, Anne Stevenson Hobbs, and Elizabeth M. Battrick. New York: Viking Penguin, 1987.

Dr. Seuss from Then to Now, by Mary Stofflet. New York: Random House, 1986.

Yani: The Brush of Innocence, by Wai-Ching Ho, et al. New York: Hudson Hills Press, 1989.

We may live in an age of mass-produced and democratizing images, but they have not yet reduced our attraction to the unique, the rare, the exquisitely exclusive. Perhaps it is because so many of the images and artifacts of our culture have been rendered commonplace, familiar, and undistinguished that we are drawn by what Walter Benjamin has called the "aura of the original" work of art— elitist as those objects may be. Certainly the 1980s generated successive waves of works with such auras, ranging from the King Tut reliques to the Gauguin retrospective, from Andy Warhol's dayglo installations to the Dreamtime paintings of contemporary Australian Aboriginal artists. Happily, too, this general fascination with the original and the iconoclastic also reached the work of artists who are best known for their children's books. Along with television documentaries about such figures as N. C. Wyeth and Maurice Sendak, the decade produced major exhibitions on the art of the

Children's Literature 19, ed. Francelia Butler, Barbara Rosen, and Jean Marsden (Yale University Press, © 1991 by The Children's Literature Foundation, Inc.).

picture book (see Gillian Avery's review in *CL* 18 of Brian Alderson's *Sing a Song for Sixpence*, the catalogue for the British Library's 1986–87 show about the history of this genre) and the work of a number of its most important practitioners. Perhaps most fittingly, the 1980s concluded with the show of a very young Chinese artist whose paintings, though not designed for picture books, nevertheless reaffirmed the narrative power of pictures.

Still, despite these impressive exhibits of the last few years, the art of the picture book is intended to be seen between the covers of a book, joined to a text on paper that one can literally touch and to the intimate experience of reading. A well-known picture from a famous children's book like, say, Edward Lear's drawing for "The Jumblies" may seem lost and feeble when it is framed and hung on a gallery wall. The pictures that Lear used to illustrate his nonsense verse were designed to have their mercurial life in an inexpensive children's book—not the carefully preserved existence of the elegant imperial folios that contained Lear's extraordinary lithographs of birds from the Earl of Derby's private menagerie at Knowsley Hall.

Of course, what we gain from these exhibits and from the sumptuous catalogues that have emerged from them is a fuller understanding of an artist whose work we may meet in and most frequently associate with the picture book. With Lear one quickly discovers, in the comprehensive exhibit that wound its way through the long narrow halls of the Royal Academy of Arts during the summer of 1985 and in Vivien Noakes's catalogue of the show, that the bird pictures and the nonsense, important as they are in our estimation of Lear today, were only a small part of Lear's *oeuvre*, though the former built his reputation and the dozen or so volumes and numerous editions of the latter paid his bills. At the time of his death in Italy in 1888 Lear left more than seven thousand watercolors and three hundred oil paintings, the majority of them landscapes from his many years of travel around the Mediterranean and farther east to such faraway places as Philae, Bassae, Benares, and Poonah. The nonsense drawings and verse were a wild, eccentric subtext, a shadow to the "serious" art that Lear was busily about; the nonsense emerged as a private safety valve from the arduous demands of his work and travels and the exasperations of his own emotional life. Their personal character helps explain why the first books of nonsense were published anonymously and why Lear wrote only close and trusted friends his famous letters with their comic drawings and uninhibited word play.

The Noakes catalogue preserves the same sense of discovery that charged the exhibition with an excitement that came from touching, again and again, these disparate poles of Lear's talent, literally within a few feet (or in the book, a few inches) of one another. For instance, at the beginning of this volume (which also contains short essays on Lear's artistic reputation from Steven Runciman and Jeremy Maas), one finds several of Lear's ornithological masterpieces, such as an early lithograph of the Red and Yellow Macaw. Noakes contrasts these immediately in her commentary with the nonsense cartoons of birds, like the bedraggled "Pink Bird" or the wary "Crimson Bird," that Lear dashed off as humorous lessons in color for child friends who claimed Lear as their "Adopty Duncle" in his middle age, long after he had done his final bird portrait. It was for these children—whose parents he had met at Certosa del Pesio, Rome, San Remo, or one of the other places where Lear stayed and painted during his many years abroad—that Lear made up new versions of his nonsense alphabets and set to music such poems as "The Owl and the Pussycat" (174).

In his own time, Lear's talent as an artist did not go unrecognized, as the essays in the catalogue make clear; and he was especially well known for the many volumes of travel books that he illustrated. He was even asked to give drawing lessons to Queen Victoria, the results of which Noakes includes along with thorough notes on this chapter in Lear's life. The queen was heartened by the fact that Lear "was very pleased with [her] drawing and very encouraging about it," and, for his part, Lear wrote a friend that he could not "help thinking H.M. a dear and absolute duck" (159–60). Somehow Lear could not translate these or other contacts into a lasting sinecure that might have made it unnecessary for him to crank out hundreds of watercolors on an assembly line in his studio. He was not skilled when it came to playing the politics of the late Victorian art world. As he himself put it with characteristic self-deprecation, with his travel-stained, paint-spattered clothes, he was "a dirty Landscape painter apt only to speak his thoughts & not conceal them" (160). One of his patrons, the Earl of Derby, for whom Lear had painted many of his best animal and bird pictures, summed up Lear's predicament with smug condescension: "in a world, where nothing succeeds like success, he has done himself much harm by his perpetual neediness . . . he has been out at elbows all his life, & so will remain to the last" (11).

But in this richly detailed catalogue, Lear has the last laugh—on the frailties of the human condition, his own follies, and the folly of fame itself. In response to a friend who had urged Lear to take more decisive steps in his career, Lear wrote one of those inimitable letters that honed the wit he put into his friendships and his nonsense: "the voice of Fashion whether it hissues hout of a Hart Cricket in a Paper, or hout of the mouth of a Duke or Duchess—ain't by no means the voice of Truth. So you see o beloved growler—your observations don't affect me a bit, who haven't got no ambition, nor any sort of Hiss Spree de Kor at all at all" (11). Long after the exhibition has come down, Noakes reminds us not only of Lear's abundant spirit and astonishing creative gifts, but also of the tension that often exists between the conflicting but complementary aspects of an artist's genius—between the varnished, formal surfaces of an oil painting, like the large canvas Lear did of the road to the pyramids at Giza and the quick, agile grace note of an owl and a pussycat playing from the other side of reason.

Unlike Lear, Beatrix Potter and her work have never really gone out of fashion, and so there has not been the need to reassess or reanimate her reputation. According to *Publisher's Weekly*, which announced its list of perennial bestselling books for children as the 1980s drew to a close, the most successful hardcover children's book is Beatrix Potter's *The Tale of Peter Rabbit*. As of October 1989, this small volume had sold over nine million copies. The next most popular book—Dorothy Kunhardt's *Pat the Bunny*—is a distant second at just under five million. A visit to Potter's home in Near Sawrey in the Lake District daily confirms her fame. Hill Top House, Potter's studio and the setting for a number of her most famous books, is a place of pilgrimage. It attracts elderly colonels in regimental moustaches who were weaned on *The Roly Poly Pudding* and wealthy industrialists who are whisked along the lanes in Rolls Royces, dowagers and busloads of dutiful youngsters, local farmers and vacationing factory workers from the Midlands, taxis full of American academics, and travel feature writers with wide-angle lenses. All are lured by the mystique of that unusual lady who drew some of the most widely recognized images in the iconography of childhood—Peter eating the carrot he has filched from Mr. McGregor's garden, Peter in tears by the garden gate, Peter scooting under the fence that claims his jacket, and others. The path to Hill Top House is so well traveled that the National Trust advertises it sparingly and strictly limits access to it, lest its fragile beauty be worn out by visitors.

Potter scholarship, which is much more than a cottage industry in England, has continued to give us over the years a steady stream of works (biographies, monographs, and, in the near future, decoded diaries and another volume of letters) that have been painstakingly and reverently researched and, for the most part, lavishly produced by Potter's original publisher, Frederick Warne. *The Artist and Her World* is the latest of those elegant volumes. A series of background essays on Potter's life and work by scholars, like Judy Taylor, who have been working in the field for some time, it was intended as a companion to the major exhibit of Potter's work that appeared first in England at the Tate Gallery in 1987–88 and then at the Pierpont Morgan Library in New York City in the summer of 1989. Even though Madison Avenue is thousands of miles from Near Sawrey, another legion of Potter fans stood in long lines to move slowly through the Morgan's grand rooms, many with magnifying glasses in hand, to examine every detail of the small, archetypal miracles that are Potter's pictures. As a rule, the pictures are so small (many of the illustrations for her books are about the size of a 3 × 5 inch index card) that their subtle brilliance comes through only in her originals, fine pen-and-ink and watercolor miniatures that even the most sophisticated photoduplication can not quite capture. Happily, the reproductions of many of the pictures in this volume are better than they have ever been, and this brings us as close to Potter's consummate art as we can get if we are not able to experience her work at first hand.

Because of the continuing interest in Potter's work, much of what appeared in this show and is contained in this volume will be familiar terrain to any student of Potter's who has worked with Judy Taylor's biography or Margaret Lane's study, *The Magic Years of Beatrix Potter*. Once more the Potters stare awkwardly (while Beatrix looks earnestly) into the camera in those now-famous family photographs, and we reach with relief the pictures of a much older Beatrix, with her serene round face, at a livestock show in one of the little villages of the Lake District after she finally managed to escape from the repressive cloud cast by her glowering parents. In one of the early biographical chapters, we see again her superb early

micological studies and those first, hesitant greeting cards of rab-
bits—her breakthrough as a freelance artist. And then, of course,
at the center of any comprehensive look at Potter are the masterpieces of her mature work: the "little books," beginning with *Peter
Rabbit* and *The Tailor of Gloucester* and culminating in the closing
chords of *The Tale of Mr. Tod* and *Cecily Parsley's Nursery Rhymes*.
Each of these works is given a brief (alas, in some cases, too brief)
discussion in a chapter jointly written by Anne Stevenson Hobbs,
Joyce Irene Whalley, and Judy Taylor. Their survey of these books
fuses elements from Potter's biography with the evolution of her
texts and pictures. We meet, for example, the real Farmer Potatoes
and see how Potter herself used photographs of people and places
as models for her illustrations; and we can observe (in her early
watercolor studies for *Squirrel Nutkin*) Potter's keen ability to adapt
a landscape perfectly to her narrative purposes.

A focal point for both the show and the companion volume is
Potter's relationship to the Lake District, where she spent her sum-
mers from childhood on and where she would eventually live herself, becoming both a part of the tradition of English artists who
had been inspired by that countryside and one of its staunchest de-
fenders against the encroachments of the developers. Elizabeth M.
Battrick's three chapters on the deep connections between Potter
and the spirit of that place are especially informative, and her stipu-
lation that profits from the sale of the book go toward a special
fund for preserving the unique character of the countryside is one
compelling reason to buy the book. But there are many others in
the thoughtful, eminently readable text and profusely illustrated
pages that make up this overview of Potter's life and works. For *The
Artist and Her World* reminds us, again and again, of Potter's stature
as an inexhaustible international resource. Her pictures, and the
small books they inhabit, remain as sturdy as the Herdwick sheep
that Potter raised, as fresh and fragile as a spring morning in the
rural world that had inspired Potter and that was already beginning to slip away when she began to paint it and to create fables
that might somehow save it from oblivion.

Despite their small size, Potter's painterly pictures are made for
galleries and public display; they are able to hang as finished works
of art, independent of the page and separate from their text. Potter
was influenced significantly by Randolph Caldecott in the construction of her own picture books, but she was not as concerned as

Caldecott was with the dynamic interplay and mutual interdependence between text and pictures. By contrast, when pictures from Dr. Seuss's books are displayed on museum walls, one sees how utterly tied most of them are to the printed page and thus to Seuss's texts. For Seuss is a true artist of the picture book, a brilliant master of that bimedial form, more than he is an artist whose visual works can (or are designed to) stand alone. Perhaps the unique interdependency that exists between Seuss's texts and pictures—and the difficulty this poses for exhibiters—may help to explain why the works of both Potter and Lear have appeared with some regularity in museums and galleries over the years, whereas Dr. Seuss has only recently had the first major, retrospective exhibition of his art in the form of a show that toured seven small museums across the country in 1986–88. Otherwise it would seem very strange that such an exhibit had not been mounted before. For, without doubt, Seuss is the most famous maker of children's books in the United States, and he also has an enormous international following: according to Mary Stofflet, the curator of the exhibit and principal author of its catalogue, "more than one hundred million Dr. Seuess books have been purchased by parents, grandparents, and children in Japan, Israel, Norway, Sweden, Denmark, Germany, Holland, Italy, Brazil, and countries of the British Commonwealth." Then she adds, almost nonchalantly, "*Green Eggs and Ham* (1960) is the third-largest selling book in the English language. Ever" (17). *Publisher's Weekly* might dispute this claim, but the same list of "all-time bestselling hardcover children's books" that placed *Peter Rabbit* first counts four Dr. Seuss books (*The Cat in the Hat, Green Eggs and Ham, One Fish, Two Fish, Red Fish, Blue Fish,* and *Hop on Pop*) among the top ten.

Not only has he been ignored by the art world; Seuss has been virtually dismissed by most scholars and critics of children's literature. Aside from a few essays, such as Jonathan Cott's short study of Seuss in *Pipers at the Gates of Dawn*, one is more likely to encounter a discussion of his work in the Sunday supplement of a newspaper. The common, knee-jerk reaction among many of the taste-setters in academic and library circles is that Seuss is "too commercial" to be taken seriously, and so he is left to the popular press, where these same critics feel his work more properly belongs in the first place.

Seuss does not wholly reject the "commercial" tag assigned to his work; in fact, as the exhibit and Stofflet's catalogue acknowledge, he began his creative career in one of the most market-driven occupations of them all, advertising. We learn from the biographical portion of *From Then to Now* that Seuss was bored with his classes in English literature at Oxford, where he had gone for graduate studies in 1925. His lecture notes soon were crowded out by the cartoons (several of which are included in the catalogue) that he doodled across the pages of his notebooks, and before long he left England and his doctoral studies for the continent and his own version of the Grand Tour. From the doodles and sketches that Seuss jokingly refers to as his "Roman and Florentine Period" one leaps out: a pen, ink, and crayon drawing of a dragon, based on the creature that Perseus slays in Piero di Cosimo's painting from the Uffizi Gallery in Florence; it is the mythic ur-beast that seems to have inspired a good number of Seuss's own monsters. Back in the States in the early 1930s, Seuss was beginning to make his living designing humorous advertising campaigns for such products as Flit bug spray ("Quick Henry, the FLIT") and Essolube motor oil. In the latter, Seuss previewed a number of characters, such as the engine-destroying Karbo-nockus and the Moto-raspus, that would evolve into several of his celebrated fantasy creatures—the Glunk and the Grinch.

Still, it was leaving the creative restraints of advertising, we learn, that freed Seuss to write his first children's book, *And To Think That I Saw It on Mulberry Street* (1937), now a classic of American picture book fantasy. The manuscript passed through the hands of twenty-eight publishers who thought "it was too different from other children's books then on the market," before reaching the twenty-ninth (Vanguard Press), which published it precisely because it was different (31). Seuss served a stint as an editorial cartoonist during the 1940s, where he sharpened the political edge to his work that would later cut through the destructive pretensions of Yertle the Turtle or the frenzied irresponsibility of "the boys in the back room" in *The Butter Battle Book*, Seuss's probing anti-war tract that received international acclaim in 1984.

Though it is adequate in covering the high points of Seuss's career and in introducing us to dimensions of his graphic art that had not been displayed before (some of the paintings he has done privately, for example, show us a Miro-esque concern for abstract form—though these, unfortunately, are not included in the book), one wishes that Mary Stofflet's text had gone further to explore Seuss's role as one of the important innovators of modern American children's literature. Though informed and cheerfully written, these textual notes leave the reader with the feeling that an opportunity has somehow been missed. Whereas most writers have only one archetypal story that they are continually repeating in various forms in their work, Seuss has three: the fable, the book of nonsense, and the fantasy. Taken together, they have helped educate several generations of readers about the wild possibilities of words, the deep reaches of the psyche, and, most powerful of all, the language of the human heart.

The vibrancy of that language, the range of that voice was given rejuvenating meaning in the exhibition of paintings by a young artist, Wang Yani, who will just be turning sixteen when this review appears. An acknowledged prodigy in her native China, where she began painting in the traditional manner with brush and ink when she was two and a half, by the age of six she had done some four thousand paintings, the vast majority of them of her favorite subject—monkeys. In the West, her extraordinary talent has been favorably and enthusiastically compared with the precocious productions of Picasso, Klee, Landseer, and Millais; and in China, which has a tradition of using monkeys as a subject for painting that reaches back into the eleventh century in the visual arts and another millenium in literature, she is viewed as a national treasure. An apocryphal story is told about how, after seeing the monkeys that Yani had painted by the time she was four, "an artist who had specialized in painting the animal decided to give up his lifelong pursuit and presented her with his personal seal, which depicts a monkey holding a peach" (16). What experts in Chinese art find amazing is her quick mastery of the technical skills of that form of painting, especially its sovereign first principle, *qiyun shengdong*, or "rhythmic vitality"—the capacity for expressing the essential qualities or characteristics of beings or phenomena in nature (17). In the Chinese tradition, this does not involve mere duplication but, rather, through a process of representation that has been called "magical realism," capturing the elemental life of a thing in just a few brushstrokes, often making use of the "accidents" of paint drippings and washes to reach this existential essence (17).

Yani's monkey paintings, which made up the core of the exhibit that toured the United States last year, are fascinating to consider in the context of a discussion about picture books because they represent in some fundamental way the ancient impulse, recapitulated in our personal development, to connect narratives and pictures. For example, each of Yani's monkey paintings has a story about the particular monkey she is depicting woven into it; these narratives are of a personal nature, fantasies she has created to talk the monkeys into being. Though the texts of these stories do not appear with the paintings, Yani's father, who is also a painter and has served as Yani's Rousseauean mentor, has carefully recorded in his journals what he has heard his daughter saying to the monkeys as she paints them. In one instance, she added a fruit tree to a painting because she knew that the monkey in it was hungry, and as she was finishing the fruit, she chided him to be patient, as it was almost ripe. In other instances the legends that she adds to the pictures, like a key line from a poem, imply the rest of the tale. On one long, vertical painting she has painted a gnarled cherry tree that has just burst into blossom. Below, on the ground, an orange-faced monkey, with its arms outstretched, leans back, staggered (it would fall on its back were it not for the curling tail that gives it balance) by the beauty of the tree and the watery mist that covers it. His sole exclamation (and the witty title of Yani's painting) is, simply: "Wow!"

Since reaching her teens, Yani has moved on to other animals—lions and tigers, egrets and horses—and it will be interesting to see if, as is suggested in the commentary for *The Brush of Innocence* (which includes essays on Yani's personal development, the tradition of the monkey in Chinese art, Yani's relationship to the broader context of Chinese painting, and the nature of the child prodigy in art), the same energy will continue and be transferred to other subjects as Yani's art develops. One also wonders whether Yani's evolution might lead her into picture book or other forms of illustration, of her own or of others' stories. For in her rare ability to communicate visually the essence of a thing in nature, she reminds us, with the sense of energy that is everywhere released in her work, of the animating force that needs to be present in any picture book. We see it unfold in Yani's scroll of a hundred dancing monkeys or in the tense, one-eyed wakefulness of a lion just ready to pounce on the gang of monkeys that have been cavorting on his back. The appearance of Yani, shortly after the death of Mao, has been viewed as representing a new spirit of vigor, openness, and experimentation in Chinese art. One also hopes that her work may serve as a harbinger for a new generation of artists who will reaffirm the dynamic form of the picture book so that we, too, may lean back bedazzled and say, "Wow!"

Class Acts

Mark I. West

The Literary Heritage of Childhood: An Appraisal of Children's Classics in the Western Tradition. Charles Frey and John Griffith. Westport, Connecticut: Greenwood Press, 1987.

Professors' publications often grow out of material originally prepared for classroom presentation, and this certainly seems to be the case with *The Literary Heritage of Childhood: An Appraisal of Children's Classics in the Western Tradition* by Charles Frey and John Griffith. If read as introductory lectures or old-fashioned appreciations, the book's twenty-eight essays work reasonably well. Written in an entertaining and informal style, they provide key information about many important children's books, introduce several forms of literary analysis, and raise some interesting questions, all in the span of around six pages each. For the most part, however, Frey and Griffith ignore the work of other researchers and critics in the field of children's literature. Combined with the brevity of the essays, this undermines the scholarly stature of the book.

Arranged chronologically, the book opens with an essay on Charles Perrault's fairy tales and concludes with one on *Charlotte's Web*. In between, Frey and Griffith discuss many of the standard works in children's literature, including *A Christmas Carol, The Adventures of Pinocchio, Little Women, The Adventures of Tom Sawyer, Treasure Island, The Wonderful Wizard of Oz, The Wind in the Willows*, and *Little House on the Prairie*. All but eight of the works discussed also appear in Frey and Griffith's massive anthology, *Classics of Children's Literature*; in fact, the first few pages from many of the essays are lifted word for word from the introductory comments that precede the selections in their anthology. Thus, Frey and Griffith begin almost all their essays with information about the author of the work under consideration and move on to an analysis of the work itself. In the process, they make some interesting connections between the authors' lives and their literary creations. For example, in the essay on *The Wind in the Willows*, they argue that Kenneth Grahame's per-

Children's Literature 19, ed. Francelia Butler, Barbara Rosen, and Jean Marsden (Yale University Press, © 1991 by The Children's Literature Foundation, Inc.).

sonal despair led him to create the idyllic world of the river bank. In their essay on Laura Ingalls Wilder's *Little House on the Prairie*, they explain which parts of the book are autobiographical and which are fictional. Frey and Griffith do not limit themselves to biographical criticism, however. As they point out in their preface, they experiment with a wide variety of approaches: "Our methods and themes are somewhat eclectic in that we vary our focus from, say, Calvinist issues in *Treasure Island*, to grown-up baiting in *Alice's Adventures in Wonderland*, to psycho-sexual readings of Andersen and Barrie, to character analysis in *A Christmas Carol*, to comparisons of tales by the Grimms and Perrault" (x).

Scattered throughout the essays are lots of questions—the sorts of questions that professors ask to spark class discussion. In the essay on *Pinocchio*, they ask, "How can it be that a tale which amounts to little else than a fanciful story of child-abuse passes for a classic especially enjoyed by children" (102–103)? In the essay on *A Christmas Carol*, the reader is asked, "Does 'Scrooge' stand in our minds for the redemptive capacities of the human heart? Or for the skeptic night of the soul" (74)? Readers may feel inclined to raise their hands and offer answers, but they need not worry if they are stumped by the questions because, as professors so often do, Frey and Griffith glibly answer their own questions. Immediately after asking the question about Scrooge, they write, "It's plain enough that Scrooge stands for a spirit of defense and self-authority, a wish to keep at bay all claims for love that might expose one to vulnerabilities and pain" (74–75).

The essays have the polish of oft-repeated lectures, but they seem to be based on notes that are beginning to yellow with age. Frey and Griffith claim in their preface that the book "freshly interprets famous works" (vii). Perhaps this means that they are deliberately distancing their interpretations from those of other contemporary scholars, but the standards of good scholarship require that they at least acknowledge the existence of other work in the field, and in many cases they include no such acknowledgements. The essay on *The Wonderful Wizard of Oz* never cites Michael Patrick Hearn's work in this area, and the essay on *The Wind in the Willows* never mentions Lois Kuznets's research. The list of omissions could go on and on. These omissions are most serious when Frey and Griffith disagree with the interpretations of important contemporary critics. In their essay on *Pinocchio*, for example, they argue that the book is "the story of a child-hero brought by a long process of ordeal, shame, and sermonizing to a thoroughly puritanical self-hatred" (99). This view is in complete conflict with the argument of Thomas Morrissey and Richard Wunderlich that Pinocchio's psychological development is healthy and realistic, at least on a symbolic level. Morrissey and Wunderlich are generally recognized as leading authorities on Collodi's book, but Frey and Griffith make no mention at all of their important scholarship.

Frey and Griffith never say exactly for whom the book is intended, though it seems to be aimed at students in children's literature classes. Although these students would probably enjoy the book's informal style, they would be better served by a more up-to-date and fully documented work. Fortunately, such a book exists. It is entitled *Touchstones: Reflections on the Best in Children's Literature* and is published by the Children's Literature Association. Nearly all the books that Frey and Griffith discuss are also covered in the first two volumes of *Touchstones*; unlike Frey and Griffith's essays, however, the entries in *Touchstones* refer to recent research on these classic children's books. This does not mean that *The Literary Heritage of Childhood* is without value; but, measured against *Touchstones*, it simply falls short.

Grace-Notes, Icons, and Guardian Angels

Ruth B. Bottigheimer

Caldecott & Co.: Notes on Books and Pictures, by Maurice Sendak. New York: Farrar, Straus and Giroux, 1988.

Maurice Sendak: Bilderbuchkünstler, edited by Reinbert Tabbert. Bonn: Bouvier, 1987.

Dear Mili, by Wilhelm Grimm, translated by Ralph Manheim. Illustrated by Maurice Sendak. New York: Farrar, Straus and Giroux, 1988.

In his unassumingly titled collection of essays, Maurice Sendak muses on illustrators like Ruth Krauss, Tomi Ungerer, and Randolph Caldecott; on authors like Adalbert Stifter and Hans Christian Andersen; and on genres that lie somewhere between pictures and words, like the transformation books of Lothar Meggendorfer and the cartoons of Winsor McKay. His humane perceptions and generous assessments of other writers and illustrators, interesting in themselves, also reflect and refract qualities which he values and expresses in his own work.

Early in his illustrating career, in an essay entitled "The Shape of Music," Sendak identified a characteristic which he called "quickening" as an essential quality in illustrations for children's books. An insistent rhythm akin to musical cadences should, he says, emanate from the image it enlivens, even where musicmaking forms no explicit part of the illustrations themselves. The harmonies and counterpoints he refers to in such artists as Caldecott resonate in his own illustrations, in the variations and repetitions of the monsters' dance in *Where the Wild Things Are*, in Else Holmelund Minarik's Little Bear books of the 1950s and '60s, or in his father's autobiographical *In Grandpa's House* (Harper and Row, 1985). In other instances Sendak depicts explicit musicmaking, as when Rosie sings in *The Sign on Rosie's Door*, or Ida plays her wonderhorn in *Outside Over There*, or the three bakers sing and dance along with Mickey in *In the Night Kitchen*. In *Dear Mili* a recumbent Mozart directs a boy

Children's Literature 19, ed. Francelia Butler, Barbara Rosen, and Jean Marsden (Yale University Press, © 1991 by The Children's Literature Foundation, Inc.).

holding an invisible violin in a double-page illustration. Looking at the illustration, we wonder how we are to understand the instrument's invisibility. Sendak himself has identified the choir as the children of Izieu, France, who were killed by Klaus Barbie and the Nazis. The children are in Paradise, Sendak has said, thus suggesting that in Paradise an instrument is unnecessary for musicmaking. But the scene may implicitly refer to Sendak's belief, which he articulates in "The Shape of Music," that "music helped unravel my imaginary scenes" and that it was "the catalyst that brought them to life" (*Caldecott* 163).

Sendak is keenly appreciative of a "quickening" musical rhythm in the work of other illustrators. "This is the key to Meggendorfer: his pictures don't merely move; they spring to life. Our little Dancing Master, by the power of music, is transformed into a gallant swain. Perfectly still, he is ridiculous. But when he moves, he is the embodiment of musical grace" (*Caldecott* 53). Jean de Brunhof's circus scene in *Le Voyage de Babar* he sees as a flat picture which "moves rhythmically in step if you keep your eyes on those stolid elephant feet, all thumpingly clumping to the same measure" (104).

Music provides one enduring metaphor in Sendak's writing and illustration, but his major pictorial metaphors are, fittingly, the book and the picture. Books appear in his published drawings on the slipcase for *The Nutshell Library* in 1962, and later Max stands on books in *Where the Wild Things Are*. Pictures are also built into many of his illustrations: Max's self-portrait as monster, Little Bear's demon, and the *Mona Lisa* in *Higglety Pigglety Pop!* To analyze and evaluate Sendak's books and pictures it is useful, even necessary, to know that he began his career as "a green recruit fresh from the analyst's couch" with scorn for "any work that failed to loudly signal its Freudian allegiance" (*Caldecott* 97). This is an allegiance which has been vital in the formulation of many of his illustrations, and quintessentially so in *The Juniper Tree*. Like the texts themselves, Sendak's illustrations present an ordered worldview for which the "Snow-White" illustration provides a clear and concise example. His composite image conflates place and time to depict a stepmother imprisoned within inchoate horror vis-à-vis her comatose stepdaughter. Since neither woman is shown as beautiful, the stepmother's jealousy would seem to be attached to inescapable life-cycles rather than to the simple sexual jealousy expressed by an aging beauty toward her younger, firmer rival. As such, Sendak's vision offers both a Freudian conception of family relationships and a supracultural vision of the human condition. Sendak clearly means to escape the "particularly American equation that manhood spells the death of childhood" (*Caldecott* 84). Not only do his essays remind his readers that his illustrations draw heavily on emotional memories of the stress and urgency of childhood; his pictures also create characters whose adult faces are shown to be subject to the superegos of ever-present and disapproving parents, as in *King Grisly-Beard* (1973) whose royal hero operates under the gaze of his mother's portrait with its decidedly downturned mouth.

Not surprisingly, Sendak's essays, written over more than twenty years, reflect various stages in the scholarship of other disciplines, notably in folk narrative. His statement that Mother Goose rhymes were "transmitted almost entirely by word of mouth" (12) should therefore be regarded as an artifact of its time (1965) rather than as quotable fact. As an illustrator, however, he speaks provocatively of Mother Goose as a text that proclaims and requires specific images, displacing the artist's vision with its own traditional view (14). It would be churlishly ungenerous to dwell on occasional and minor errors of fact, for the essays as a group delight the reader with their incisive criticism and their literary sensitivity.

There is also a fascination with Sendak's work on the other side of the Atlantic, where psychological approaches to children's literature have an equally strong hold. The essays in the collection edited by Reinbert Tabbert address Sendak's illustrations of specific books (Griswold, Lange, Thiele, Hildesheimer, Criegern); the relationship between two of his books and their re-creations as operas (Cech); his Freudian rejection of the *Struwwelpeter* morality (Tabbert); and his Grimm illustrations (Knecht). Of particular methodological interest is Hans Halbey's discussion of metalanguage in the picture book, in which he suggests that the system of encoded iconic messages underlying visual communication in advertising also inheres in Sendak's work. His findings are based on his direct questioning of children about their perceptions of illustrations, and the result adds a welcome and long-overdue element of empiricism into semiotic theory.

Placing Sendak's work in a different context, that of Western European painting, Axel von Criegern identifies Sendak's historical sources, like Matthias Grünewald, Heinrich Füssli, and Philipp Otto Runge (especially the *Hülsenbeck Children*). On the same subject, Robert Rosenblum's *The Romantic Child from Runge to Sendak* (Thames and Hudson, 1989) documents and establishes an equivalence between the abducted child in *Outside Over There* (55) and the child in Runge's *Hülsenbeck Children* (7). The rest of Criegern's essay on the iconography of the unconscious could be expanded profitably by referring to Heinz Rölleke's related essay on models and sources, "Tales from Grimm—Pictures by Maurice Sendak: *Entdeckungen* and *Vermutungen*" in *Brüder Grimm Gedenken* 2 (1975): 242–45.

Complete with audiovisual sources and studies in English, French, and German, Tabbert's volume also offers a much-needed bibliography, since Selma G. Lanes's *The Art of Maurice Sendak* (1980), until now the standard reference for Sendak's work, lists no secondary literature. Tabbert's bibliography is not exhaustive, however; one notes, for example, the absence of Jennifer Waller's "Maurice Sendak and the Blakean Vision of Childhood" (*Children's Literature* 6 [1977]: 130–40).

On the negative side, the illustrations in Tabbert's volume are few in number and poorly reproduced. As counterexamples, one thinks admiringly of the carefully executed illustrations in the East German *Beiträge zur Kinder- und Jugendliteratur* or longingly of the handsomely printed single issue of the American journal *Image and Maker*, which was dedicated to the illustrations of children's books. Though it survived for only one issue, the reproductions in the latter set a standard which one hopes will someday return to scholarly publications about children's literature.

Grimm's *Dear Mili*, illustrated by Sendak, is a much-heralded and remarkable publishing success. Of its initial print run of 250,000 copies, 230,000 were sold before publication. The discovery of the Grimm manuscript and its subsequent sale by the New York antiquarian children's book dealer Justin Schiller occasioned a flurry of transatlantic scholarly charges and countercharges which made front-page news in London and New York newspapers, surely a rarity in children's literature scholarship. A British Grimm scholar claimed that Farrar, Straus and Giroux had spent 29,000 dollars needlessly, because German archives were awash in unpublished and free-for-the-taking Grimm manuscripts—without, however, adding that many of these manuscripts, unlike the text of *Dear Mili*, were either fragmentary or of little literary or publishing merit, whereas others, like those in *Grimm's Other Tales*,[1] diverged in many respects from the moral and social vision which Wilhelm Grimm built into the collection over five decades. Originally scheduled to appear in 1985 during the bicentenary celebrations of the Grimms' births, *Dear Mili* would seem to have forfeited little public interest by a three-year delay.

The designs, sketches, and final illustrations for *Dear Mili* were exhibited simultaneously with romantic drawings from East German collections in a major exhibit at the Pierpont Morgan Library in New York City during the fall of 1988. One of the artists displayed, Philipp Otto Runge, served as an artistic model for Sendak as well as a literary model for the Grimms. Sendak quotes Runge visually just as the Grimms quoted him stylistically, for they regarded (mistakenly, as it happens) Runge's two prose contributions to *Grimms' Tales* as paradigmatic for tales from the folk. Runge's paired legacy to Sendak and the Grimms lends a pleasing symmetry to the fact that Sendak previously illustrated a selection of Grimms' tales in *The Juniper Tree and Other Tales* and has returned to a Grimm narrative in *Dear Mili*.

Dear Mili was composed in late 1816, relatively early in Wilhelm Grimm's career. Elements of the story characterize and prefigure Christian values and Christian narratives as they subsequently emerged in the Grimms' collection: a young and innocent girl alone in the woods; her orderly housekeeping for a woodland male; the threatening forest as a dangerous locus where wild animals, tempests, and sharp stones inspire fear; a plucked and rootless flower; a joyful (and early) death; and a scaffolding of Christianized imagery, here Saint Joseph and guardian angels. Thus, the tale fits into a familiar and established worldview in *Grimms' Tales*, although it is less well known that girls and women fare peculiarly badly in tales with a Christian cast, a fact which is as true of *Dear Mili* as it is of "The Old Man Made Young Again," "Our Lady's Child," or the religious legends.

Sendak's color illustrations for *Dear Mili* differ radically from, and are less foreboding than, the black-and-white ones he did for *The Juniper Tree*. The differences may derive in part from the dating of the texts, for the social and moral values implicit in *Grimms' Tales* became ever more uncompromising and harsh in the course of their fifty-year editing history. In contrast to the texts of *The Juniper Tree* with their embedded ethic of misogyny and the futility of work, Sendak has quite clearly understood the complex tale of *Dear Mili* as optimistic in its intent and outlook. It must be pointed out that, for many readers, its optimism will be compromised by the little girl's death immediately after her reunion with her aged mother, although other readers may well comprehend their sudden death as a joyful event presaging eternal life, as Wilhelm Grimm himself undoubtedly did. The sharp difference between the illustrations of *The Juniper Tree* and *Dear Mili* is also manifested in Sendak's coloristic responses to the different texts. His black-and-white drawings for *The Juniper Tree* parallel the narrow and bounded world they depict. In *Dear Mili*, on the other hand, the pictures appear to have been composed on three levels: putty-colored backgrounds that contain images of death are overlaid with muted pastels which emphasize life-affirming elements, while a third level of images in some pictures is colored red to represent more dramatically the color of life. Red appears first with, and grows ever more intense in the presence of, the little girl's protector, Saint Joseph, and red persists in the illustrations until she returns home during a symbolic sunset heralding the end of her own and her mother's earthly lives while apparently—because of the life-associated reds of its composition—promising life beyond.

The material of *Dear Mili* appears to offer a teleological vision of the well-lived or the grace-attended life ending in Paradise. Perhaps for this reason, it elicits responses from readers which have little or nothing to do with its illustrations. Among the dozen or so readers of the book that I have polled, there is a close correlation between belief (or disbelief) in an afterlife and assessment of or feelings about the book. Believers like it a great deal and skeptics dislike it intensely—certainly an instance of worldview taking precedence over bibliographic or aesthetic discernment. But what is indisputable is the bibliographic quality of the book. *Dear Mili* lives up to those standards that Sendak sets for himself and others in *Caldecott and Co.*: it is distinguished by excellent pictorial and typographic reproduction as well as the pleasing fragrance of acid-free paper. With *Dear Mili* there is, of course, much more—namely, those exquisite pictures from an illustrator whose images have captured and continue to hold the imaginations of children and adults in the second half of the twentieth century.

Note

1. Ed. Wilhelm Hansen, trans. Ruth Michaelis-Jena and Arthur Ratcliff, illus. Gwenda Morgan (1956; reprint Edinburgh: Canongate, 1984).

Reading an Oral Tradition

Jack Zipes

Inside the Wolf's Belly: Aspects of the Fairy Tale, by Joyce Thomas. Sheffield: Sheffield Academic Press, 1989.

Though in many ways an informative and perceptive study of different thematic aspects of the fairy tale, Joyce Thomas's *Inside the Wolf's Belly* is also disturbing and misleading. It tends to rehash phenomenological, Jungian, and Freudian notions about the wholesome and holistic nature of fairy tales without questioning whether these notions are valid. Moreover, Thomas disregards most of the recent historical, sociological, and feminist critiques of fairy tales as though they had no bearing on our understanding and reception of fairy tales today.

Her book is divided into six chapters which focus on the aspects of the fairy tale that she believes are crucial for understanding the "essence" of the fairy tale: the human at the center, since, as she says, "the hero is the tale" (17); fantastic effigies; animal helpers and monsters; landscapes and things; and language, form, and structure. Simply stated, her main thesis purports that all fairy tales are concerned with the "humanization" of a protagonist, who must learn to acquire characteristics that she or he lacks to become whole. Along the way, other figures, animals, and landscapes are designed to assist the protagonist in his or her quest. Moreover, the language and style of the tales serve to reinforce the notion of "humanization." In this regard, Thomas follows in the tradition of Max Lüthi, whose works have treated the phenomenological features of folk and fairy tales. However, unlike Lüthi, who covers a wide tradition of folktales, she refers primarily to tales in Margaret Hunt's translation of *The Complete Grimm's Fairy Tales* and Joseph Jacobs's *English Fairy Tales*, with some casual comments on tales by Basile and Perrault. As she states in her preface,

> My foremost concern is with the tales themselves, as narrative, as story. These are the *Volksmärchen* as fairy tales, products of anonymous tellers that were orally transmitted from one gen-

Children's Literature 19, ed. Francelia Butler, Barbara Rosen, and Jean Marsden (Yale University Press, © 1991 by The Children's Literature Foundation, Inc.).

eration to another until fixed in print. Taking my cue from other scholars, I employ both "fairy tale" and "Volksmärchen" to designate those oral creations best distinguished from other folk tales by the presence of the "faerie"—wonder, magic, marvels experienced as reality. [9–10]

Thomas is at her best when she interprets individual fairy tales in detail, for she is a sensitive critic who has a fine appreciation of the symbolic language and subtle meanings of the fairy tales. Thus, her discussions of "Snow White" (69–75), the animal-helper tales (123–36), "The Frog Prince" (157–60), and "Rumpelstiltskin" (227–232) are all stimulating, but not because they support her overall theory. Rather, they reveal just how insightful Thomas is as a reader. Her interpretations are valid readings of the texts, but her theoretical premises are, bluntly put, vacuous and erroneous.

To begin with, Thomas claims to study folk fairy tales—that is, the oral tradition—and yet almost all her examples are from the literary tradition. There have been some excellent studies by Heinz Rölleke, Maria Tatar, and Ruth Bottigheimer that have demonstrated how the Grimms composed their own tales from different variants and how they relied on *literature,* not on the oral tradition, for their collection. Yet Thomas does not even allude to these studies or to the problematic nature of the so-called folk-fairy tales she claims were preserved and transmitted by anonymous tellers. Her references are almost always to a literary tradition: Basile, Perrault, the Grimms, and even Jacobs. And in the case of the Grimms, she has chosen the most archaic and faulty collection on the market; for Hunt's work is filled with incorrect titles and inaccurate translations.

It seems to me an amazing *tour de force* (French for chutzpah) to try to develop a phenomenological and descriptive theory of the contents of the oral fairy tale when the critic relies mainly on *literary* sources and when she also makes generalizations about all folktales but focuses primarily on a tiny group of tales extensively revised by the brothers Grimm. Moreover, though Thomas talks about the reality of the wondrous symbols of the tales, she has little sense of history and does not draw parallels with the real conditions of their origins and development as, for instance, Bengt Holbek does in his remarkable study *Interpretations of Fairy Tales* (1987).

Even more disturbing than the meager scholarship, and perhaps a result of it, are frequent statements about the *true essence* of *the* folk-fairy tale, sometimes referred to in German as the *Volks-märchen*. For instance, I do not know what to do with references to the "true *Volksmärchen*" (103, 105) or such statements as this: "Like myth, fairy tales function for us as a mesocosm, a sort of middle cosmos coming between ourselves and the world outside. Mediating between microcosm and macrocosm, they help us bring the two into accord. . . . Myths, legends and fairy tales represent the pure essence of story; as such, they possess a therapeutic, health-instilling value" (281). The tales, which Thomas herself has selected, may function for *her* in this manner, but they certainly do not function for every-one in the same way. Nor are they always "healthy," if we look at some of the sexist, racist, and conservative political aspects of the tales that she discusses. Drawing on the ideas of Campbell, Jung, and Bettelheim (who would not want to be associated with either Campbell or Jung), Thomas blends some of their notions together and concocts a conclusion that comes close to viewing *the pure fairy tale* as our salvation at a time when the world is filled with chaos. Not even my five-year-old daughter, who loves fairy tales, is inclined to make a religion out of the tales, especially the Grimms' tales. She has a healthy suspicion that something is wrong with them and would like to know why. Like my daughter, I have a healthy suspi-cion that, if something is wrong with the fairy tales, then something cannot be right with Joyce Thomas's approach and her discovery of their pure essence.

What Is the Use of a Book without Pictures?

Anne Higonnet

Les abécédaires français illustrés du XIXe siècle, by Ségolène Le Men. Paris: Editions Promodis, 1984.

"What is the use of a book without pictures or conversations?" asks Alice in Wonderland. In her original, probing, and meticulous book *Les abécédaires français illustrés du XIXe siècle*, Ségolène Le Men takes up Alice's query, which she cites. She investigates the foundations of nineteenth-century French children's literacy and discovers there not only conversations but also pictures.

Le Men's own alphabet book is based on an impressive collection of some 765 nineteenth-century examples from the Bibliothèque Nationale. Le Men analyzes her sources with exemplary rigor. Though occasionally she lapses into unnecessary charts and categorizations riddled with confusing ambiguities and exceptions, she almost always maintains her sense of the overall project and its cultural context. Indeed, *Abécédaires français* helps us see its subject in a completely new way precisely because it situates its material in relation to broad social and epistemological issues.

The book is divided into three parts, each of which incisively addresses a different issue. Part 1, "The Conditions of Educational Practice," studies the material conditions of literacy. Who produced alphabet books? How were they distributed, and to whom? Who was taught to read, and by whom? By giving attention to such factors as the invention of lithography in 1796, Le Men immediately situates her subject in the real world of individuals, institutions, technology, economics, and government policy. Learning to read, Le Men begins by showing us, happens partly as a function of historically and culturally specific circumstances. She reminds us to take into account such phenomena as the new nineteenth-century inclusion of a child's first lessons among maternal duties, which encouraged mothers to use alphabet books. This gender factor was exploited by another nineteenth-century French phenomenon, the

Children's Literature 19, ed. Francelia Butler, Barbara Rosen, and Jean Marsden (Yale University Press, © 1991 by The Children's Literature Foundation, Inc.).

entrepreneurial publisher eager to expand his markets by promoting alphabet books.

But Le Men—whose background, like the books she studies, is of an "intersemiotic type" (146)—goes on in Part 2, "Reading's Technical Apprenticeship," to show exactly how the alphabet book inculcates literacy. The most methodologically innovative passages of *Abécédaires français* analyze not only the pedagogies of the written word and the image but the relation between the two. The very belief in a radical difference between the meanings and effects produced by images as opposed to words gave rise to the nineteenth-century French alphabet book and ensured its cultural coherence.

According to these books the image preceded the word. The image belonged to the playful consciousness of the small child, whereas the word marked the child's entry into the realm of reason. Prior to the nineteenth century, Le Men explains, reading was unrelentingly taught through Cartesian "analytical" methods, based entirely on rationality and memorization. The introduction, then, of images into alphabets both signaled and produced a "synthetic" method of learning based on association and a mutual reinforcement of play and reason.

Proponents of the new method claimed of images that "this kind of thing exerts a powerful attraction over children: nothing captures their gaze nor rivets their attention more rapidly than this first gaze of the mind that fecundates our intellectual qualities" (145). The new synthetic method had its adamant detractors, however, chiefly among religious orders whose control over French primary education was being eroded by exactly those forces that enthusiastically adopted the new method: republican schoolteachers or administrators whose triumph finally came under Jules Ferry in the late 1870s and early 1880s.

Le Men traces the genealogy of the synthetic method as a pedagogic attitude back through Kant, Rousseau, and Locke. More unusual is the genealogy she provides us of belief in the semiotic efficacy of the image. The great precedent, model of all future illustrated alphabet books, was Comenius's 1658 *Orbis Pictus*. Comenius asserted that the power of the image resided in its ability to signify the whole and to convey its meaning to the senses: "The foundation of all this consists in well *representing to our senses tangible objects* . . . certainly there is nothing in reason that was not before in the senses, and consequently, it is the foundation of all wisdom, all eloquence and all good or prudent action, to carefully exercise the senses in the proper conception of the differences amongst natural things" (178).

Thus Comenius articulated the belief that, though the image was necessary to reason and could be rationally apprehended and analyzed, nonetheless the image and its meanings occurred earlier, more fundamentally, and more sensually than the word and its meanings. Being somehow less representational, the image guaranteed the reality of its representations. The image taught what Le Men calls a "lesson of things" (177). This belief lies deeply embedded in our modern Western mentality and has been responsible for the ideological character of the cultural functions differentially assigned to the visual and verbal arts, especially to painting.

When in Part 3 of her book, "General Reading Subjects," Le Men then shows us how the pictures and the texts of alphabet books interacted to accomplish constructions of gender, work, class, and "nature," she does much more than explain alphabet books. She is showing us how a belief in the "natural" meaning of images itself ratifies the cultural meanings proposed by texts, a lesson we could bring to many other forms of visual culture.[1] As the image in alphabet books evolved from the detached emblem to the inclusive scene, and as the image sometimes brought the letter into its territory, even entwining itself around the letter, its message proved that the text was "right" and showed to whom the text applied. Together image and text enunciate what Le Men calls in the case of frontispieces a "metalanguage" (290).

To cite a prominent instance, alphabet books distinguish between the "useful" and the "lazy"—terms, respectively, of the highest praise and condemnation. The "arts and crafts" were "useful" because they contributed to a civilization based on the values of ancient Greece and Rome. In one particularly revealing example published in 1834, an image makes its points both thematically and spatially; among "little workers" we see fine artists in the foreground, artisans in the middleground, and peasants in the far distance. As Le Men puts it so well: "This tripartite organisation of perspectival space corresponds to the hierarchy of utility of the crafts which assigns to agriculture a foundational and primordial role, to the crafts a medium and therefore perfect degree of utility, and to art the hyperbole of utility that becomes luxury and re-finement" (209). One might even say that the image's perspectival devices themselves construct the places where human activities are perceived.

This perception, of course, occurs from the point of view of a patriarchal middle class. Le Men gives the example of an 1851 plate illustrating "Work" that by 1863 had acquired Paris monuments in the background and a bust of an emperor in the foreground—clear references to Napoleon III and his rebuilding of Paris, now "natu-ral" parts of what "work" looks like (227). As the century goes on, "work" gradually comes to include buying and selling, particularly in small shops, but heavy industry and proletarian labor remain invisible.

To each class and to each sex its attributes. Alphabet books show men and women doing different kinds of tasks, and learning differ-ent kinds of skills. An *Abécédaire instructif des arts et métiers*, published around 1840, shows on one page boys of the artisan class engaged in chiseling stone and hewing wood and on another, a bourgeois boy drawing an antique statue while his female counterpart studies the piano, a polite feminine accomplishment (208). Even animals are enlisted in the alphabet books' lessons, housed in the bourgeois institution of the municipal zoo, where they are classified by an om-niscient science or paired into happy couples, the females tenderly caring for their young.

Lest we doubt that images could be so heavily invested with mean-ing, Le Men points to their self-consciousness. Under the letter "I" especially, the image illustrates itself being looked at, producing a "mise en abîme" (58). Le Men ends her book on a similar note, with a description of an image that shows a bored child yawning over a straight text and a happy child poring over an illustrated alphabet book.

By the time we reach this conclusion, we have learned that Alice's question about the use of a book asked more than it might seem to have. The issue is not just how alphabet books use images with words but how, more generally, nineteenth-century culture de-pended on alliances of images and text, and how those alliances be-came the means by which a child mastered language. Le Men shows us why Alice wanted a book with both conversations *and* pictures.

Note

1. In his "The Post-Modern Alphabet: Extending the Limits of the Contemporary Alphabet Book, from Seuss to Gorey," (*Children's Literature Association Quarterly* 14: 3 [Fall 1989]: 115–17) George R. Bodmer notes the breakdown of the postmodern alphabet book's coherence and the increasing tension between image and word. I would suggest that this signals a fundamental re-evaluation of the meanings of the image induced by our postmodern computer and television-age awareness that images as well as words can be constructed, organized rhetorically, and orchestrated for ideological purposes.

Dream Children

Jan Susina

Jessie Willcox Smith: A Bibliography, by Edward D. Nudelman. Gretna, Louisiana: Pelican Publishing Company, 1989.

If L. Frank Baum's Dorothy can be considered the American Alice, then Jessie Willcox Smith is certainly the American Kate Greenaway. America's most prolific and best-known female illustrator, Smith illustrated between 1888 and 1932 more than sixty books and hundreds of magazines.

Edward Nudelman has carefully collected and arranged in chronological order every book cover of every first edition, with excellent, full-color reproduction, in this visual bibliography, which gives detailed bibliographical information, including pagination, collation, issue date, physical description, paper type, issue notes, and publication notes. The bibliography includes many additional book illustrations, as well as sections which show a rich array of illustrations in periodicals (a Smith illustration appeared every month on the cover of *Good Housekeeping* from December 1917 through April 1933) calendars, posters, advertisements, and prints. For those interested in Smith's illustrations, and those who collect Smith's work, this bibliography will quickly become an essential research tool. While I was in the process of reviewing the proofs, I received a book catalogue which cited an item according to the "Nudelman Bibliography."

But seeing so much Jessie Willcox Smith all at once—there are more than three hundred fifty illustrations, most in color—has its cost. Like Greenaway, Smith is an acquired taste. Either you like all these beautiful but static children or you don't. The terms frequently used to describe Smith's style—"sensitive," "soft," and "sentimental"—can cut both ways. Hers is an extremely idealized version of childhood, rich in both sweetness and light; viewing this collection becomes a sort of pictorial binge in a candy store. Yet Nudelman's brief introduction suggests some valuable ways to view such a large body of work.

Children's Literature 19, ed. Francelia Butler, Barbara Rosen, and Jean Marsden (Yale University Press, © 1991 by The Children's Literature Foundation, Inc.).

Whether or not one is enchanted by Smith's romanticized view of childhood, one cannot help but be impressed by her industry and determination to succeed as a female illustrator when the profession was essentially dominated by men, such as N. C. Wyeth, Edmund Dulac, Arthur Rackham, Maxfield Parrish, and Kay Nielsen. Smith, along with Violet Oakley and Elizabeth Shippen Green, was a member of Howard Pyle's first class at the Drexel Institute. Although she had studied with Thomas Eakins at the Pennsylvania Academy of Fine Arts, Pyle was her most influential mentor. Nudelman suggests that Pyle's greatest contribution to Smith was color appreciation, but she certainly acquired his keen sense of illustration's commercial feasibility as well. Her collaborations and strong friendships with Oakley, Green, and Henrietta Cozens are important aspects of her career as a female illustrator which too frequently have been overlooked by those seeing her solely as a children's book illustrator. The women formed Cogslea, an all-female artist community where they lived and worked together. Smith's frequent images of mothers and children might fruitfully be compared to those of her contemporary Mary Cassatt.

Nudelman suggests that some of Smith's finest illustrations are those which appeared in the 1916 edition of Charles Kingsley's *Water-Babies*. Smith considered them her best work and bequeathed the set of twelve original oils to the Library of Congress. This is the only known group of paintings Smith illustrated for a single book that has remained intact as a group. Critics and collectors have followed Smith's lead in praising the illustrations for *The Water-Babies*, but they are, at least to me, not the text's best set. Though certainly superior to those tepid ones produced by Noel Paton in the original 1863 edition, they lack the exuberance and vitality of Linley Sambourne's 1886 set, which seem the ideal match for Kingsley's digressive prose. Nor do they have the comic and elegant line of Heath Robinson's 1915 edition. So to me, Smith's set is, at best, third-rate. I much prefer her stunning 1901 and 1902 Bryn Mawr calendars, done in conjunction with Green, to any of her book illustrations.

The value of Nudelman's bibliography is that it brings together the vast, and at times uneven, body of Smith's illustration so that her development as an artist, and her adaptation of styles, can be explored.

Literature Is Not All That Glitters

Hernan Vera and Carol Reinermann

Bibliography of the Little Golden Books, compiled by Dolores B. Jones. Bibliographies and Indexes in American Literature, Number 7. New York: Greenwood Press, 1987.

In 1987, Western Publishing celebrated the printing of the billionth Little Golden Book by reissuing the imprint's best-seller, *The Poky Little Puppy*, by Janette Sebring Lowrey, which was among the first twelve titles that inaugurated this series in September 1942. The marketing success of Little Golden Books stands in stark contrast, however, to its failure to be accepted as serious children's literature. Little Golden Books are regularly ignored by reviewers, librarians, and teachers. As Selma Lanes points out in "All That's Golden is Not Glitter," one of the very few essays to have been written about the books, they are dismissed as not being books at all but, rather, mere "products" or "merchandise," and, even worse, artistic "treachery" or literary "junk food." Though more than eight hundred different titles in over a dozen languages have been published in the series, making them, arguably, among the most accessible children's books in the world, only one has received any special recognition from the children's book community: *I Can Fly* by Ruth Krauss (illustrated by Mary Blair), which was designated an "Honor Book" in the *New York Herald Tribune*'s 1951 Spring Book Festival. It is perhaps not surprising, then, that the first bibliography of the Little Golden Books, an indispensable tool for research on this series, did not appear in print until 1987.

Perhaps the major difficulty of the bibliographer's task arises from the sheer popularity of the series and the many editions that a number of the books have gone through in their publication histories. But Jones's *Bibliography* provides a comprehensive list of all Little Golden Book titles from the beginning of the series in 1942 through 1985. Included are the titles issued in the Little Golden Book format itself as well as those issued in the various subseries that have appeared over the years, such as Giant Little Golden

Children's Literature 19, ed. Francelia Butler, Barbara Rosen, and Jean Marsden (Yale University Press, © 1991 by The Children's Literature Foundation, Inc.).

Books, Little Golden Activity Books, and Walt Disney Books. The bibliography contains exhaustive information, along with numerous indexes that help the researcher to negotiate the often complex and extensive publication histories of many of the Little Golden Books and their relatives. These multiple listings make it possible to locate a group of works by the same author or illustrator quickly and also to determine the order of publication of a sequence of books.

One of the factors that has sustained the commercial success of the Little Golden Books has always been their inexpensiveness; they sold for a quarter in 1942, and the highest priced volume in 1988 was still only $1.29. In spite of their low price, however, the production quality of the books has remained relatively high, since basic costs weigh less on each copy than on those of smaller editions. With their sturdy covers and bright illustrations, Little Golden Books are designed for younger children; but, as Selma Lanes has noted, they have an immediate appeal to all ages—in part because, over the years, some of our better illustrators and authors (among them, Margaret Wise Brown, Trina Schart Hyman, Ruth Krauss, P. L. Travers, Leonard Weisgard, and Garth Williams) have contributed works in the series.

By examining Little Golden Books as cultural artifacts, we can identify and explore those ideas which have been passed along to a large proportion of the population—children—at stages in their development when they are most malleable and sensitive. Because these books are largely commercial undertakings (unlike folk and fairy tales) they appeal to what their publishers believe is a relatively simple, conventionally accepted and therefore salable moral standard. Compare, for instance, the anarchic lack of rewards for virtue in "Little Red Riding Hood" with the 1945 Little Golden Book *Tootle the Engine* (text by Gertrude Crampton and pictures by Tibor Gergely). In *The Lonely Crowd*, David Riesman analyzed *Tootle the Engine* in order to demonstrate how many important attitudes and values can be transmitted through such seemingly unimportant literature for children. As countless children learn, little Tootle was more interested in jumping the tracks to find flowers in the field than he was in following the wheels of the well-behaved engines. The desperate engine schoolmaster decides to teach Tootle a lesson with the help of the citizens of the town of Engineville, where the school is located. Out in the field, Tootle finds red flags and stop signs that force him to halt no matter which direction he looks. Bewildered, he returns to the tracks where a green flag held by his teacher invites him to come back to town. He promises he will never stray from the tracks again and is rewarded by the cheers of his teachers and the town's citizens. Riesman notes that the story shows children how wrong it is to depart from the straight and narrow discipline of the track, that freedom and approval are to be found by following society's green lights. In this way, he argues, children learn about self-control and more subtle forms of cooperation. Adults, as represented by the townspeople who erect the stop signs and red flags, appear as those manipulating the child into conformity and then rewarding him for it. As a point of contrast, Reisman observes that "Little Red Riding Hood," which can also be read as a cautionary tale, displays little of the adult tolerance or the rewards for virtue contained in *Tootle*.

Because Little Golden Books have reached such an extraordinary number of households, they can be assumed to be a representative part of the experience of more men and women than, say, a collection of Caldecott Award winners. Thus, the dismissal of these books by critics and scholars reflects an attitude of the cultural arbiters in the past half century that avoids any engagement with the actual experience of buying or reading a book for the parents and children in our society—an experience that includes, for the majority of our population, at least one and possibly many Little Golden Books. For Little Golden Books, regardless of what the literary critics' opinion of them may be, are bought as books. Working-class parents who spend $1.09 on a Little Golden Book for their children do so with as much conviction that they are buying a book as do professional parents who pay fifteen dollars for the latest award-winning book for their youngsters. Both types of parents are acquiring for their children an object that, in Western culture, carries unique and highly charged meanings as a symbol of intellectual, ethical, and social development.

Today, we take for granted the presence of Little Golden Books and paperbacks in our supermarkets and drug stores among an assortment of consumer objects. We think nothing of picking up the latest best-seller novel or diet manual ourselves as we go through the checkout line. Before the time of Little Golden Books, however, buying a book necessitated a trip to a bookstore, often downtown. Even without statistics on the proportion of the population that took that special trip to the bookstore, it is safe to say that it was significantly lower than the number of those who visited a supermarket or drug store during any given week. Even today, when there are bookstores in practically every shopping mall and commercial district, it is the checkout lanes that put the book, quite literally, within the reach of everyone's hand.

In "novelty stores" and "five and tens," Little Golden Books joined baseball cards, cube books (big-little books), and comic books (which had appeared in the 1930s), as part of a group of cheap reading materials and other objects manufactured for children's direct consumption. But the importance of this children's market lies not so much in its magnitude as a part of the American economy as in the role it plays in helping to instill in the child the habits and values associated with reading and literature that he or she will draw on as an adult purchaser of books. Jones's bibliography provides one of the basic tools for a long overdue appraisal of Little Golden Books, which have remained, for nearly a half century, a virtually untapped body of material for social scientific and cultural research.

Dissertations of Note

Compiled by Rachel Fordyce

Adams, Joan E. "A Comparison of Significant Adults in Books with an Adolescent Protagonist Written by Recommended Authors and Judy Blume." Ed.D. diss. United States International University, 1989. 217 pp. DAI 50:1237A.

Adams analyzes twenty realistic works of fiction, published since 1969 by "recommended" authors, in terms of "background descriptors, roles and verbal interactions." She also analyzes the work of Judy Blume to determine whether or not her treatment of adults is consistent. By comparing the results of both analyses she finds that Blume is more likely to have a female relative or parent who is white and middle-class as a dominant character than the recommended authors and that Blume's "mothers spoke more than twice as many lines as did her fathers"—an inverse proportion when compared with recommended authors. Adams also shows that Blume uses "a variety of types of interaction" but that each is limited "to one or two lines."

Alaimo, Kathleen. "Adolescence in the Popular Milieu in France during the Early Third Republic: Efforts to Define and Shape a Stage of Life." Ph.D. diss. University of Wisconsin, 1988. 413 pp. DAI 49:3843A.

Alaimo argues that adolescence, as a concept "distinct from youth, is a modern idea" and that it flourished in France at the turn of the century. She notes that "attempts to give social meaning to adolescence were initiated by educators, social reformers, politicians beginning in the 1870s and [they] remained an active effort through World War One." While France during a somewhat conservative Third Republic did not support a full-blown "adolescent experience" Alaimo believes that a study of the topic is significant not only because she is able to trace the inception of the idea of adolescence, and many of the moral judgments associated with its definition, but also for comparative purposes. It is worthwhile to compare early responses to the concept with those prior to World War II in Germany and Austria and subsequent responses in Eastern European countries.

Allingham, Philip Victor. "Dramatic Adaptations of the Christmas Books of Charles Dickens, 1844–8: Texts and Contexts." Ph.D. diss. University of British Columbia [Canada], 1988. n.p. DAI 49:3728–29A.

The two purposes of Allingham's dissertation are to explore the extent to which Dickens was involved in the "officially-sanctioned dramatizations of the Christmas Books, 1844–8" and to discuss the methods used by his adapters. He analyzes the texts of Edward Stirling's *Christmas Carol*, Mark Lemon's *Haunted Man*, C. Z. Barnett's *A Christmas Carol; or, The Miser's Warning!*, and Albert Smith's *The Battle of Life* to indicate that Dickens was innovative as well as astute in his suggestions for dramatizing the plays. Allingham also compares "the relationship between the final printed text of each novella, that of the corresponding official adaptation, and the original manuscript of the play." He provides texts for all sanctioned adaptations in an appendix.

Alqudsi, Taghreed Mohammad. "The History of Published Arabic Children's Literature as Reflected in the Collections of Three Publishers in Egypt, 1912–1986." Ph.D. diss. University of Texas, Austin, 1988. 223 pp. DAI 50:285–86A.

Alqudsi notes that modern Arabic children's literature "is moving toward

Children's Literature 19, ed. Francelia Butler, Barbara Rosen, and Jean Marsden (Yale University Press, © 1991 by The Children's Literature Foundation, Inc.).

realism," although it remains predominantly didactic and moralistic. And though "Egypt's economic dilemma, poverty, pollution," and relations with other countries are common topics in every Egyptian home, "none of these topics seems to appear in children's books." War as a topic is also avoided while "publishing of religious themes is increasing."

Anzul, Margaret Howe. "Exploring Literature with Children within a Transactional Framework." Ph.D. diss. New York University, 1988. 309 pp. DAI 49:2132A.

Anzul worked with fifth- and sixth-grade students in weekly lecture-discussion sessions to analyze to what extent pupils' sophistication in the discussion of, and aesthetic appreciation for, literature increased over time within a "naturalistic," transactional setting. She concludes that successful strategies include "helping students assume ownership of the discussion, pursu[ing] topics of intense interest to them, and direct[ing] their attention back to the texts to see what had evoked individual responses." She concludes that teachers of literature are more successful using an inductive than a didactic mode.

Arewa, Olufunmilayo Bamidele. "Tarzan, *primus inter primates*: Difference and Hierarchy in Popular Culture." Ph.D. diss. University of California, Berkeley, 1988. 336 pp. DAI 50:474A.

This dissertation in cultural anthropology deals with sociocultural aspects of the 1912 Edgar Rice Burroughs novel as well as the comic books, films, and other examples of popular culture it engendered. Arewa finds that "Burroughs' Tarzan . . . reflects long debated views on nature, nurture, and evolution" in terms of the noble savage, wild men, and apes. He is concerned with the image of Africa that is portrayed in various Tarzan renditions as well as the unprecedented popularity of the material in the face of "images imbued with racism and sexism." He notes specifically that "in reaching a mass audience world-wide, Tarzan's images have the capacity to influence the realm of daily existence and social action."

Atkins, Jean Pollard. "The Use of Young Adult Literature to Teach Writing." Ph.D. diss. University of Kansas, 1988. 280 pp. DAI 49:3289–90A.

Atkins notes the rise of illiteracy in this country and the decline of an ability to teach writing well. She configures the dissertation to exemplify the principles of good writing and revising while she focuses on five basic rhetorical modes: definition, explanation, description, narration, and comparison and contrast. "The study's results are the proposed teaching strategies on fourteen young adult novels and two adult novels read widely by adolescents," although the intended audience for the books as well as the instruction in writing is adolescent. She finds the use of young adult literature particularly effective for teaching purposes because its major themes are maturation and development— both characteristics of good pre-writing and writing.

Backstrom, Ellen Lees. "The Effects of Creative Dramatics on Student Behavior and Attitudes in Literature and Language Arts." Ed.D. diss. University of California, Los Angeles, 1988. 204 pp. DAI 49:3243A.

Working with an eighth-grade class Backstrom studied the effect of creative dramatics on "self-worth, on attitudes towards reading literature, and towards the creative dramatics curriculum itself." Her results suggest that immersion in creative dramatics improves students' cooperation as well as their attitudes toward themselves and their teacher and, consequently, their "retention of reading and language arts skills." She also concludes that students who are given more decision-making opportunities improve their ability to think critically. The dissertation strongly suggests that "teachers and students should combine the functional, daily classroom learning with life experiences to produce a lasting impression." Through the process of applying creative dramatics to reading material, students are preparing themselves for life-long learning experiences.

Banks, Carol P. "Playwriting for Different Age Levels." Ph.D. diss. New York University, 1988. 279 pp. DAI 49:2023–24A.

Banks seeks to identify the major limitations of plays for young audiences and, by comparing the processes for writing plays for different ages, to overcome some of those limitations. She includes an analysis of two plays about Joan of Arc which she has written for audiences of different ages, a brief biography of Joan of Arc, and a comparative study of plays about Joan of Arc by Anouilh, Shaw, and Brecht. Based on her experience she disagrees with the common notion that there is no fundamental difference between writing plays for adults and writing for young audiences, particularly in terms of material, structure, length, and "poetic vision."

Brown, Neil Levan. "The Status of Wordless Picture Books, 1977–1986." Ed.D. diss. Temple University, 1989. 195 pp. DAI 50:870A.

Brown is concerned primarily with the content, mechanics, and format of wordless picture books. By comparing books produced between 1960 and 1976 and between 1977 and 1986 he concludes that there is an emphasis on realism in the more recently published books, particularly in works by Tana Hoban, John S. Goodall, and Mitsumasa Anno; that most recently, wordless picture books have become more sophisticated, appealing to an adult audience; and that in bibliographic sources and checklists the definition of "wordless picture books" is ambiguous because many listed books contain words or text.

Browning, Clifton, Jr. "Delphi Technique: A Method for Distinguishing between a Realistic and an Unrealistic Portrayal of Death and Dying in Adolescent Literature." Ed.D. diss. Auburn University, 1988. 185 pp. DAI 50:1194A.

The goal of Browning's dissertation is "to establish criteria to evaluate death-related adolescent literature." Using the results of a study conducted with social workers, oncologists, nurses, physicians, the clergy, counselors, funeral directors, and members of families that had recently experienced the loss of a close member of the family, Browning defines the major aspects of death-related realistic and unrealistic literature. He defines realistic fiction as that in which death is accepted honestly, in non-heroic terms, and where the causes of death are analogous to typical childhood and adult causes, including suicide. "Unrealistic plot elements and themes include denial of dying and death . . . ignoring the side-effects of certain medical treatments (especially chemotherapy), lying to the critically ill," embracing unnatural funereal rituals, obscuring fact with religious belief, "portraying death romantically or heroically, and feeling embarrassed about suicide."

Crume, Mary Adams Tanzy. "Images of Teachers in Novels and Films for the Adolescent, 1980–1987." Ph.D. diss. University of Florida, 1988. 296 pp. DAI 50:138A.

Crume predicates her thesis on the idea that "literature and film serve as vehicles for portraying and transmitting a culture, its values and attitudes." She tests the commonly held notion that teachers are maligned in fiction and popular arts, "depicted as fools, villains," and other unflattering stereotypes. Dealing with American novels and films produced between 1980 and 1987 she concludes that portrayals of teachers are diverse, although fiction writers tend to treat teachers more sympathetically than film writers. She notes that both mediums "presented a mixed view of American schools that minimized their academic functions and highlighted their roles as social settings and battlegrounds." Essentially Crume finds that teachers are not consistently impugned in either medium, although filmmakers are less sympathetic to the profession and the people in it than novelists.

Evans, Charlene Taylor. "In Defense of 'Huckleberry Finn': Anti-Racism Motifs in 'Huckleberry Finn' and a Review of Racial Criticism in Twain's Work." Ph.D. diss. Rice University, 1988. 199 pp. DAI 49:3025–26A.

Evans begins her dissertation with a historical analysis of nineteenth- and twentieth-century censorship of Twain for his "themes of violence and rebellion" and his "racism." She believes that Twain is maligned on both counts because his audiences do not understand the latent irony in *Huckleberry Finn*. Nor do they comprehend that Twain's characters are "imprisoned by their social milieu" and consequently obliged to portray divided selves to be true to both self and society. Hence it is imperative to remember that "Huck's intuitive self is juxtaposed to the conflicting internalized mores of the society. . . . This duality represents the double consciousness that permeated nineteenth century America." Evans concludes that *Huckleberry Finn*, and its counterpart *Pudd'nhead Wilson*, are both anti-racist, that in each Twain is consistent in his treatment of race, and that "the power of social fictions and the fear of isolation and social ostracism are recurring themes which illuminate the problem of race and morality, thus revealing the complexity of the racial situation [in] America."

Fortuna, MaryAnn. "A Descriptive Evaluative Study of Children's Modern Fantasy and Children's Science Fiction Using a Well-Known Example of Each." Ed.D. diss. Temple University, 1988. 111 pp. DAI 49:1696A.

Fortuna applies principles established in Charlotte Huck's *Guides for Evaluating Children's Literature* and *Children's Literature in the Elementary School* to C. S. Lewis's *The Lion, the Witch, and the Wardrobe* and Madeleine L'Engle's *A Wrinkle in Time* to determine whether or not children's science fiction should be classified as children's fantasy. "There have not always been clear distinctions between the two." She concludes that "although there are a number of similarities between the two genres, science fiction should not be confused with fantasy" because fantasy is based on magic and the supernatural; science fiction is based on scientific knowledge or quasi-scientific beliefs.

Grossmann, Maureen Ellen. "Small Beginnings: The Recovery of Childhood and the Recovery from Childhood in the Victorian Novel." Ph.D. diss. University of California, Berkeley, 1988. 276 pp. DAI 50:952A.

Grossmann deals particularly with *Jane Eyre, David Copperfield, Great Expectations*, and *Mill on the Floss*—works of the major novelists of the Victorian period—to determine how these authors use specific childhood incidents and mind-sets either to allow their characters to grow through and build on the experience of childhood or, through repetition of the childhood experience, to "continue to produce a child self."

Gulotta, Donna Sheinberg. "Fairy Tales and Arthurian Legends in the Novels of Henry James: The Emergence of Self." Ph.D. diss. State University of New York at Buffalo, 1988. 161 pp. DAI 50:449A.

Gulotta predicates her study on the fact that "the theme of the individual fighting to free himself from family entanglements and make his own way in the world is the central theme of fairy tales and legends" as well as of the works of Henry James. She deals specifically with the Grimm fairy tales, "which James loved," and the Arthurian legends as recounted by Wace, Chrétien de Troyes, and Malory. She notes that James employs standard aspects of fairy tales to construct his plots: the reliance on an outsider or "magical agent" to effect change, the process of maturation in the hero, "the confusing web of family life," and the use of the tale to educate and integrate the reader/listener into a societal point of view. She concludes that the "successful completion of James's novels, like fairy tales, results in either marriage or self-knowledge."

Harrison, Barbara. "Moral Intensity and Heroic Possibility in the Postwar Children's Novel." Tufts University, 1988. 211 pp. DAI 49:3360A.

Harrison's "argument is that there is implicit in many post–World War II children's novels a profound moral consciousness, and that the books are significant not only in form and structure" but "in terms of the human awareness they promote, awareness of the possibilities of life." In a three-part dissertation Harrison focuses on works that discuss the Holocaust and what it did to existing definitions of tragedy, then on works that can still be discussed with existing definitions of tragedy, and finally on works in which "hope and innocence are rekindled." She predicates her discussion on the understanding that authors assume that their young readers can deal with abstract notions of "justice and injustice, complacency and commitment, freedom and responsibility" and that they are concerned with the definition of heroism "in a world awesome in its age-old patterns."

Haynes, Carol. "The Explanatory Power of Content for Identifying Children's Literature Preferences." Ed. D. diss. Northern Illinois University, 1988. 181 pp. DAI 49:3617A.

Haynes used a large sample of fourth-grade boys and girls, across four states, to determine their literary preferences. She notes that girls appear to prefer mystery, suspense, realistic fiction, and fantasy; boys prefer mystery, suspense, science fiction, and science, although both prefer stories of high adventure, particularly if couched in the form of a mystery. She further notes that there is little or no difference between girls' and boys' watching or reading literature. Haynes concludes that children's preferences "can be explained better by content than by [the] literature classification often used by teachers, librarians, and researchers. . . . Traditional genre may be too monolithic in that children do differentiate within a single genre" but they do not differentiate between reading or viewing literature by preferring one over the other.

Johnson, Dianne Anita. "For the Children of the Sun: What We Say to Afro-American Youth through Story and Image." Ph.D. diss. Yale University, 1988. 255 pp. DAI 50:1345A.

Johnson's interdisciplinary inquiry in American Studies "explores the various forces, literary and extra-literary, which undergird the development" of a "canon" of Afro-American children's literature—a literature most frequently written by Black authors but not necessarily for an exclusively black audience. Specifically she attempts "to define the relationships and tensions between Black children's literature, Black adult literature, and mainstream American children's literature."

Kantar, Andrew Klekner. "The Indian Series Books for Boys by Dietrich Lange: A Critical Study of the Application of Natural History in Fifteen Novels Published between 1912–1930." Ph.D. diss. University of Minnesota, 1988. 241 pp. DAI 49:3646A.

Kantar's study analyzes "Lange's instructional and literary application of natural science and the wilderness to instruct his young readers." He also compares Lange's didactic approach with that of other writers of wilderness fiction and with contemporary novels based on natural history.

Lac, Christine Marie Andrée. "A Comparative Study of Louisa May Alcott and Sophie de Ségur (Rostopchine)." Ph.D. diss. University of Nebraska, Lincoln, 1988. 250 pp. DAI 50:437A.

After illustrating the similarities in background and upbringing between Alcott and Ségur, and contrasting them with such contemporary nineteenth-century writers as Hawthorne, James, Sand, Balzac, Eliot, and Flaubert and such twentieth-century writers as Duras, Walker, Ehrdrich, and Condé, Lac concludes that Alcott and Ségur "have a more established kinship with very contemporary twentieth century women writers, especially minority writers, than to the male writers of the nineteenth century." She further suggests that the writing of Alcott and Ségur is "ideally suited to the audience of the young or the powerless, an audience with which the canon has not been truly concerned very often."

Luke, Allan A. J. "Dick and Jane in Canada: A Critical Analysis of the Literacy Curriculum in British Columbia Elementary Schools, 1945–1960." Ph.D. diss. Simon Fraser University [Canada], 1987. n.p. DAI 50:865A.

Luke's dissertation surveys the post–Second World War literary judgments that were passed on to children: "a selective tradition of ideologically-based values, knowledges and literate competencies."

Monroe, Suzanne Stolz. "Images of Native American Female Protagonists in Children's Literature, 1928–1988." Ph.D. diss. University of Arizona, 1988. 274 pp. DAI 50:89A.

Having surveyed sixty picture books and novels written for children over the past sixty years, Monroe concludes that the image of native American female protagonists is a traditional one as presented by both native and non-native American writers. Her research "confirms the need for more books featuring Native American female protagonists; more books depicting protagonists from diverse tribal backgrounds, in contemporary settings, urban environments and literate contexts; more books building on the oral tradition and legends of the Southwestern tribes; more involvement of Native American authors, illustrators and publishers in children's literature; and more mentoring of Native American developing authors."

Murray, Thomas J. "J. M. Barrie and the Search for Self." Ph.D. diss. Harvard University, 1988. 266 pp. DAI 50:450A.

Murray is concerned that Barrie's critical acclaim has been consistently marred because biographers and critics alike consider him "more for his personality than for his work." This is particularly pertinent because Barrie himself "sought to obscure and mythologize" his life and work. Using Heinz Kohut's theory of "self psychology," Murray "argues that Barrie was the victim of parental narcissism." Primary works discussed are *Tommy*, *Peter Pan*, *A Kiss for Cinderella*, and *Little Mary*.

Noel, Roberta Christine, "The Borrowed Cup of Courage: A Descriptive Comparison of Archetypes Presented by Male and Female Authors in Fantasy for Adolescents." Ed.D. diss. Gonzaga University, 1987, 345 pp. DAI 49:2206A.

Noting the demise of physical rites of passage in contemporary life, Noel hypothesized that "psychic rites of passage become more important and may be encouraged through the reading of tales of high fantasy which, like the ancient myths and folktales, explore the world of the unconscious through symbolic imagery." She found that definite rites of passage were evident in all the novels she studied, that female heroes were more prevalent in novels since 1965, and that "author gender had no effect upon the choice of hero, nor upon the rites of passage experienced by that hero on the journey to adulthood."

Schindler, Richard Allen. "Art to Enchant: A Critical Study of Early Victorian Fairy Painting and Illustration." Ph.D. diss. Brown University, 1988. 297 pp. DAI 49:2430–31A.

Schindler "examines the significance of fairy subjects in the development of early Victorian art," particularly its associations with "literary themes, theatre, and folklore; its narrative principles; and its metaphors for the artistic imagination." He notes also that "fairy imagery benefited from the emergence of ballad collections, folklore studies, and fairy tales."

Shin, Eun Ja. "Young Children's Use of Decontextualized Language as a Function of Parents' Mediation of Storybook Reading." Ed.D. diss. University of Michigan, 1989. 144 pp. DAI 50:1555–56A.

Shin concludes that young children are most likely to be able to use decontextualized language if they come from literate homes in which children are read to and books are readily available. She also determines that "repeated readings of the same book facilitates the child's independent reading."

Simpson, Roger. "A Triumph of Common Sense: The Work of Sir John Tenniel (1820–1914)." Ph.D. diss. University of Essex [United Kingdom], 1987. 505 pp. DAI 49:1605A.

This dissertation in fine arts gives a critical history of Tenniel's long career from the decoration of the Houses of Parliament through his work for *Punch* and the "great high satire of his *Alice* work, a triumph of English common sense." Simpson views Tenniel's greatness as the creation of "a traditionalistic cosmos in which the past permeated and enriched the present."

Stokes, Kathy Jo. "Children's Journey Stories as an Epic Subgenre." Ph.D. diss. University of Nebraska, Lincoln, 1988. 160 pp. DAI 50:131A.

Stokes compares six fantasies written for children with *The Faerie Queene* and *Pilgrim's Progress* and notes striking similarities between the journeys within them. She also notes that "the works are about language as names and words have special power and the importance and misuses of language are illustrated." Ultimately what binds together these works for children and adults is the desire of the authors to teach. "The epic tradition of didacticism in the works of centuries ago is brought gracefully into contemporary fiction."

Sullivan, Dale Lee. "A Rhetoric of Children's Literature as Epideictic Discourse." Ph.D. diss. Rensselaer Polytechnic Institute, 1988. 306 pp. DAI 49:3204A.

This dissertation in speech communication is concerned with epideictic rhetoric, "a form of rhetoric traditionally devoted to educating the young in orthodox values and reinforcing those values among adults." Sullivan views children's literature as "a powerful instrument for rebuilding our cultural life world." The primary focus of his study is on C. S. Lewis's *The Chronicles of Narnia* because "they were designed to combat A. J. Ayer's emotive theory of values by educating children in just sentiments and by introducing them to the Western literary heritage."

Tobin, Barbara Joan. "The Responses of Early Adolescent, White Australian Readers to Selected Cross-Cultural, Folklore-Based Fantasy Novels by Patricia Wrightson." Ed.D. diss. University of Georgia, 1989. 377 pp. DAI 50:1586A.

Tobin observes that in the 1970s and 1980s Australian children's author Patricia Wrightson developed "a new approach to creating stronger, more convincing Australian fantasy writing. She rejected the imported Old World folklore that lacked the power of authentic magic to interpret this land, in favor of the indigenous spirits of the little known Aboriginal folklore, that she wove into her contemporary fantasies." Unfortunately Tobin concludes that most white Australian readers either miss totally or misconstrue the clues Wrightson presents that would allow the audience to read her novels as fantasy based on Aboriginal experiences and folklore. She makes recommendations "for increasing the depth and integration of learning about Aboriginal culture."

Wamsley, Dorothy Katherine Davis. "Adolescent Self-Concept: An Analysis and Comparison of Selected Young Adult Fiction and Current Theories of Adolescent Psychology." Ph.D. diss. Ohio State University, 1988. 277 pp. DAI 50:108–09A.

Using a selection from the University of Iowa's *Books for Young Adults'* polls taken between 1979 and 1985 as well as self-concept theories derived from Erik Erikson, David Elkind, and Morris Rosenberg, Wamsley compares the theoretical notion of "teenage self-concept in young adult novels with the views of some leading authorities in adolescent psychology." She concludes that young adult novels are excellent realistic vehicles by which adolescents learn about themselves. Equally important, "being able to have an increased understanding of the adolescents as persons gives teachers and curriculum designers improved insights for developing more effective and relevant materials and experiences for learning."

Williams, Anita Spencer. "The Elderly in Children's Fiction: A Content Analysis of the Treatment of the Elderly in Children's Books Published between 1960–1972 and 1973–1986 for Primary Grades Kindergarten through Three." Ed.D. diss. Temple University, 1989. 208 pp. DAI 50:875A.

Using a content analysis methodology Williams investigates early childhood realistic fiction to determine to what extent portrayals of the elderly have changed since 1960. She analyzes sixty books in terms of occupational roles, leisure activities, status of mental and physical health, status of social well-being, and the quantity of age-related material. She concludes that "the portrayal of the elderly in both time periods was generally positive and contained minimal amounts of ageistic or stereotypic material." While the study does not indicate any great differences in subject matter or treatment between the two periods, there is some indication that more recent literature presents "more positive and realistic images of the elderly."

Young, Diane Elizabeth. "Restraining the Wild Child." Ph.D. diss. Stanford University, 1988. 234 pp. DAI 49:3712A.

Young deals with the dichotomy in Western and Eastern literature between the classical notion of feral children as "heroes of civilization" and the Enlightenment view of the child as uncivilized. She studies *The Origin of the Species*, *De l'éducation d'un homme sauvage*, *Rapport sur le sauvage de l'Aveyron*, *Journey through the Kingdom of Oude*, *The Diary of the Wolf-Children of Midnapore*, *Tarzan of the Apes*, *The Jungle Book*, *Gazelle-Boy*, and Truffaut's film *L'Enfant Sauvage*.

Also of Note

Antelyes, Peter Alan. "Tales of Adventurous Enterprise: The American Narrative of Western Economic Expansion in the Age of Irving." Ph.D. diss. Columbia University, 1986. 391 pp. DAI 50:137–38A.

Bach, Raymond E. "The Sacrificial Child: A Phenomenological Study of a Literary Theme." Ph.D. diss. Stanford University, 1988. 273 pp. DAI 49:3714–15A.

Brown, Barbara Mahone. "The Human/Machine Distinction in Children's Para-Social Experiences with Communication Technologies." Ph.D. diss. Stanford University, 1989. 154 pp. DAI 50:820–21A.

Butler-McGranaghan, Sylvia M. "Fairy-Tale Motifs in Early Works of Thomas Mann." Ph.D. diss. University of Pennsylvania, 1988. 151 pp. DAI 50:151A.

Cojuc, Juan-Ricardo Wolfowitz. "Children's Perception of Television as a Function of Various Modes of Parental Guidance." Ph.D. diss. University of Michigan, 1988. 204 pp. DAI 49:2009A.

Ford, Elizabeth Anne. "Nursery Tea: Child Characters in the Novels of Virginia Woolf and E. M. Forster." Ph.D. diss. Kent State University, 1989. 230 pp. DAI 50:1663A.

Giddings, Jeremy Lane. "Innocence and Instinct: The Figure of the Child in Modern Japanese Fiction." Ph.D. diss. Harvard University, 1988. 298 pp. DAI 50:446A.

Homan, Paul W. "Spatial Form and Humor in the Old French Fabliaux." Ph.D. diss. University of Kansas, 1988. 142 pp. DAI 49:3358A.

Howard, Catherine. "Children's Librarianship: A Descriptive Study of the Responsibilities Found in Job Announcements and Written Job Descriptions, Compared with Perceptions of Successful Candidates." Ph.D. diss. Indiana University, 1989. 187 pp. DAI 50:1123A.

Little, William Kenneth. "Inventing Circus Clowns: The Irony of Parody and Pastiche in the Modern European Circus." Ph.D. diss. University of Virginia, 1988. 565 pp. DAI 50:186A.

Locke, Jill L. "The Effectiveness of Summer Reading Programs in Public Libraries in the United States." Ph.D. diss. University of Pittsburgh, 1988. 186pp. DAI 49:3539A.

Luce, Stanford L. "Jules Verne: Moralist, Writer, Scientist." Ph.D. diss. Yale University, 1953. 363 pp. DAI 50:698A.

Merrill-Mirsky, Carol. "Eeny Meeny Pepsadeeny: Ethnicity and Gender in Children's Musical Play." Ph.D. diss. University of California, Los Angeles, 1988. 256 pp. DAI 49:2445A.

Passigli, Richard Arthur. "Adolescent Adaptation to the Social Environment in Twentieth Century American Literature: A Psychoanalytic Inquiry." Ed.D. diss. University of Massachusetts, 1989. 585 pp. DAI 50:1267A.

Pecora, Norma Odom. "The Business of Children's Television." Ph.D. diss. University of Illinois at Urbana, Champaign, 1989. 280 pp. DAI 50:1471A.

Peterson, Barbara Leach. "Characteristics of Texts That Support Beginning Readers." Ph.D. diss. Ohio State University, 1988. 381 pp. DAI 49:2105A.

Petrini, Mark Julien. "Children and Heroes: A Study of Catullus and Vergil." Ph.D. diss. University of Michigan, 1987. 160 pp. DAI 49:3714A.

Reed-Nancarrow, Paula Elizabeth. "Remythologizing the Bible: Fantasy and the Revelatory Hermeneutic of George MacDonald." Ph.D. diss. University of Minnesota, 1988. 235 pp. DAI 49:1811A.

Salgo, Deborah Frances. "Cohesion in Children's Fictional Stories: Transitivity and a Goal-Directed Causal Analysis." Ph.D. diss. Stanford University, 1988. 226 pp. DAI 49:3708A.

Shanken Skwersky, Serena. "The Dialogical Imaginings of Adolescent and Youth: Discourses on Gender, Language, and Power in Student Literary Magazines from 1900 to 1929." Ph.D. diss. University of Pennsylvania, 1988. 396 pp. DAI 50:276A.

Ssutu, Patricia Chih-Ping. "Children's Theatre Management: Financial Management and Promotion Strategies." Ph.D. diss. University of Kansas, 1988. 303 pp. DAI 50:1140A.

Taylor, Myra Gwen. "A Comparison between Big Books and Traditional-Sized Books in the Kindergarten Reading Program." Ed.D. diss. Montana State University, 1988. 141 pp. DAI 49:2167A.

Witek, Joseph Patrick. "'Stranger and More Thrilling than Fiction': Comic Books as History." Ph.D. diss. Vanderbilt University, 1988. 270 pp. DAI 50:688A.

Contributors and Editors

RUTH B. BOTTIGHEIMER is the author of *Grimms' Bad Girls and Bold Boys: The Moral and Social Vision of the Tales* and numerous articles on folk narrative, children's literature, and illustrations. She is currently writing a book on the history of children's Bibles. She teaches at the State University of New York at Stony Brook.

FRANCELIA BUTLER, founding editor of *Children's Literature*, has recently published *Skipping around the World: The Ritual Nature of Folk Rhymes*.

JOHN CECH is the book review editor of *Children's Literature*. He teaches in the English department at the University of Florida. He is the author of a book for children, *My Grandmother's Story*, which will be published in the fall of 1991, and has recently completed a book about the works of Maurice Sendak.

JANE DOONAN was originally trained as an art historian at the University of Leeds, and then York, where she subsequently conducted research in the field of medieval alabasters. She is currently head of the faculty of English and drama in an English comprehensive school. She has published a number of articles on picture-book art and artists, mainly in *Signal: Approaches to Children's Literature*, and she regularly reviews new picture books.

JACQUELINE F. EASTMAN teaches children's literature, English, and French at Talladega College. She is currently working on the Twayne series *Ludwig Bemelmans*, and she has recently published an article in the *James Joyce Quarterly* revealing Joyce's indebtedness to "the language of flowers."

RITA FEOLE, a recent graduate of the University of Connecticut, worked as a freelance writer for a local newspaper and is presently pursuing a Master of Science degree in special education.

RACHEL FORDYCE, former Executive of the Children's Literature Association, is the author of four books, the most recent of which is *Lewis Carroll: A Reference Guide*. She is the dean of humanities and social sciences at Indiana University of Pennsylvania.

CHRISTINE DOYLE FRANCIS, at the University of Connecticut, has recently completed curriculum guides on Gerald McDermott's and E. L. Konigsburg's books. Her research emphasizes the relation between feminist and myth criticism and children's literature.

SUSAN R. GANNON is professor of literature and communications at Pace University, Pleasantville, N.Y. She has recently written on Robert Louis Stevenson and is collaborating on a book on Mary Mapes Dodge.

ANNE HIGONNET teaches in the art department of Wellesley College. She is the author of a biography of Berthe Morisot and is completing a study of Morisot's images of women.

NANCY HUSE teaches English and Women's Studies at Augustana College, Illinois. She is currently working on the Twayne *Noel Streatfeild*.

SYLVIA PATTERSON ISKANDER teaches English at the University of Southwestern Louisiana. She is currently working on a series of articles on Anne Frank.

JEAN I. MARSDEN teaches English at the University of Connecticut. She recently edited *The Appropriation of Shakespeare: Post-Renaissance Reconstructions of the Work and the Myth* and is currently writing a performance history of *Cymbeline*.

PAULO MEDEIROS, who teaches comparative literature at the University of Massachusetts, has recently completed a dissertation on the theoretical implications of eating and drinking in relation to Western textuality.

William Moebius has taught in the department of comparative literature at the University of Massachusetts since 1967. He heads the International Committee of the Children's Literature Association and is completing a book of essays on children's literature of which "Room with a View" is a part.

Perry Nodelman teaches English at the University of Winnipeg. He is the author of *Words about Pictures: The Narrative Art of Children's Picture Books* and *The Pleasures of Children's Literature* (forthcoming).

Carol Reinermann studied sociology at the University of Florida, where she was involved in a research project that examined Little Golden Books using the developmental model of Erik Erikson. She currently resides and works in Cincinnati, Ohio.

Barbara Rosen, who teaches at the University of Connecticut, has published on witchcraft, children's literature, and Shakespeare in performance.

George Shannon is the author of several books for children, including *Lizard's Song* (1981), a young adult novel, *Unlived Affections* (1989), and the critical study *Arnold Lobel* (1989). He lives in Eau Claire, Wisconsin.

Ann Marie Succi is a recent graduate of the University of Connecticut. She is currently planning future studies in English literature and hopes to attend graduate school in the fall of 1991.

Jan Susina teaches English at Kansas State University and is the editor of *Logic and Tea: The Letters of Charles Dodgson to Members of the G. J. Rowell Family*. He is currently working on a study of nineteenth-century fairy tales for children.

Hernan Vera is an associate professor of sociology at the University of Florida. He has written on the Chilean folk art form, the arpillera (see *CL* 15), and has been involved in research on Little Golden Books from an Eriksonian perspective. He is currently at work on a book about the French sociologist Marcel Mauss.

Mark I. West teaches children's literature at the University of North Carolina, Charlotte. He has written *Children, Culture, and Controversy* and *Trust Your Children: Voices against Censorship in Children's Literature* and has recently edited *Before Oz: Juvenile Fantasy Stories from Nineteenth-Century America*. He is currently working on a book about Roald Dahl.

Ian Wojcik-Andrews teaches children's literature at Eastern Michigan University. He has published on the relation between children's literature and Marxist criticism.

Jack Zipes teaches German literature and folklore at the University of Minnesota. His most recent publications include *The Brothers Grimm: From Enchanted Forests to the Modern World* (1988) and two translations, *The Complete Fairy Tales of the Brothers Grimm* (1987) and *Beauties, Beasts, and Enchantment: Classic French Fairy Tales* (1989).

Awards

The article award committee of the Children's Literature Association publishes a bibliography of the year's work in children's literature in the *Children's Literature Association Quarterly* and selects the year's best critical articles. For pertinent articles that have appeared in a collection of essays or journal other than one devoted to children's literature, please send a photocopy or offprint with the correct citation and your address written on the first page to Dr. Gillian Adams, 4105 Ave. C, Austin, TX 78751. Papers will be acknowledged and returned if return postage is enclosed. Annual deadline is May 1.

The Phoenix Award is given for a book first published twenty years earlier which did not win a major award but has passed the test of time and is deemed to be of high literary quality. Send nominations to Alethea Helbig, 3640 Eli Road, Ann Arbor, MI 48104.

The Children's Literature Association offers three annual research grants. The Margaret P. Esmonde Memorial Scholarship offers $500 for criticism and original works in the areas of fantasy or science fiction for children or adolescents by beginning scholars, including graduate students, instructors, and assistant professors. Research Fellowships are awards ranging from $250 to $1000 (number and amount of awards based on number and needs of winning applicants) for criticism or original scholarship leading to a significant publication. Recipients must have post-doctoral or equivalent professional standing. Awards may be used for transportation, living expenses, materials, and supplies, but not for obtaining advanced degrees, for creative writing, textbook writing, or pedagogical purposes. The Weston Woods Media Scholarship awards $1000 and free use of the Weston Woods studios to encourage investigation of the elements and techniques that contribute to successful adaptation of children's literature to film or recording, or to developing materials for television and video. For full application guidelines on all three grants, write the Children's Literature Association, c/o Marianne Gessner, 22 Harvest Lane, Battle Creek, MI 49015. Annual deadline for these awards is February 1.

Order Form   Yale University Press, 92A Yale Station, New Haven, CT 06520

Customers in the United States and Canada may photocopy this form and use it for ordering all volumes of **Children's Literature** available from Yale University Press. Individuals are asked to pay in advance. We honor both MasterCard and VISA. Checks should be made payable to Yale University Press.

The prices given are 1991 list prices for the United States and are subject to change. A shipping charge of $2.75 is to be added to each order, and Connecticut residents must pay a sales tax of 8 percent.

Qty.	Volume	Price	Total amount	Qty.	Volume	Price	Total amount
___	8 (cloth)	$40.00	_____	___	14 (cloth)	$40.00	_____
___	8 (paper)	$13.95	_____	___	14 (paper)	$13.95	_____
___	9 (paper)	$13.95	_____	___	15 (cloth)	$40.00	_____
___	10 (cloth)	$40.00	_____	___	15 (paper)	$13.95	_____
___	10 (paper)	$13.95	_____	___	16 (cloth)	$40.00	_____
___	11 (cloth)	$40.00	_____	___	16 (paper)	$13.95	_____
___	11 (paper)	$13.95	_____	___	17 (cloth)	$40.00	_____
___	12 (cloth)	$40.00	_____	___	17 (paper)	$13.95	_____
___	12 (paper)	$13.95	_____	___	18 (cloth)	$40.00	_____
___	13 (cloth)	$40.00	_____	___	18 (paper)	$13.95	_____
___	13 (paper)	$13.95	_____	___	19 (cloth)	$40.00	_____
				___	19 (paper)	$13.95	_____

Payment of $_____ is enclosed (including sales tax if applicable).

Mastercard no. _____

4-digit bank no. _____ Expiration date _____

VISA no. _____ Expiration date _____

Signature _____

SHIP TO: _____

_____

_____

See the next page for ordering issues from Yale University Press, London.

Volumes 1–7 of **Children's Literature** can be obtained directly from John C. Wandell, The Children's Literature Foundation, Box 370, Windham Center, Connecticut 06280.

Order Form   Yale University Press, 23 Pond Street, Hampstead, London NW3,
                   2 PN, England

Customers in the United Kingdom, Europe, and the British Commonwealth may photocopy this form and use it for ordering all volumes of **Children's Literature** available from Yale University Press. Individuals are asked to pay in advance. We honour Access, Visa, and American Express accounts. Cheques should be made payable to Yale University Press.

The prices given are 1991 list prices for the United Kingdom and are subject to change. A post and packing charge of £1.75 is to be added to each order.

Qty.	Volume	Price	Total amount	Qty.	Volume	Price	Total amount
——	8 (cloth)	£40.00	_____	——	14 (cloth)	£40.00	_____
——	8 (paper)	£13.95		——	14 (paper)	£13.95	_____
——	9 (cloth)	£40.00					
——	9 (paper)	£13.95	_____	——	15 (cloth)	£40.00	_____
——	10 (cloth)	£40.00		——	15 (paper)	£13.95	_____
——	10 (paper)	£13.95	_____	——	16 (cloth)	£40.00	_____
——	11 (cloth)	£40.00	_____	——	16 (paper)	£13.95	_____
——	11 (paper)	£13.95	_____	——	17 (cloth)	£35.00	_____
——	12 (cloth)	£40.00	_____	——	17 (paper)	£11.95	_____
——	12 (paper)	£13.95	_____	——	18 (cloth)	£35.00	_____
——	13 (cloth)	£40.00	_____	——	18 (paper)	£10.95	_____
——	13 (paper)	£13.95	_____	——	19 (cloth)	£35.00	_____
				——	19 (paper)	£10.95	_____

Payment of £_____ is enclosed.

Please debit my Access/Visa/American Express a/c no. _____

Expiry date_____

Signature_____ Name_____

Address_____

See the preceding page for ordering issues from Yale University Press, New Haven.

Volumes 1–7 of **Children's Literature** can be obtained directly from John C. Wandell, The Children's Literature Foundation, Box 370, Windham Center, Connecticut 06280.